More Praise for Michele Mitchell and
The Latest Bombshell

"Insightful and hilarious, *The Latest Bombshell* is a novel that is About Something: politics, honor, charm, loyalty, and human nature. Denizens of Washington, D.C., and small towns everywhere will recognize this cast of characters, from the feisty heroine to the friends and fiends that surround her. A terrific read!"

—Laura Zigman, author of *Her*

"Michele Mitchell's j'accuse not only wonderfully captures the various blood sports of Washington, but gives us Kate Boothe—a bright, funny, and spirited heroine with a literary future."   —Jeffrey Frank, author of *The Columnist*

Michele Mitchell is a correspondent for *NOW with Bill Moyers* on PBS, and was political anchor and senior political correspondent for CNN *Headline News*. She has written editorials for *The New York Times*, and commentary for *The Washington Post* and National Public Radio's *All Things Considered*. She began her career on Capitol Hill. She lives in Brooklyn, New York.

THE

LATEST

BOMBSHELL

· A NOVEL ·

MICHELE
MITCHELL

A PLUME BOOK

PLUME
Published by the Penguin Group
Penguin Group (USA) Inc., 375 Hudson Street, New York, New York 10014, U.S.A.
Penguin Books Ltd, 80 Strand, London WC2R 0RL, England
Penguin Books Australia Ltd, 250 Camberwell Road,Camberwell, Victoria 3124, Australia
Penguin Books Canada Ltd, 10 Alcorn Avenue, Toronto, Ontario, Canada M4V 3B2
Penguin Books India (P) Ltd, 11 Community Centre,
Panchsheel Park, New Delhi–110 017, India
Penguin Books (NZ), cnr Airborne and Rosedale Roads,
Albany, Auckland 1310, New Zealand
Penguin Books (South Africa) (Pty) Ltd, 24 Sturdee Avenue,
Rosebank, Johannesburg 2196, South Africa

Penguin Books Ltd, Registered Offices: 80 Strand, London WC2R 0RL, England

Published by Plume, a member of Penguin Group (USA) Inc. This is an authorized
reprint of a hardcover edition published by Henry Holt and Company, LLC. For
information address Henry Holt and Company, LLC, 115 West 18th Street, New York,
New York 10011.

First Plume Printing, July 2004
10 9 8 7 6 5 4 3 2 1

Ⓡ REGISTERED TRADEMARK—MARCA REGISTRADA

The Library of Congress has catalogued the Henry Holt edition as follows:
Mitchell, Michele.
The latest bombshell : a novel / Michele Mitchell.—1st ed.
p. cm.
ISBN 0-8050-7321-3 (hc.)
ISBN 0-452-28544-5 (pbk.)
1. Women political consultants—Fiction. 2. Americans—Italy—
Fiction. 3. Washington (D.C.)—Fiction. 4. Rome (Italy)—Fiction.
5. Treason—Fiction. I. Title.

PS3613.I86 L3 2003
813'.6—dc21   2002038817

Printed in the United States of America

For Sonya,
and the Bellavista Franciacorta

THE LATEST BOMBSHELL

1

THE SCANDAL

Start at the beginning. I actually hate that phrase. If I start from the Big Bang, the *beginning*, I risk arrest in Kansas. Besides, no one ever really means it when they say, "Start at the beginning." What they mean is, "Start from the point relevant to *me*."

Well, how about this: I was in Rome when it happened. I had spent two months tripping through the Venetian fogs until heading south to the Eternal City, with the handsomest man in the world carrying my suitcase. In fact, he was waiting for me that calm, cool night at the wine bar, undoubtedly with plates of cheeses and olives, and I was late.

So there I was, teetering through the cobblestone streets in heels the clerk in the smart shop off the Piazza del Popolo had no right to sell me—grace is not one of my assets, and the odds were not good (some American is *always* fracturing her ankle in Rome)—when I happened to catch an elderly tourist braying "Damn Commie spy!" while crumpling a copy of an English-language newspaper. "Commies" are a little retro these days; spies, however, are not. I was intrigued enough to grab for the front page just as the man started to lob it through the air into the trash. The man stared—I did wobble dangerously in my effort—and then he steadied me with his arm in the courtly manner of another era. "Selling secrets!" he exclaimed, shaking his head. "And in this day and age! That's not just spying. It's wrong—morally wrong. It's treason!"

I nodded, because he was not looking for any other response, and left him there, grumbling, near the statue of a man burned at the stake for believing the earth revolved around the sun.

I planned to consume copious amounts of *prosecco* at the Enoteca l'Angolo Divino, on the corner, appropriately, of a narrow street just off the Campo dei Fiori, with its walls lined with bottles and twenty tables, carefully labeled and crowded with attorneys, hipsters, and the odd lost sightseer. I pushed open the wood and glass door, and Roberto immediately raised his chin in my direction. He sat at one of the polished tables, splendid in a checked blue shirt, his suede jacket draped across my chair. The bottle of bubbly was on the table and open.

"You're late," he said, pouring me a glass.

"I attacked an old man for his newspaper," I replied.

"But you buy one every morning," Roberto said.

"Today I got shoes." I waggled patent leather at him. Nearly five months in Italy had taught me, if nothing else, that there is nothing like a well-chosen pair of shoes to knock a man off his game. Sure enough, Roberto reached for an olive and settled back, and I scanned the front page in peace.

Well. So. The State and Defense departments of the United States had discovered that someone had been sending confidential documents detailing movements of various special forces divisions. The information was sensitive but vague; whoever paid for it must have been disappointed. And whoever sent it must have been a colossal idiot, since it went via e-mail (electronic espionage—how trendy!). But because it was meant for an attaché in the Chinese embassy, and because the country was currently in the grip of a hunt-the-bastards details-be-damned hysteria, I knew the story would have, as they say, legs.

"Look at this," I said. "I can only imagine how your father must be reacting."

"Me, too."

Roberto laughed but then frowned slightly at the thought. His father recently had risen, as expected, to the rank of China's ambassador to the United States. They didn't talk much. Roberto used his mother's last name and embraced her country and had his reasons for doing so.

He folded my hand in his. "We can find other things to discuss." And then he smiled.

I pushed aside the newspaper. After all, an "egregious breach of national security"? How many times had we heard *that* one? There was a usual course: find the culprit, jail the culprit, sentence the culprit. Didn't involve me. Pass the *prosecco*. I was on vacation.

. . .

The straight-up holiday had been Venice. Yes, I stood in Venice, on the Bridge of Dresses, a wine bar on each hand. Perhaps not as poetic as the Bridge of Sighs, with its palace and prison, but infinitely more fun. We had met on the airplane from Washington to Rome, and a week or so after dancing alone around the spun-sugar city (sinking on rotting wood but still a fine place to recover from an election cycle), Roberto "just happened" to find himself in Venice on business. He took me beyond the fish market to a restaurant where the pot-bellied and greasy-haired chef looked distinctly like my childhood conception of a pirate. We ate piles of tiny fish, still with faces (the French fry of the sea, according to the chef), and drank the house wine while Roberto regaled me with stories of an ill-fated bear hunt in Siberia and a successful excursion to Cuba to learn guitar. That night, he didn't even try to kiss me. Eventually he got around to it, and then it was off to Rome.

La bella confusione, as they say, with motorcycles and taxis, buses and trolleys swirling around cake layers of ancient columns and modern concrete slabs. Roberto worked on his architectural writings on an ornately carved desk with gold and silver fittings in his apartment just off the Piazza Navona, while I—well, I halfheartedly attempted to learn Italian and thought about trying to drum up some business. I sort of enjoyed the blissful ignorance of not understanding the babble around me. Still, every morning, on my way to Bar Sant'Eustachio, I picked up a copy of *La Repubblica* (and, for good measure, the *International Herald Tribune*).

And so, the day after the big news broke, I spent an hour in the rose-gold light, poring over the headlines and plowing through several cappuccinos and a croissant. Good God, the beast was having a field day with this scandal. Who-oh-who-oh-*who* could the horrible treasonous creature be? The beast gnawed happily because, while the Chinese might have pledged their solidarity with Americans in squelching terrorism, that didn't really mean anything. The timing could not have been worse for the alleged scoundrel. I don't need to remind anyone of The Moment when we literally collapsed into the next era (just as, nearly sixty years before, there had been the Hiroshima Summer).

I am a political consultant. Which is why, as I paged through the newspapers, I thought, Here we go. You know, frankly, I would love to say that those who conceive political pitches and then market candidates to the public are utterly brilliant. Nothing would please me more. But most of the time we're just trying to stay ahead of the media and one another. Let's face it: The best any of us could come up with for our candidates the previous fall was "I'm running for America's Security." Because I knew, and everyone else in the business knew, that we were going to need a scapegoat by the next election cycle if our guys were to keep their jobs. The rest was left unsaid, but it was clearly implied: If we couldn't find a scapegoat, we would have to invent one.

Little treasonous scallywag, I thought, as I sat at the café, surrounded by scrubbed, bright buildings, who are you? Run, run, run, because you're going to hang. And then I returned to my coffee.

In the afternoon, as usual, I wandered over to the wine bar. All right, the *enoteca*. My "office," where I would perch on a stool near the smooth counter, picking at prosciutto under the wood-beamed ceilings, or at the table marked with a number 1, with my papers scattered across the top. Occasionally a legislator would drift in between sessions in the parliament building just five minutes away and join me for a few glasses, which was enough to convince me that I was actually accomplishing some business. Mostly, I just liked the place.

So there I was, sitting at my table tucked under the shelf of the owner's grappa collection, drinking whatever lip-staining red he had decided to pour for me, when my beloved partner, Jack, walked in.

He came straight to the point, not even acknowledging the months that had passed without so much as a postcard. I didn't wonder how he had managed to track me down. I simply looked up at him as if this was the most natural place to resume our conversation and listened as Jack leaned across the rickety table and said, "They've found their traitor. One of your old pals."

I stared at him. He looked no worse for the seven-hour flight, his shirt only slightly rumpled, but then Jack firmly believed in the religion of good fabric.

"You've been following this Mao thing," he said, gesturing at the newspapers on the table, "the Chinese attaché? The one who supposedly paid somebody for our military secrets."

"Sort of. I just heard about it," I said.

They're saying it's Lyle Gold who did it."

"Lyle Gold?" I repeated.

"So they've decided."

I started laughing. "Oh, come on, Jack! That's just—"

"And they're calling it treason," Jack interrupted. He was serious.

"Against what?" I waved to the owner for another glass of wine. "Since when does Lyle know anything about the military? He covers Capitol Hill!"

"Actually, babycakes, his beat for the last two years has been the military."

I shrugged, nonplussed. It wasn't as if I kept tabs on all my former boyfriends. "All right. Instead of ticking off members of Congress, he's been ticking off soldiers."

"And the State Department," Jack said. "He managed to embarrass them a few times too."

With a slight clink, the owner placed red liquid in front

of me, warning, "This is too strong to drink so early in the day."

"You're the one who gave it to me in the first place," I reminded him.

"When I thought you were drinking one glass," he said.

"What about me? Can I get one too?" Jack asked. The man examined him closely, but a wink from me gave Jack clearance. Another glass was grudgingly set out.

Fortified now, I had questions. "So he made people mad. What else is new?"

"He embarrassed the hell out of the military several times," Jack said. "The thing in Algiers. Remember hearing about that? About a year ago—we were busy with the Taylor campaign down in Biloxi. But there was that 'incident' with special forces, where thirty people died and about two hundred rebels just disappeared. The guy who got the story was Lyle."

"But he hates to travel," I murmured.

"He probably didn't enjoy it," Jack said. "He did find out that the guns the Algerian soldiers used were given to them by the CIA. Neat, eh?"

"I don't remember this happening at all," I said.

"That's because like most Americans you don't pay any attention to what's happening overseas," Jack pointed out. "Except for flight specials."

Jack hated it when I went on vacation. I called it "limiting media exposure," because if too many newspapers give you too much good press, you can bet that you are being set up for a fall. Jack didn't buy into it, though. Three years ago, when I limited my exposure after an election cycle with a timely visit to the Caribbean, Jack burned all our office stationery. Of course, when I returned with the tidbit that dwarfs were considered good luck in the Dominican Republic, he reprinted it. We were consulting for a Dominican politician, and I had made sure to sign up every dwarf on the island to appear at a campaign rally. Our client won.

Jack drew a thick envelope out of his leather briefcase and slid it across the table. VANZETTI & BOOTHE shimmered in gold embossing. I had to give him points for presentation. Tidied in chronological order were newspaper clippings, television transcripts, hard copies of Internet documents. Spilling out first: the headline, SPECIAL OPS TROOP MOVEMENTS SOLD TO CHINESE BY REPORTER. Lyle's face, edged sharply in black and white, stared out from the page. Here was one I hadn't seen before—I leaned closer and noticed the name *Albergo del Senato* across the top. Of course: a fax. Jack was never one for wasting time. "Today a reporter for . . . placed under arrest . . . under suspicion of. . . ." Clinically written, just as I had learned in one of the nation's finest journalism programs (to this day, my father grouses about the hundred grand he spent for a bachelor's degree that I "never use"). Inverted pyramid style, the most important facts squashed up front. But then:

> Pentagon sources say that Gold has worked covertly for the Chinese, passing on U.S. military secrets for at least $1.2 million through the Chinese embassy in Washington, D.C. His coworkers began to suspect Gold when he purchased a $500,000 townhouse in Georgetown and a sports car. "We started to wonder how he could afford all that on a journalist's salary," said one.

I looked up at Jack. "Is this the best they've got?" I asked. "Come on! We know Lyle's cheap. His idea of luxury is searching for the perfect lobster roll."

Jack swirled the wine in his glass. "Well, they—"

"And his finances are impeccable! Every extra cent he had went into the market; he cleaned up in the bull run. He can afford that kind of house. He used to talk about his thirties being the right time to have a mortgage." I was working myself into quite a state, until the thought occurred: We were dealing with Lyle here.

"Did you get to the part about the attorney general being pissed at him?" Jack asked.

That would put Lyle in fine company. The attorney general was a shallow man whose mission in life was to ban alcohol from all airline flights. He had a six-foot-high replica of the Statue of Liberty in his barn in Iowa that he had built himself out of barbed wire. It wasn't difficult to antagonize him. But Lyle had gone for extra credit, tracking the story of the thousands of people—students, mostly—

detained in jail for overstaying their visas or being in the wrong place at the wrong time but never charged with a particular crime, just *suspicious*. And these were suspicious times, which often translated into prolonged stays in solitary, often shackled and usually without access to lawyers. Or at least this was Lyle's version of the situation. I read through the notes Jack had so carefully compiled, and I was inclined to believe him. Lyle did not want to be president someday, whereas it was well-known that the attorney general did. Ambition always raises a red flag.

"Lyle also said some . . . dumb things," Jack told me.

"Surprise, surprise," I muttered.

"Really, Kate. He outdid himself. He actually questioned the patriotism of the attorney general."

"Good for him! The guy is a lunatic," I said.

"He also questioned the White House for sealing its public records," Jack continued. "He questioned the antiterrorism czar for using government aircraft to fly to Aspen to sell his seven-million-dollar house. And that's just for starters."

Now I knew why Jack had come. Here was the scapegoat, all right, and what a fine one! Lyle Gold, with his dour frowns and artless protestations of innocence, was perfect for the role. I knew this better than most. When I was twenty-six, I had been on the receiving end of his particularly tasteless breakup technique. He would rub his pale forehead as if it pained him and then, rapid-fire, list off a girl's faults—"I can't date you anymore because, well, you're

too selfish, you're too frenetic, you didn't help me pack"—
and so on for at least thirty reasons, ending with "I'm saying
this so that it helps you." It helped me, all right, straight
into a bruised ego and a frenzy of work.

This is how my job operates: I run media campaigns.
When a politician hires us, I figure out an angle, package it,
and sell it. Jack handles all the polls and voter information.
Then, together, we come up with a political strategy. Occasionally, we do this for corporations. It was exactly the same
rundown we used to do for a much larger firm, just five
years ago, when we shared an office. Now that we had our
own, we knew the drill. What it comes down to is examin-
ing a situation with the manipulative eye that our profession
demands and then weighing whether or not we have a shot.
That is how I would have read Lyle's file if I possessed any
sense at all.

Instead, the articles made me wince. Lyle may not have
been the nicest guy, but he wasn't a bad person. What was
happening to him—good God, just calling him a traitor in a
political year was a sure-fire winner, this era's equivalent of
red-baiting. I pressed my lips together. Not for nothing
have we been called a republic of opportunists.

"We need a big win," Jack said, getting to the point of
why, exactly, he had seen fit to fly all the way to Rome.
"Business is all right, even without you around, but things
are getting tight. You know that. And if we're ever going to
land a heavy-hitting national campaign, we need something

like this. This would be the biggest challenge we've ever had. If we take it and we win, we're *made*."

"And I thought you were here out of the moral goodness of your heart," I said.

"I don't like the guy, never have, and to be honest he's not doing himself any favors with his behavior," Jack said. "But in the big picture, we could do the right thing *and* the profitable thing. They aren't mutually exclusive." He paused a moment. "Kate, I can't do it without you." It had to kill him to say that. But he went on. "You're the one who can talk to the press. You're the one who looks the best on TV. And you're the one who can get those guys on the Hill to do anything." He always brought *that* up. But it had been a long time since I pushed through legislation. Almost ten years, in fact.

"What does Lyle say about us taking this on?" I asked.

Jack didn't reply immediately. He gazed intently at the sediment in his wineglass.

"Does he even know you're here?" I lifted my eyebrows.

"He's got other things, other worries—he—oh, come on, Kate. You know how these things work."

"Does he want any consultants figuring out strategy for him?" I pressed.

"I know he does," Jack said.

"He's asked other people," I realized aloud.

"A few." Jack did not even blink.

I burst out laughing, rapidly figuring the situation. "And

what happened? They all turned him down, didn't they: How do you know he'll even want us to make an offer? He might have some other firm lined up by the time you get back."

"No one else will take it," Jack said quickly. "The odds are too long and people are too scared."

I didn't ask the question that hung in the air: *What about Roberto?* If Jack and I took this on, I would breathe nothing else for as long as it lasted, and one could only imagine how the implications would affect the son of the Chinese ambassador to the United States. The inevitable relationship dissection by the media would hardly be fair, but who cares about fairness, right?

"His lawyers may not want an ex-girlfriend representing him." This seemed quite a salient factor, in my opinion.

"Better than no one," Jack shot back.

"Not true. I'm baggage. I'm a distraction."

"That might work in this case." Jack shrugged. Damn him, I thought, may he not get lucky for a week. Because Lyle Gold was not going to be pleased about any proposal coming from me. I hadn't spoken to him in years.

"I need to think about this," I said.

"What's there to think about? If you don't come now, you'll regret it."

"If I do come now, I might regret it." Indeed. Media pile-on factor: extremely high. Right-thing factor: probable. Grateful-client-and-burnished-reputation factor: not likely.

Jack flushed a deep red, almost the same shade as the wine he had been drinking.

"Fine, then." He exhaled. "I'll be around until tomorrow evening." His shoes clicked on the terra-cotta tiles as he left.

The proprietor was studying me from the corner of his eye. "Kate, do you want a bottle to take home for tonight?" he asked tactfully.

"Better make it two," I said.

. . .

Roberto had an apartment at number 37 on the Via di Parione, across from an antique bookstore. The walls were the color of old wax, and I had to lean my shoulder against the thick wood door to shove it open. The property had belonged to his mother. His mother's home, his mother's name, his mother's sculpted features: It was difficult, really, to see the Xianxu in him, he had managed through determination and attitude to excise it so thoroughly. He couldn't even speak Mandarin. And when I met him on the airplane, he was wearing a blue velvet suit, something only an Italian could pull off properly.

Yes, the great lottery in life is the airplane: You never know who you're going to end up with as a seat companion. Once, on a flight from Indianapolis to Newark, I ended up next to a kid who was ultimately destined for Luxembourg, extradited on check fraud. He had mossy teeth, he smelled like a barn, and he talked endlessly about the science-fiction comic book he wanted to write. That was one end of the spectrum. At the other was Roberto. Maybe because I was so focused on getting the melatonin-wine proportions precise, I didn't say a word until the onion soup was served. It wafted rich, even for airline food, and I thought, That soup smells really good.

To my horror, as my seatmate turned to face me, I realized I had actually said the words aloud. I tried to recover— "I really . . . like onion soup"—but he smiled easily and replied, "It does smell good. Much better than it tastes." Roberto would always maintain that "That onion soup smells really good" was my pickup line.

The door clicked open now, and I heard his heavy step on the parquet flooring. Roberto was hard on shoes, wearing through soles every few months. His gray overcoat sparkled with raindrops from a late-afternoon shower. "Forgot the umbrella," he said, tousling my hair, and the world fell away for a moment. "What's all this?" He gestured at the scrawled notes from my conversation with Jack.

"I have something to talk to you about," I began. "Jack is here. He wants me to go back to D.C."

I walked him through the situation. Roberto listened carefully, his almond eyes narrowing. He had known nothing himself, of course. His father had a different life now, with a new wife. But knowing him to be a proud man, Roberto could hardly imagine his father stooping to deal with a lowly reporter. Certain journalist types made it into the circle, the ones with sharp wits, polished manners, and custom-made tuxedos. Lyle was witty, but with a tendency to dribble as much food out of his mouth as he had in it, and he owned perhaps one decent suit.

Roberto considered all of this, and then he asked the big question: "Do you believe Lyle Gold is guilty of these things?"

I sighed. "I'm not sure yet."

"Can you hire someone to investigate?" he asked.

I thought, Yes, there is a safe idea. There were bound to be unchecked corners. But then I heard myself say, "But I don't think he is guilty." It was the unavoidable truth. The Lyle Gold I knew was pompous, cold, and brusque, but he didn't even cheat at Go Fish.

"Something is missing," I insisted.

"Is this fact or feeling?" Roberto asked.

I went over to the desk and flipped through the papers again. I had done this so often that day that a latticework of thin cuts laced my fingers. "It's just outright odd. There's no evidence I can see that Lyle had any direct access to information about troop movements."

"He had sources," Roberto said, "and he had access to the State Department and the Pentagon."

"Limited access. It's not like reporters can run amok in those places."

"He could have found a way. He's a smart guy."

"Yes, but then they supposedly figured out he was the bad guy by tracing the e-mails sent to the Chinese attaché back to him. If Lyle's so smart—and he is pretty sharp—why would he be that stupid?" I demanded.

"One of the most intelligent men I have ever known was my roommate at the university, and he couldn't use a microwave oven."

"So what do I do," I said tonelessly.

"What can you possibly do? Kate, you're one person. You're not expected to shoulder the burden of the world. Besides, he has lawyers, no?"

Roberto had a point. But I still drank most of the two bottles that night.

2

VILLAIN OF THE CENTURY

The grand jury indicted Lyle Gold in record time. The next morning, Roberto handed me the newspapers, filled with gleeful accounts gleaned from the jurors: Gold remaining in his chair, frozen in cold restraint; Gold listening impassively to the testimonies of military officials and former colleagues and even a few erstwhile girlfriends (who seemed delighted finally to get *their* shot at listing *his* character faults); Gold leaving the courthouse, dropping the mask of indifference to issue a monotone mantra: "I am innocent. I am innocent. I am innocent." The crowd outside, jeering and booing and even turning their backs.

"I thought what happens in an American grand jury is sealed," Roberto mused.

"These things have a way of getting out," I explained.

"If you cannot show warmth of the soul, you cannot

win," Roberto said, and he went into the kitchen to make coffee.

Lyle's fate, with the public at least, *was* sealed. He had started at a disadvantage, since, as I knew firsthand, he not only hated gratuitous emotion but didn't have the stomach to fake it. Instead of passionately denouncing his detractors, which might have aroused sympathy, he defended himself with all the flair of a burnt-out museum curator. Watch any three-hour cycle of twenty-four-hour news, and you can figure out that the media love to see a spirit break. An entertaining display of pathos translates into higher ratings. Give the press what they want, and you might even elicit some decent coverage. Lyle, however, no doubt clung stubbornly to the belief that by virtue of the fact that *he said* he was innocent, the government and the media and the people would realize the terrible error that had been made. Lyle had amazingly shoddy instincts about his colleagues. I shook my head, because he should have known that the ensuing outrage would be poisonous.

Which it was. Melvin Gluck, the bloated film producer who fancied himself a political player, was one of the first to speak out. "It seems to me that if I were in his skin and I really was innocent, I would rebel. I would struggle or shout." Others had equally fatuous contributions. The fresh-faced conservative commentator (a noted fall-on-his-face drunk) offered, "Maybe he hasn't been convicted yet, but the grand jury indictment is all the proof we need. It's cut and dried! Clean and clear!" The pinched liberal commentator (who also drank too much and did not practice discriminating sleeping arrangements) went even further. "You've got to be an idiot not to see the wretch is guilty." It was all there, literally in black and white, along with the verdict from a blow-hard congressman from (naturally) New York. "He's got no wife, no child, no love of anything, no human or even animal ties, nothing but an obscene soul and a black heart."

No one had really doubted the outcome, except perhaps Lyle himself. But still, it was dumbfounding to see such a rush to judgment based on sensational accusations and thin evidence and to realize that a people as diverse as Americans could seemingly be so wholly united against one man. A very special series of elements—media saturation, a united core, a hint of war—had been required to lock out differing opinions. So it was easy to join up. Righteous finger-pointers, no matter what sins they had committed, could never ever be accused of betraying their country. At least, this is how I read it.

No doubt there *was* a traitor. Military and state secrets had been leaked to the Chinese by *someone* on the inside. My guess was that the someone could be found in the State Department or in the Pentagon. But who wanted to consider that possibility?

I sighed. No denying the strength of the public case against Lyle; the instant adoption of that damning word, *traitor,* spoke volumes. No mention of espionage, which was much more common and modern. *Traitor* was a masterful stroke. The geniuses in the federal government who bestowed the term understood its power. It evoked a whitewashed era, long since past, when words like *honor* still meant something, and it conjured up ghosts of the most reviled—Benedict Arnold, the Rosenbergs, Alger Hiss—still burning with the word. *Traitor!* The cry led to the gallows, the firing squad, the electric chair, depending on the technological enlightenment of the day. And now here it was again.

■ ■ ■

"Did you see the magazine covers by your coffee place?" Jack had reached me on my cell phone. I was on my way to buy cheese. I froze at the sound of his voice. "Lyle's all over the place: 'America's Traitor.' "

"I saw," I muttered.

"Did you hear what the Cajun Fox said?" This was our first and most favorite client, a congressman who had easily won his reelection campaign. "He said, and I quote: 'Sure I want the death penalty erased. But everyone will understand that the law should, by necessity, be the last resting place, if Lyle Gold is a traitor.' Yep. And there's this editorial in the *Orange County Register*; it's a beauty, Kate. It says, 'We are a population of millions; China is over a billion. Mr. Gold may have thus done more damage to our national security than anyone in our history, for the Chinese clearly intend to end the American Century and to seize it for their own.' The Chinese Century. Might want to ask Mr. Wonderful what he thinks."

"Where are you?" I demanded, looking around. Bureaucrats and politicians scurried between government buildings, not far from Bar Sant'Eustachio.

"On some street with a lot of fancy stores. You should see this place. Even the cops are dressed better than me."

I could hear the whir of Vespas and the chatter of window shoppers beyond his voice, and despite my rapidly deflating mood, I smiled. Via Condotti—of course. Good ol' Jack, when we had attended the inaugural ball this last time, he had turned up in a tuxedo nicer than most of the gowns.

"Don't spend your entire paycheck," I warned.

"Hell, sweetheart, why do you think I want to take on Gold?" And then he hung up.

■   ■   ■

Roberto had spent the day fielding calls about his father. He was rubbing his eyes when I returned (without the promised cheese), but he nonetheless insisted that we attend the American ambassador's reception for Frank Gehry that night. Usually Roberto steered clear of such events. But his interest in the great man won out over potential discomfort.

"I want to meet Gehry," Roberto said, "and I don't

particularly care what anyone says to me about my father."
This was brave of him, I thought, considering the gossip-
riddled world of the diplomatic circles from which he
descended. His mother's father had been the Italian ambassador to China. Such a sweet little story: a dark-eyed young
daughter, sophisticated beyond her years, falling madly for a
dashing Chinese attaché; a courtship in Beijing against a
thrilling backdrop of cherry blossoms and Cold War
intrigue. The marriage had soured by the time Roberto was
born, and the divorce was relatively quiet. But his father's
trajectory into the upper echelons of diplomacy and his Italian grandfather's continued prominence in the same circles
ensured Roberto's own place in that insular society. The
moment we walked into the ambassador's residence, the
chummy back pats began.

This particular American ambassador, in what could be
interpreted as a crass display of personal wealth, had
eschewed the usual diplomatic digs for a villa in an exclusive
neighborhood, on Aventine Hill, with a staggering view
of the city. A peek through the front-gate keyhole yields a
very famous view of St. Peter's Cathedral, with the dome fitting perfectly. Tourists in the know make the drive just to
peer through. But the world-weary guests attending that
evening's festivities ignored such a treat, much more intent
on walking the corridors lined with Caravaggios and
Basquiats (the ambassador's wife thought it showed depth to
have Italian masters and American sensations side by side).

The mosaic floors of angry gods had been pieced together in Trastevere. And the rich heavy draperies were as good a Fortuny reproduction as any I had ever seen. Roberto rolled his eyes at all this—"more Italian than the Italians," he murmured in my ear—while yet another European Union official tugged at his elbow.

The political soirees I was accustomed to were packed with congressional members and staffers in basic black, wielding greasy mini-quiches and wilted broccoli platters and the usual opening line, "So, who do you work for?" The diplomatic world took some adjustment. Since ambassadors paid for the parties themselves, there was a direct correlation between their financial worth and that of the food. At this party, uniformed waiters served skewers of lamb, and the champagne they poured was Pol Roger—Winston Churchill's favorite. And unlike my scene, there were no deals overtly being cut in these glorious rooms. The chatter dealt with summering in Sardinia, the rate of the euro, and the latest faux pas by the German ambassador, whom no one seemed to like.

I reached for a glass of champagne from a waiter's silver tray. I knew this game. Surely it isn't only Washington and other capital cities that practice the fine art of subterfuge (I understand that small towns are equally adept). Everyone is seeking something—a phone number, an account, a piece of legislation—and usually offering a favor in return. You play the game even with those you despise. After all, knowledge is power. And then there are exceptions, the fixtures who seem inoculated by virtue of position, who can do anything.

No one at the Gehry reception was going to shun or insult Roberto. I watched him, nodding and smiling solemnly at the businessmen and politicians who approached, hands extended. I hadn't done too badly after all.

"Oh, Kate, did you hear about Lyle Gold?" asked the ambassador's wife, draping an arm around my shoulder and offering me another glass of champagne. I hadn't finished my first, but far be it from me to let that get in the way. This was one reason I could never pass as an Italian woman. I look like one—I am of a Mediterranean palette, with resolutely straight brown hair that I push behind my ears or pull up in a ponytail, olive skin, hazel eyes (which I think appear green if I draw a thin line of violet on my upper lid). Yes, I nearly struck the mark. But Italian women rarely drink, whereas in my world, the ability to imbibe and still manage to do business is regarded as an essential negotiating skill.

"I couldn't help hearing about it," I replied.

"Yes, yes. I'm sure you couldn't." She nodded at Roberto, who stood on the other side of the room with her husband. "Everyone's saying he'll surely be found guilty." Her heavy diamond earrings flashed as she leaned toward me conspiratorially, because after all I had known her back when she was a mere congressional scheduler. "You know, death is too good for his kind, if you ask me."

"And what kind would that be?" I wondered.

"Oh, you know. Not *ours*." She arched her eyebrows significantly. "Did you hear about that lieutenant and the grand jury? I guess you wouldn't have—it was all very hush-hush—but such a handsome man. And quite a performance. It sounded like something straight out of a movie. He's a marine."

"A marine. Really. The newspapers didn't say anything about him. What did he say?" I asked, humoring my hostess, because what could a marine lieutenant—a mere cog—possibly have to offer a grand jury that was so earth-shattering?

"Oh, my husband says it was all very dramatic," said my hostess, her eyes wide with delight. "Joseph Henry—that's the lieutenant's name, the one in military intelligence—he said he knew a former military aide from Russia who told him there was an American, one quite close to the government, who was spying for the Chinese. And then he stood up from his chair, pointed at Lyle Gold, and shouted, 'And that traitor is right there!' "

The ambassador's wife uttered each word with relish. She liked stories. I had a good one to share with her: how her husband had landed his job by providing the president with a list of relatively discreet, soft-tongued ladies. But why ruin her night?

"Was the Russian aide at the grand jury, too?" I asked.

"Oh, no. He died. Mob hit, I heard. You know how vicious the Russian mafia is." She shook her head.

"Not really—" I began, but her attention had drifted. She had spotted an industrialist from Turin, and with a wave of her red-tipped fingers she scuttled off to give him the update. I brought my glass to my lips. How handy that such an important source like an unnamed Russian was now, sadly, deceased. Oh, well. It had nothing to do with me. I took another sip from my glass, but I couldn't shake off the nagging thoughts. I have spent enough time in Washington to know certain aspects about the military. It is the one substantive alternative culture we have: its own housing, justice, way of thinking. Those who dedicate their lives to it don't do so to get rich; a marine serves the national interest, not his own. The national interest these days seemed to lie in proving Lyle Gold was a traitor. How trustworthy, then, could the testimony of this Joseph Henry be?

"A pity, isn't it, these idiots who keep landing ambassadorships?"

I knew that voice. I smiled broadly as I turned. "Reiff Prouty!"

He nodded. "The one and only. Still having bloodies and finger sandwiches at the Hay-Adams?"

I rolled my eyes. Once—once!—I had met him for tea at the lovely venerable hotel across the street from the White House. It seemed like such an elegant thing to do and, after all, Reiff was a cosmopolitan kind of guy. But he was still a *guy*, which meant he started laughing when the plate of salmon and cream cheese sandwiches was put in front of us. "This is like flying coach and getting those miserable snack bags," he had said. To compensate, I had bought him several stiff Bloody Marys.

"I haven't been in a while," I told him. "I've been in Rome."

"A lover, I'll guess." Reiff flashed teeth so perfectly white I wondered if he had them bleached. He had always been acutely aware of his appearance. His head was large for his body, but women rarely noticed. He kept his hair short and combed forward, slicked with expensive gel. He even had his eyeglasses custom-made to enhance his cheekbones.

"As a matter of fact, I'll introduce you." I nodded toward Roberto, who stood with the ambassador in a cluster of tuxedos.

"Roberto Picchi? Well, well, Kate. Not bad." Reiff tilted his glass my way.

"And what are you doing in Italy?" I asked.

"Funny thing, this State Department. It sends me overseas for work."

"Wrong sea, though."

His eyes darkened. "Yes," he answered, finishing the cocktail. "But you remember that story."

Oh, did I! Over tea, he had poured forth the bitterness of watching colleague after colleague (none, in his humble opinion, as qualified as he) attain exalted, exciting positions as attachés. He could excuse Moscow, Tokyo, Berlin—even Paris and Mexico City. But not China. He spoke passable Mandarin, after all. To tell this to me, practically a stranger, was a terrific risk in the cloistered worlds we moved in. But it seemed he couldn't stop himself. I decided immediately to avoid getting sucked into his micro-ecosystem; it was evidently always raining there.

He would have had a reasonable shot at a middling career, at least. He had a bit of family wealth, a distinguished name, and an Ivy League degree (this last one, just barely). But he wanted the status of an international power broker. One tried-and-true rule: Visible ambition never wins votes. Reiff badly wanted China. It was easier to believe that unseen forces were working against him than to face the fact that he was his own worst enemy.

"It's an interesting time for you to be with him." Reiff nodded toward Roberto. "His father is in the news a lot these days."

"His father is not a good topic of conversation."

"Do they talk much?" Reiff asked.

"I wouldn't know," I lied.

Reiff smiled, not kindly. "Oh, Kate," he said, "if people know you're fucking the son of the Chinese ambassador, you might as well get something out of the connection."

I tightened my grip on the stem of the glass. "Believe me, I get something out of it, sweetheart." I winked, desperately racking my brain for a change in subject, and remembered that a former college professor of mine had landed at the State Department not too long ago.

"I was wondering if you've run into a woman at work. Joan Picquart."

"I've heard about her. One of the assistant secretaries. She literally saved the face of her equivalent in Japan. He started to faint during yen negotiations, and she caught his arm just as he went down. Great story. Why?"

"She taught the toughest class I had in college," I said.

"Well, she's got the ear of the secretary of state. Her office is right next to his. Tell you what: Buy me a drink at the bar at the Eden, and we can talk about it more."

"Deal," I said. "Tomorrow at seven."

Roberto had been watching warily, over the ambassador's shoulder. As soon as I moved away from Reiff, he swept in. "I don't like him," he said quietly.

"How would you know? You've never met him."

"I don't have to. I don't like his look."

"And what would that be?" I laughed.

"That is a man who is looking to get something from you," Roberto said.

"How does that make him different from any other man?" I asked.

"The lady is a cynic."

"Actually, I think he's using me to get to you," I said. I was joking, but it hit a nerve. Even as Reiff chatted with other adjutants, he kept looking our way. "He asked about your father."

Roberto glanced at me sharply. "Oh, really? Who is this man?"

"Reiff Prouty."

"Rife with what?" Roberto asked.

"Frustration, mostly." I raised my glass, and Roberto clinked his against it softly. There it was, that knight-in-shining-armor chivalry that makes Italian men so charming. But then Frank Gehry himself wandered by, alone, and kissing my hand quickly, Roberto was off after him. I could have followed too, but this was Roberto's chase.

So I whisked another glass from a waiter (the secret to avoiding a headache is to press the bubbles to the roof of your mouth with the tip of your tongue before swallowing) and stepped through an arched doorway. The room I entered was slightly smaller than the gaily-lit one I had just left; its thick walls muffled the party chatter. Elegant oil-rubbed leather chairs and sofas shone in the flickering candle-light. The room was so dim that I almost didn't notice, nestled in one of the chairs, none other than Danny Daly. I had never met him, but of course I had read all about him. You can't get through a civics class without running across the resilient Danny Daly, with his brightly disappointing career—marine sergeant, congressman, senator, two-time presidential candidate (once losing by the largest landslide in American history). Since then, he had been relegated to the occasional book tour and professorial stint, so I was surprised to see him here. Rome seemed out of context. But there he was, his watery blue eyes regarding me expectantly. I cleared my throat and said, "Senator Daly. I'm Kate Boothe. I'm a consultant in Washington."

He took my extended hand—"Of course, of course"—
and nodded with the studied familiarity of a natural politician.

"What brings you here?" I asked, sitting in a chair
beside him.

"Oh, the president asked me to help out on the EU talks
next week. Any bit of work for an old one like me, it keeps a
fellow waking up in the morning." A smile spread across his
plump, rosy cheeks.

"Well, you're missing all the action in there." I nodded at
the crowded room beyond the doorway.

"I doubt it," he said, waving his hand. "Nothing of
consequence ever happens in Rome anymore." His eyes
twinkled mischievously. It struck me that he looked an awful
lot like Santa Claus. No wonder he never made it to the
White House. We don't usually elect cuddly leaders.

"They're all talking about Lyle Gold," I said.

Daly shook his head. "It's a shame, a real shame."

"Which piece of it?" I asked.

Daly lifted a stubby finger. "The rush to judgment," he
said. "What is happening with that young man: too many
persuasive people telling the public to believe one thing.
But that doesn't mean everyone will buy into it."

"Do you think it's possible," I began slowly, "to convince
people he might be innocent?"

"Anything is possible."

"Really?"

Daly stared distractedly in front of him. For a moment, I thought he had lost his thought or perhaps even forgotten I was in the room. But then he said gravely, "A situation like Lyle Gold—well, that troubles me. I have spent my entire life respecting and upholding the Constitution. There are rights, and there is a process. It makes me sadder than you can imagine to watch it get trampled now. And for what? Because we have found the Villain of the Century? No, no—it's opportunism by scared, weak men and women. I start to wonder what I have done with my life, to have worked so hard for so many years, and now for what?" He sighed like a man who had been disappointed by many people. "Remember this moment, my dear," he said. "It will haunt us."

"But what would you do?" I demanded, my voice rising an octave. "I happen to think he is innocent. But how could anyone argue *this* one out, with all the Yankee-Doodle flag-wavers scoring their points?" I looked at my half-consumed glass. "Isn't it convenient for the friendless traitor to appear now?"

"*La belle époque* has faded." Daly nodded.

"And along comes the scapegoat that so many people need," I concluded.

Daly chuckled at me but then grew sober. "Be careful," he cautioned. I did sound a bit hysterical. "That sounds like you're implying someone has set him up. Conspiracy theories are never charming."

The old man leaned in; he was as close to me as he could be without falling into my lap, and he gripped my hand in his papery one.

"Listen to me, young lady," he whispered fiercely. "Everyone I cared for is gone. I outlived them, and the fruit of it is an accursed memory of what they stood for: imperishable courage. Can you imagine it? Ah, they had it but never knew it until they fought in the wars. You say there's no war now for *you* to fight in? You're locked out of it all, no way to test yourself? Don't believe that. There are many fronts. And *this* is part of that war, or it will be if you go forward. It is a new battle of attrition that will go to the side that has the last man. They shall not pass. Remember that. *They shall not pass.* That is how you win."

I tried to pull away, but he was still clasping my hand, shaking. He made me repeat his words. *They shall not pass.* What the hell did that mean? But Daly was finished. He released me, retreating back, I thought, into the shadows of previous glories as I made my way back to the main room. As I stepped through the doorway, however, the ghosts must have grabbed at him, because Daly called out in a hoarse rasp, "Come on, you sons o' bitches! Do you want to live forever?"

． ． ．

I hadn't been missed at all. Roberto was preoccupied, still standing with the ambassador and Gehry. I realized I had left my glass of champagne in the room with Daly, so I took another from a passing waiter.

A friend of mine worked for Nixon in his waning days, and she once told me, "You want to see someone who regretted not doing the right thing, look no further. It ate him alive." Oh, fine, some people might say that was too generous an out, but surely even Nixon had regrets. I wondered if my grandfather did, representing Johnny Russo. Granted, they were never able to pin anything on the guy, but the mob is the mob. Wouldn't it be ironic—or at least fitting—if the kid from the long line of lawyers, the one who didn't quite cut it for law school, the one who began her a career on a dare, could be the only person who had a shot at an innocent man?

Yes, yes, I really could do it. Jack had known for certain before I did; he wouldn't have dragged himself here in the first place if he didn't.

Come on, you sons o' bitches! Do you want to live forever?

I guess not. I put down the half-consumed glass, walked over to Roberto, and told him I was flying home.

3

THE SECRET DOSSIER

I stood next to Jack in the sterile metro stop, the concrete arches soaring over our heads, survelliance cameras blinking, and digital signs flashing NEXT TRAIN, 3 MINUTES. What the D.C. mass transit system lacks in aesthetics it compensates for in safety; there hasn't been a violent crime on it in thirty years.

I had been back only two days, my body was still heavy with jet lag, and I hadn't finished unpacking. Roberto had dropped me off at the airport in Rome with a parcel of Sant'Eustachio coffee, wrapped in brown paper. "Come back when it's gone," he said. It was a small package. When I met Jack at the gate, he thrust his hands deep into the pockets of his leather coat and muttered, "Mr. Wonderful isn't coming?"

"Don't be mean," I had said. "He's got a job, too." Jack had rolled his eyes but, mercifully, kept his mouth shut.

Quite a feat, considering the flight was over eight hours, by the end of which my face was pale and puffy, my eyes shot with telltale red. I knew better than this. A governor's widow once told me to cry in the shower so my face wouldn't swell.

Oh, I had come back to a mess. Over a million people out of work, including a chunk of reporters and producers, and if there is one creature worse than a fame-loving journalist it is an unemployment-fearing journalist. Foreclosures and personal bankruptcies had replaced irrational exuberance in the headlines. If it had looked bad when I left for Italy, it was downright ugly now.

Most people don't read newspapers. Journalists do. So reporters report for reporters: a tight, controlled circle. A few cardinal rules, though. Number one is: Protect your own. Think of the television hostess, the one with the soothing voice and the smooth complexion, who in her youth rendezvoused with a White House press chief *and* a secretary of state. Or the floppy fop reporter, famous for the nights he spent broadcasting from beneath a desk in Baghdad during bombing raids, who now tempers his nightly newscasts with three martinis. These aren't ringing any bells? Of course not. Cannibalism is strictly frowned upon.

But there is a way to get kicked out of the pack: if the others are scared. And they were scared. Certainly the White House spokesman had shaken them up, only two years before, when he warned them to "be very, very careful" with what they said and wrote.

So the one entity that should have watched Lyle's back—his newspaper, for which he had slaved through seventeen-hour days and routinely aborted vacations—abandoned him. "We had a scorpion in our shirt," wrote the editor in chief, a legendary investigative journalist who had brought down a presidency decades ago. He added, in a printed apology to his paper's readers, "Gold is a man without honor who operated out of hostility and contempt."

The frenzy was in full swing, complete with ready-made headlines, FOOL'S GOLD! and TARNISHED GOLD. The press had been merciless in its single-minded pursuit of their common goal: Gold needed to be sufficiently and publicly damned, sacrificed to save the integrity of all the good journalists in the world.

I had a pretty clear mission: All I had to do was figure out who had framed Lyle and then get him (or her, or them) to confess—and somehow, in the process, flip public opinion.

Right. I squared my shoulders, which were still stiff from the plane, and scanned the résumé of Lyle's attorney. At least he had managed to get one name on his side. Edgar Demange was a fossil, but he certainly had notched an impressive string of victories. He had specialized in the tough cases, kicking off his career by defending a gospel singer who had killed the man he claimed stole his girlfriend.

Some might say Demange got a lucky break when Hollywood adapted the kid's story to create a hugely popular television series, but Demange was plain good, too. I remembered hearing my grandfather say as much. And this from a man with a coup of his own. Getting Giancana Outfit cohort Johnny Russo acquitted of murder by reason of temporary insanity induced by *E. coli* still stood as one of the least likely outcomes in recent trial history.

Odd cases beget odd behavior. Before Gold, in his dotage and semiretirement, Demange had been busy carving out a new role for himself as the patron saint of that vastly underrated vegetable, the potato ("Everything on our dinner table is derived from the potato"), but occasionally he remembered his roots and returned to law.

"I think this guy might be a little eccentric," I told Jack.

Jack gulped his deli coffee. "He's old guard, Kate. Old guard, new guard. We've got 'em all with this. Which reminds me—I've found us a new contact: John Jaures. Great guy. War correspondent for *USA Today*; now he's in the D.C. bureau. I think he's our man to put on the unchecked angles."

"You want to feed a new guy all our inside stuff—well, once we've *got* inside stuff?" I demanded. "You've lost it. No way."

"He's hungry, Kate. He's back in town after five years and he wants a big story. He's not tainted like the rest."

"I was thinking about Maurice Barres." I was loyal to Maurice, who, after all, had written the first item about our firm:

We hear that Washington's hottest non-couple, the beautiful brainy Kate Boothe and ladykiller Jack Vanzetti, are
hanging out their shingle on K Street.

Neither description was exactly accurate, but this was the
quote that decided our image.

"Come on," Jack cajoled. "Maurice is great, but we need
someone fresh, someone who isn't cozy with the rest of the
press or the pols. Maurice is in the club. We need someone
who'll owe us, not the other way around. Plus, this guy's
been shot at and shot up; he had guns at his head and the
shit beaten out of him in Peshawar."

"If a war zone's the prerequisite for this, we're in bigger
trouble than I thought."

"We'll have dinner at my place tomorrow," Jack said. "I'll
make risotto."

Risotto was Jack's tool of, alternately, seduction and
negotiation. It was the one thing he took his time with, and
he liked to ply me with it whenever we were divvying up our
workload. In this case, it was fairly obvious. I would take the
lead on the Gold affair while Jack handled our other clients.
Either way, we would have no lives beyond the office if Lyle
Gold and Edgar Demange signed on to our plan.

. . .

Demange, who lived in New York City, had borrowed office
space near Capitol Hill. This was an unusual choice. Most
Washington lawyers huddle downtown. But the location

made sense: direct access to Congress and all the other influence makers. Still, considering the glamorous digs Demange must have lorded over in his heyday, this was a comedown. The room was in the basement of a nonprofit foundation, the rust-colored carpeting pocked with cigarette burns and littered with files and law books. A wilted fern—how do you kill a fern?—stood near a metal desk, and a phone was ringing nonstop. Demange himself was nowhere to be found. We stood for a few moments, listening to the phone ring.

"The old guard doesn't believe in answering machines," Jack observed. And of course, just then, we heard Demange's gravelly voice behind us.

"We believe in answering *services*."

"Maybe you should get one that works," Jack said under his breath.

Demange brushed past us to his desk. "Sit, sit. Can I get you some water, Jack? And Kate. I presume you are the famous Kate."

"You're the famous one, Mr. Demange," I replied.

He wasn't looking at me, but he nodded his head approvingly. "True, true. Don't believe that inane Warhol statement about fifteen minutes. Fame is a constant effort." He handed each of us thin paper cups of water. There was a white hair floating on the top of mine. The cup was shaped like a cone; I couldn't even put it down on—well, there was no table—the floor. I discreetly poured it into the fern.

"So you think you can help Lyle," Demange said.

"We know we can," Jack replied. "I laid it all out in my proposal."

Demange sat down in his chair, which creaked ominously. "How fortunate for us. What leads you to believe Lyle has any interest in hiring you?"

"He's been indicted," Jack said.

"Not convicted."

"Let's be honest about that," Jack countered.

"Look, my young friend." Demange leaned forward. "I'd been around the block a hundred times before you were even born. It's not going to be enough to kick sand into a few faces."

"What does that have to do—" Jack was looking distinctly cranky. My cue to interrupt.

"Now, wait a minute," I began. "We're not saying you need us to win in court. That's your realm. But this is a two-front war you're fighting. We're here to help out on the PR front."

Jack crossed his arms and looked at me. Demange was clearly enjoying this.

"What we want, Mr. Demange, is your—and Lyle's—permission to start the rehabilitation, so to speak. We're good at this. You've got our record. And, as you know," I said, "considering how helpful a certain television series was in getting you a retrial once upon a time, public opinion can help swing a lot of other things your way. Our objective is to be winners as far as *public opinion* goes."

Demange folded his hands on his stomach, thoughtfully

pursing his lips. "Miss Boothe," he began, "I know about the privacy law you got passed ten years ago, when you defended that young man accused of date rape. Nice work, elegantly done. Must have made your family proud. And I knew your grandfather, God rest his soul. I know your father, your uncles."

I had not been aware of this, and to be truthful I found it disconcerting. My family had never had any connection to my business before, and now would not be the ideal time to break the precedent.

"So you're not following in their path," Demange continued, "but I would wager, after what I've seen, that you're as wily as they are. Plus, you're skinny, and you're easy on the eyes." He paused and stared pointedly at me. "This is one of the most futile cases I have ever seen. I am not saying I think Lyle Gold gave precious secrets to the Chinese. I'm too old to defend another guilty bastard. I don't need the money and I don't need the acclaim. I accepted this case with one reservation: I would be the first to judge Lyle Gold if I found any evidence that made me question his word. But what I underestimated was the fact that people don't simply doubt his innocence but vehemently believe in his guilt.

"I know the Boothe boys. They've got the mettle for this. You come from the same stock, but I don't know if you do. You'll take a hit. Because you're a girl, it'll be worse. But on the plus side, the people who are eviscerating Lyle aren't expecting you. They may not know what to do when a sharpie with legs steps up. They'll figure it out, though. How do I know that when it gets bad you'll stick with us?"

It was a fair question. I didn't mind, but Jack was a study of indignation. I had to respond quickly.

"Mr. Demange," I began, "like my uncles, I run marathons."

"Do you finish?" he asked.

"Always." The fact that I had finished five in under three hours and forty minutes would undoubtedly be lost on this audience. "It's all in the training."

Demange seemed convinced. "Go to it," he growled. "You need Lyle's permission; I'll make sure you get that. I'll give you what information I have. You see what you can do with it."

. . .

Jack thought the meeting had gone well. Oh, sure it had. But now I was obligated to call my parents with a full update; they were under the impression that I was still in Rome, attending cooking school. I had spent most of the past decade proving my independence, and I didn't see them very often. Coming from not one but two lawyers, the string of inevitable questions about who I was dating and how I was eating inevitably felt like a cross-examination. I did call often, offering short, superficial assurances of my general well-being. But now I was going to have to give them the mother of all briefings before they heard from

Demange directly. I shuddered. Well, maybe I didn't have it so bad. Jack's father is a rocket scientist.

Jack had a meeting on the other side of Capitol Hill, and so there I was, standing in his taxi's wake and stewing in my thoughts, when my foot was very nearly pierced by a stiletto. It belonged to Mimi Ryan.

"Hi, sweetie!" She tossed her hair over her shoulder. I inwardly cringed; I had forgotten how shrill her voice was. "It's been a while. How pretty you look!"

That was a lie. Jet lag had given me the coloring of an aspirin. But it was typical. Mimi (pronounced *Mah*-mee; her mother was from Louisiana) had always been an air-kiss cotillion aspirant. She was an amazingly successful recruiter for our sorority, although we tried not to talk about *those* days too much.

"You look very nice too," I replied. And she really did, aside from the obvious signs of an eating disorder. It is said that the camera adds ten pounds, which is why Mimi started sticking her finger down her throat after every meal. Jack, toward the end of their ill-fated fling, asked if she had rickets. But Mimi loved the pundit circuit and made the sacrifice.

Mimi curled her scarlet lips into a smile. "I haven't seen you for a long time. Rumor had it you went into rehab or something."

I returned the gesture. We might have our differences now, but back when we were decent and young, Mimi had, in truth, saved me. After graduation she had resolved to join the Junior League, land a powerful husband, and become a media sensation, not necessarily in that order. I had been rejected by every law school I had applied to, my childhood home in Lincoln Park became a cookie-cutter prefab in the suburbs, and my grandfather had decided I should marry the son of his law partner. When Mimi told me she was leaving Chicago for the nation's capital, I immediately hitched a ride.

It was a debt she felt had not been repaid. I decided to let the rehab comment slide. Anyone who went back as far as Mimi did was entitled to a little slack. "Just some much-needed zen time. I've been in Italy."

Mimi nodded perfunctorily. "Oh, yes. Nice. We've all been caught up in this Gold affair. I'm sure *you* know all about it, naturally." She giggled. "I'm doing some polling on it now for the White House."

I was impressed. A White House connection was a big deal. Mimi played it for all it was worth. With a flourish, she checked her watch, which was gold and studded with dia-monds. "Uh-oh—I'm late for a meeting there right now, in fact. I'd say call me when you get a chance, but these days it's easier if *I* call *you* when *I* get the chance." She bussed my cheek and waved as she walked away. "Give my best to Jack!"

I had one person (besides my parents) on my must-contact list for the afternoon. Maurice Barres was surprised to hear from me, but his voice turned weary when he gleaned the reason for my call.

"This is really resurrecting the dead," he told me.

"There are people on TV I haven't seen for years. Your old girlfriend Mimi Ryan is all over it."

"Of course she is," I said. The chattering class never changed much; the seating chart was merely rearranged once in a while. But then Maurice lowered his voice; I could barely hear him over the din of the newsroom.

"This is getting whipped up for a reason," he said. "This is Truman Pace's rainmaker."

That was one factor I hadn't considered: Truman Pace, the Mouth That Roared, according to his syndicated radio show. The acidic old burnout wore sweater vests, which ordinarily suggest a certain degree of affability; cashmere can take the edge off the devil. But it didn't much help Truman. Half the time, he mumbled so thickly—the result of a decadelong cocaine binge—that you couldn't understand him. But sometimes, when he was having an on day, the radio still sizzled. He used to be much bigger, over a decade ago, influencing politics and pop culture. So like many others, Truman must have seen in Lyle Gold an opportunity for renewed relevance.

"Oh, and there's something else," Maurice said. "Hollywood's gotten involved."

"As always." I sighed.

"No, they're not trying to prove they're smart this time. This is all about being patriotic, if you can believe that. There's money being raised all over LA against this Gold guy."

"Are you kidding?"

"They're falling all over themselves to prove how American they are," Maurice said. "Hey, you know what it's like these days. Here's a guy who most people think committed treason. How many people do you know who have had affairs or stolen something? But treason—well, that's different. It's a scandal we can all feel good about, even puff ourselves up with superiority. No one's felt that way about themselves for a long while. Nothing seems to be going right—except that this bad guy has been caught red-handed."

I paused, guessing the answer before I asked. "Who's behind the Hollywood effort?"

"Gluck."

Melvin Gluck, the producer with a famously vile temper (legend had it that he once threw a Chagall at his vice president of marketing, who was pregnant at the time), could always be counted on for contributions at every election cycle, but he definitely expected a return on his investment. He had a lot of money and a taste for power.

Truman Pace and Melvin Gluck. Lyle didn't stand a chance. But it was even worse than I thought. I phoned everyone I could think of: the jolly political columnist, who laughingly described the antics of Pace and company but soberly added, "This is where the rubber meets the road"; the music photographer, who told me that from her Brooklyn neighborhood to concerts nationwide, she had seen every stripe of person denounce Lyle; and the society matron—my father's childhood sweetheart—who viewed the situation from her Park Avenue apartment and reported little doubt among the swells that Lyle was guilty ("This has been better than a face-lift for a lot of people"). I sat back in my office, rapping a pen against the edge of my desk. Last man standing, all right.

■   ■   ■

"You'll never guess who I saw today," I told Jack, leaning on his stainless-steel bar stool. "Mimi Ryan."

Jack was uncorking a bottle of wine. He screwed his mouth into a tortured grimace. "Ah, the toxic bachelorette."

I laughed. Washington women didn't know what hit them with Jack. There was no mistaking the milk-fed midwestern roots, but this only added to his appeal—saved him, in truth, from crossing the line into the domain of the overly slick. No hair gel or trendy eyeglasses for Jack; he relied on a good haircut, a strong chin, and a classic sartorial sense to separate him from the pack.

And excellent taste in wine. He poured me a glass of a dry white, and as I lifted it to my lips I suddenly remembered one loose end still dangling in Rome.

"I forgot to cancel drinks with Reiff," I said. "I was supposed to meet him at the Hotel Eden."

"Who?" Jack was vigorously hacking up red and white onions.

"The guy in the State Department who hates his life," I reminded him.

But Jack was preoccupied, throwing the onions into the pot. "You know what that is?" He pointed at the pieces while stirring. The skins began to brown and soften in the olive oil. "*That's* love."

"My last taste of it?"

"You know it, babycakes." Jack kept his eye on the contents in the pot. He swirled his glass of wine for a moment, then tossed in four handfuls of arborio rice. Jack's apartment had the requisite bachelor gear—black leather couch, chrome tables, copy of *Atlas Shrugged* strategically placed near his bed (because, he maintained, girls read *Atlas Shrugged*, not *The Fountainhead*)—but his kitchen defied stereotype. What do most guys have in their cupboards: potato chips, beer, crusty mustard jars? Even Roberto only occasionally procured a box of pasta. Jack painstakingly brewed his own chicken stock every two months. What better way to a woman's heart?

"So," Jack began casually. "You heard from Roberto yet?"

"An e-mail." Disappointing, but thoroughly to be expected in this day and age. I know a couple who became engaged via the Internet.

"Hmm." Jack poured me another glass of wine. He looked at it carefully. "Good *cuisse*. Unusual in a white, but sexy. Very sexy." Thankfully, the ringing buzzer interrupted his wine commentary.

John Jaures. The man walked in with three Cohibas, threw them at Jack, and announced, "My illegal drug of choice." He looked just like you would imagine a post–Cold War correspondent: shaggy hair, unshaven cheeks, khaki pants, and a blue T-shirt with IRON CITY BEER stamped across the front. Draped over his arm was the stereotypical trench coat (he had left the flak jacket at home).

At thirty-four, Jaures had already landed in most of the hot spots. In fact, if you flip through that book *The World's Most Dangerous Places*, you've pretty much seen the itinerary. He had (I would later learn) a scar on his upper right arm from a bullet in Bosnia, which he incorporated into a tattoo of the French Foreign Legion Second Division patch (their doctors had saved him). After stints in Kazakhstan and Uzbekistan, he chain-smoked Russian cigarettes, which reeked but, he claimed, gave him a hell of a buzz. And he evidently hadn't reacquainted himself with the American custom of using deodorant. He told me later this was because for two years in Kosovo he had used an old pickle barrel as a bathtub, and after twenty-four months of stinking like pickles he wanted to smell like himself. But at the time all I could think was, *This* is the guy we're counting on in the media?

John handed me a piece of paper. "My good-faith gesture." It was a photocopy of a letter. Handwritten, which is unusual enough these days, and copper-plate penmanship at that:

My very dear friend,

Last night I ended up calling the doctor, who has forbidden me to go out. Since I am unable to visit you tomorrow, I am asking you to my home in the morning, since G has brought me many things of interest and since we have only ten days we will have to divide the work.

Try, then, to tell the ambassador that you can't go up.

All yours,
Mao

"Who's Mao?" I asked.

"A top aide to Ambassador Xianxu, but obviously Mao isn't his real name," John said.

"*His* name?" I asked.

"The staff is mostly male. What I do know is—"

"Who writes crap like My very dear friend?" Jack interrupted, looking over my shoulder while he stirred.

"The envelope was addressed to an aide at the Pakistani embassy," John continued. "Saeed Khan."

Jack and I stared at him. "You're kidding," I said finally.

"Sordid, ain't it?" John leaned back in the chair. "This would be a key piece of the so-called smoking gun, or *dossier*, as they're calling it in certain branches of our government."

An American was accused of selling military secrets to a Chinese diplomat who was having an affair with a Pakistani adjutant. How titillating that it was a gay affair; that alone made it a nightmare for the embassies of Pakistan and China (imagine the reports back to Islamabad and Beijing). What made it a nightmare for *our* government, aside from the selling of secrets, was the inevitable geopolitical ripple effect.

"Where did you get this?" I demanded.

John smiled. "I never reveal my sources, Kate. Bottom line, though, is that someone *did* get hold of relatively sensitive documents, and those documents *did* end up in the hands of the Chinese. My questions are: Who did it and what did he give?"

"And you don't think Lyle is the guy," I said.

"I'm leaning toward no," he replied. "I think this is an inside thing. Lyle's good, but he's not that good."

John shoveled risotto with his fork, bits of half-chewed rice falling from his open mouth, as he told us about the "secret dossier" that the military, through Lieutenant Joseph Henry, claimed to have assembled on Lyle. To the best of John's knowledge, no one outside of intelligence— even the grand jury—had gotten more than a glimpse of the documents. The letter to Saeed Khan was the one bit that had been leaked to him. A single character *G* hardly seemed indictment-worthy, but that was just my humble opinion.

"I'm still trying to figure out who all the players are," John admitted. "March Madness is easier to follow."

"Why is the military involved?" Jack asked. "Isn't the FBI checking it out?"

"You know how streamlined these things get," John said sarcastically. "Twenty-two different federal agencies claim to be investigating it, as usual. But because of the Special

Ops angle, it seems to have fallen primarily to military intelligence. The State Department is involved too, since it was a deputy secretary who was one of the first to see the e-mails."

"What about the White House?" Jack refilled his glass.

I mentioned running into Mimi. John didn't seem surprised. "Straight out of the playbook. She's polling for August Mercer."

"These days, he *is* the White House," Jack said.

The power behind the throne, I guess you would say. August Mercer was brilliant, a big reason the current president was where he was to begin with. Mercer officially served as a White House adviser, but in reality he controlled everything from policy to fund-raising. He had made his fortune through a direct mail company, which he sold when he joined the president's campaign. *Direct mail* is another way of saying *junk mail*, since that is what most Americans do with campaign literature. Nonetheless, Mercer believed with certainty that he was put on this earth and into a position of power to improve the lives of his countrymen through absolute morality, and his zeal translated into some ruthless campaign maneuvers. He was unlikely to be a fun guest at dinner parties, but if *I* ever ran for office I might hire August Mercer. The man was a miracle worker.

So he had commissioned a project from Mimi. That didn't sound like Mercer. What was in it for him?

"We know it's not because he wants to get laid," John said. "That guy's a monk."

"He must not want it too secret. Mimi always blabs any

information she gets on television." The thought came to me as I spoke the words. "There you go."

"Instant media without the bother of a press release," John said. "Marvelous."

Jack poured us each a glass of grappa. "But why does someone like August Mercer even concern himself with this?"

"That could be my story right there," John said. "Or at least one of them."

As we clinked our glasses together, I tried not to think about Roberto. After all, I had work to do. Clearly, he realized this and quite considerately, then, hadn't called.

. . .

Peel an onion. Jack once had me take apart twenty Vidalia beauties for a dinner soiree he was throwing. It was a painstaking process, and not unlike what I did for a living. Take the Gold case: At the core, someone sold secrets; one layer, someone wanted that person to be identified as Lyle; another layer, others wanted to *believe* the traitor was Lyle; and so on. With each filmy piece ripped away, it became increasingly evident that all the elements were stacked against us. It wouldn't be enough for me to simply smile nicely and suck up to the right people. I needed to find out why the White House was conducting polls on Lyle Gold. I needed to get to August Mercer.

Now, Mercer had no reason to meet with me. I wasn't important in his world—in fact, I wasn't even on his radar screen. Why would a senior adviser to the president, the head of the newly created Office of Strategic Security Initiatives (a fancy way of saying he had carte blanche), so much as deign to talk with me?

Fortunately, my very best friend, Lili, happens to be the maître d' at the finest restaurant in town. Everyone who is anyone wants a table at Le Sénateur, the home of "*la cuisine du diplomate*," to quote Lili (subtle restaurant names rarely soar in this town; politicos and their ilk delight in places such as the Capitol Grille and the Caucus Room). The players in Washington might dismiss a maître d' as "the help," but Lili held a measure of power. If you wanted to eat at the restaurant—and everyone did—you had to go through her. That made the restaurant a marvelous way of tracking people.

Four days later Lili called me at the office. "Happy early birthday! Guess who's on the books today?" I made a note to give her a bottle of Krug for that one.

I was wearing a lightweight cashmere sweater and decided to add a scarf that my mother had given me as a birthday present last year; I had never worn it, because Hermès seemed uptight, especially when dappled with perfume bottles, but I dug it out of a deep desk drawer. "Loose and off-center," Jack advised, knotting it for me. And then I trotted off in the patent leather heels that I first wore the night Roberto and I had *prosecco* (they still weren't broken in; patent leather takes forever). Thus armed, I arrived at the restaurant at exactly the same time as the guest chef from France. The little man marched up to Lili, pointed to his glossy cookbook, which was graciously displayed at the front, and announced, "Zees ees zee book. I em zee cook. *Allons-y!*" She winked at me as she led him to the kitchen, along with the string of jet-lagged line cooks who accompanied him. So it was her second-in-command who took me to my table, which just happened to be right next to August Mercer's.

He was dissecting a pheasant, deep in conversation with renowned attorney Kent Brewster. This was another break; I knew Kent from various conversations in greenrooms around town. Talk-show panels are a marvelous way of networking.

Kent Brewster was just as plump as Mercer (no wonder universal health coverage never went anywhere; who in Washington wanted to subsidize all these walking heart attacks?) and he enjoyed some of the power, since he had pried pols of all stripes out of jams. He didn't acknowledge me, though, until Lili's version of the plowman's lunch—a plate of Blue Point oysters and a glass of champagne—hit my table. It was her favorite and best ice-breaking trick. Sure enough, Kent slid a bemused glance my way and paused between mouthfuls.

"It sure is a sad day when a beautiful young woman lunches alone, Katie," he said in his raspy voice.

"Don't worry about me, Kent," I replied. "The chocolate-covered strawberries come later."

August Mercer cracked a smile. "I don't believe we've met," he said.

"You haven't met the loveliest woman in Washington?" Kent was in full-blown good-ol'-boy form.

"Only in Washington?" I smiled as I lifted the glass of champagne.

"Well, August, I think we need to rectify this. Kate's one of the sharpest young bucks—well, does, I suppose—on K Street."

"So why don't I know you?" Mercer asked.

"You know our girl. Remember Frederick Banks?" Kent nudged him with his elbow.

"Remember him"—Mercer stabbed a fork into his pheasant—"I hired him."

Oh-my-oh-my, did my ears prick up. This was getting good.

"This is the young lady who saved his ass," Kent said.

Mercer regarded me a bit more closely. "Really? That *is* interesting."

"So what is my first client doing for you these days?" I asked, lifting an oyster to my lips.

"Working in my office," Mercer said vaguely, still staring at me.

"Freddy's a smart guy," I said. "In fact—"

The squat French chef himself suddenly barreled over to my table, slinging a small plate of caviar and crème fraîche pastries. "Zees eez for you," he announced sullenly. Lili must have put him up to it, I thought, and he clearly resented the fact that I wasn't anyone important. I smiled at him and, because I wanted him to realize I appreciated the gesture, mentioned that I thought his restaurant was better than any of the competition, including Les Crayères, a famous place in Reims that Lili had once dragged me to.

The chef squinted at me. "Where?"

"Les . . . Cray*ères*," I repeated hesitantly. It had Michelin stars! I decided to throw out the name of its chef. "Gérard Boyer."

The chef paused a moment, then, with a glint of recognition, he said, "Oh, Les *Cray*ères." As if one syllable made such a difference.

"Thank you . . ." I trailed off as he spun around and quickly walked back into the kitchen. I decided it might not be a bad idea to work on my pronunciation before attempting to drop any names again.

Kent Brewster and August Mercer were frowning in the direction of the kitchen.

"Damn frogs," Mercer said, gulping from his martini glass.

"We've saved their asses enough times over the years," Brewster added. "Don't you think twice about Frenchie, Kate. I don't like his food much anyway."

"Oh," I said. "That's too bad. I was going to offer you some of these." I gestured at the plate.

"In the interests of diplomacy," Mercer said, scooping up several pastries. "Kate, you should swing by my office sometime. See Freddy."

"Oh, Mr. Mercer, I would love to," I replied. "And I'd really love to meet with you too."

He passed me his card and said, "Call me."

Just like that, I was, possibly, useful to him. God bless good food. Maybe Jack was on to something, after all.

4

ALL YOURS AND ON THE MOUTH

I am not a morning person, which puts me at a disadvantage in a city like Washington. The bright-eyed bushy-tailed ones skip to their desks at dawn; I limp in a couple of hours after that, clutching my coffee. I hadn't gulped nearly enough of it when I saw the front page of the *New York Post* on my desk the next day. DEATH OF A DIPLOMAT blared the headline above the photo of a dashing young man, one Saeed Khan.

It can't be, I thought, setting down the cup. Khan was a common Pakistani name. So was Saeed.

Of course the *Post* would cover a subway accident—and this was a lurid one. The handsome young diplomat, based out of Washington, on his way to city hall to pick up his marriage license with his fiancée, who happened to be the daughter of the Pakistani ambassador to the United

Nations. His fiancée said he had felt faint, although hung over is more like it, since he had been out the night before with his friends for the distinctly American custom of celebrating the end of bachelorhood. He wasn't used to drinking much, of course. He told his fiancée he wanted to walk a bit to shake off the queasiness. They were in the Times Square station, the platform packed with grim commuters and bewildered tourists while a Russian played Chopin on his violin for quarters. The fiancée lost sight of Saeed Khan as he wandered away. A few minutes later, they found him on the tracks, crushed.

I must have grimaced. Just then Jack strolled in, his hair windblown (I bought plane tickets after every election cycle; Jack saved up and finally landed an Alfa Romeo). "You heard?" he asked, pushing his sunglasses up over his forehead.

"Lightning strikes. Subway accidents happen." I tried to sound casual. "There's not necessarily something sinister behind this."

"Maybe he killed himself," Jack suggested, "instead of getting married."

"Or maybe he fell," I said.

Jack shrugged. "Whatever. John's up in New York, checking it out."

"Saeed Khan could be just a sad footnote to the story," I said.

Jack waited a moment before he spoke. "John managed to get an interview with Khan before he died."

I raised my eyebrows. Maybe Jack was right about Jaures. "What did he say?"

"The only thing John would say is that we ought to check the Mao–Khan correspondence very very carefully, because that's what he's doing, too." Jack tossed his cup into my wastebasket before walking down the hall.

. . .

Deaths, of course, are bad. In my line of work, you can't help but think of conspiracies, induced suicides, murder. But I was not about to buy into this conceit quite yet. It was, I told myself, simply Saeed Khan's fate to fall off the platform, just as it was Lyle's fate, by virtue of his disposition and his profession, to be accused of treason.

Then again, according to the *Post*, that bastion of journalistic accuracy, Lyle Gold had been seen frequently in Saeed Khan's company. A convenient detail for the tub-thumpers like Truman Pace, who spent the morning's show railing against the barren soul known as Lyle Gold. I threw a wadded-up piece of paper at the radio. Lyle probably had been developing Khan as a source. That is how it is done.

I stared at a new piece of paper, sparkling clean, next to the stack of notes I had been amassing over the past few days and tapped my pen on the desk. All right. At the heart of the Gold Affair lay the actual accusation, on top of that, the grand jury indictment. Then there was the war fought out in the press and in politics. The layers were forming. Think onions.

Two key departments were involved: State and Defense, departments that traditionally loathed each other. The e-mail originated within the State Department; it contained military information. Now consider the Pentagon, shaken for nearly thirty years by a history of vague battles, lost wars, and secret skirmishes, not to mention a string of humiliations—questionable arms deals gone awry, soldiers slaughtered in unexpected pockets of urban warfare—so well documented by the media (and by Lyle Gold in particular, I found, as I finally read through my ex's journalistic accomplishments). Even now, in this hyperpatriotic climate, the military was wary of the press. Extremely selective information, spoon-fed to the public, was fine; no information was even better. Not many people, journalists or otherwise, objected to this. To do so appeared unseemly.

I uncapped the pen and wrote down one name: Lieutenant Joseph Henry. The key player in Lyle's indictment, whose job fell under military intelligence, Henry understandably would have been concerned about a rat in his midst. And if he had higher aspirations, times were very good indeed for the ambitious. Henry, a loyal marine, no doubt had observed the upward trajectory of other military-cum-diplomat types who had cut to the head of the line via three simple steps: Unquestioningly fulfill one's duty; make a few connections in diplomatic circles; use these connections to secure a nice private-sector offer upon retirement.

I started paging through the stack of research. There had to be something to point me in a direction, *any* direction.

To my delight—I get a thrill from the little things—I stumbled upon a quote that Henry had given shortly after Lyle's indictment. "Like many people, I become concerned when principles are at stake. There are those who are the standard-bearers, and we must rise to the occasion." Well, here was something I could work with, stretch and pull. Few people regard "standards" as flexible. An established code must be protected by those who by virtue of their upbringing, social standing, and sympathies are qualified as guardians. These wise men, the old boys' network, see themselves as the embodiment of such principles; it is their birthright.

I flipped back quickly to an article that mentioned, fleetingly, the deputy secretary of state, upon whose desk the Mao–Khan correspondence had landed. Here was a man who, interestingly enough, had received the appointment through a professional friendship with August Mercer. The deputy secretary claimed that, despite this tie, he believed he could become that rare individual who rises above party affiliation to permanent State Department status. Well now, this deputy secretary might observe the world from above the slope of his patrician nose with an unshakable sense of personal destiny, but he had already presided over *three* near disasters. A man with a blemished record, if he wants to keep his job—not to mention make it to the next regime—needs an unmistakable triumph, something that splashes his name in a kinder, brighter light across the newspapers. Instead, he had a spy.

So imagine the man's reaction to the lurid Mao–Khan letters: *"When will you come to bugger me? My darling, all yours and on the mouth,"* and then the reply! *"Yes, little red dog, I shall come for your pleasure. Oh, the filthy beast. All yours, still coming, Mao."* It was a little much for me, but I am sure it works for someone. I did think, though, how marvelously ironic: The actual espionage might have taken place through e-mail, but it was correspondence doing business amid a flurry of love letters, all sent through the postal system and occasionally hand-delivered, that tipped off the State Department that something was terribly amiss.

Most people convinced of the moral superiority of their position, when finding themselves with their backs against the wall, will have no trouble rationalizing what they do in order to preserve that position. I was reminded of a lecture given years ago by my most difficult professor, Joan Picquart, now of the State Department herself, in which she expounded on this very subject. *"Those who believe in moral absolutes use a whole series of alibis, which to them are not 'alibis' per se; they believe these alibis to be the truth; therefore, these people are not lying."* At the time, I had wondered what kind of people she was talking about. Not anymore.

. . .

I left my office, figuring I would head over to Le Sénateur. I would be a bit early for lunch, but no matter. It was a Thursday.

A brigade of briefcases marched through downtown, as

men in uniforms of khakis, blue blazers, and red ties and women in fruit-colored suits festooned with large gold buttons hurried from one "urgent" meeting to the next. But one figure stood out. There is a marked difference between a blazer-khaki ensemble and a dark tailored suit, especially in the spring. The lone suit, standing in front of the Corcoran Museum, bore an uncanny resemblance to Reiff Prouty. I stopped for a moment—my instinct was, in truth, to duck, since I *had* stood him up for drinks. But Reiff disappeared into the crowd before I had the chance to do the honors. I blinked. Maybe I was seeing things.

Lili was conducting a final check of the reservation list when I walked into the restaurant. Uniformed busboys scuttled from one cream-linen-covered table to the next, rattling silver and glass. Lili weaved through them and met me at the door, her naturally blond hair tied in a fashionably disheveled knot.

"Tell me you're not eating here," she said, chewing the color off of her lips. Right before every lunch and dinner rush, she is always nervous. She had already ruined her nails.

"At the bar," I said helpfully.

"Oh, thank God. We're so overbooked. The FBI director's wife called to reserve a table for lunch. Who calls an hour before lunch for a reservation? But I don't feel very good about having to tell her no." Lili laughed faintly. She was scanning the empty restaurant, mentally choreographing the seating arrangements. It was a joke between the two of us that it was not for nothing that her last name was Parry.

Lili and I had met on a bike tour of Champagne four years earlier. We had been the only single girls—well, young women—who dared to cycle *sans* significant others over the rolling chalk hills of northern France and learn all about the bubbly wonders from the locals.

"Oh, also you should know that irritating little man is already on his second martini." Lili had lowered her voice and was nodding toward the rest room. Then she hurried off to the front of the room to mull over her book again.

The bartender gave me a warning glance as I slid onto a leather stool, but before I could register its significance a sagging sack of a man plopped himself in the seat next to me.

"My *my*, Miss Katie Boothe, how *brilliant* to see *you* here." Lewis Tap, a lobbyist from Texas who spoke, incredibly, in a British accent, brushed a lock of sandy hair from his eyes. He opened his mouth, and I steeled myself. "I have a new *joke* for you," he said. He always did, some ribald tale he evidently thought made him look clever.

"If I buy you a martini, will you not tell it?" I asked. The bartender coughed and slid me a glass of champagne.

"Only if it's a *dirty* martini." Lewis Tap giggled. "Kate, have you heard about this *spy* business? It's the most *exciting* thing to happen in this town in *ages*."

"The Lyle Gold situation." I nodded.

"Well, *I've* heard something *you* probably haven't." Lewis Tap's tiny blue eyes glittered. "About Mao. The Chinese switch-hitter."

"I thought he was gay," I said, draining my glass.

"No no *no*. He cut *quite* a swath up and down Massachusetts Avenue, if you know what I *mean*: men, women; it didn't matter as long as they were *pretty*." Again, the giggle. "And he is possibly the *sloppiest* spy in the *history* of espionage."

Lewis sipped loudly for dramatic effect.

"You know *how* the State Department got their hands on all those *graphic* love letters? From Mao's *wastebasket*! It's true! He had the habit of throwing away *everything*: love letters, even hard copies of e-mails—and for God's sake *who* runs off hard copies of e-mails and then throws them *away*, into the trash can at his desk? At *least* he could have tossed the scraps in a *different* trash can! So our aspiring little spy, depending on his *mood*, I suppose, would tear up papers in six bits or four. He did this with copies of his *own* letters and with letters he received from his myriad lovers, including—" and here Lewis Tap raised his martini glass in salute—"the *unfortunate* Saeed Khan."

I sat silent for a moment. Lewis Tap is a lot like a tabloid; much as I want to dismiss everything that comes out of his mouth, his tales usually hold at least an element of truth.

"Is Mao still at the embassy?" I asked.

"Oh, *no*. No, the ambassador dispatched *him* back to China, *pronto*."

"And among these letters was the damning *G* missive," I said.

"*Evidently*." Lewis leered. "And a hard copy of an e-mail from Lyle Gold *himself*."

"And how did the State Department get all these letters?"

"A very patriotic cleaning lady," Lewis said. "That's what I heard."

A *cleaning lady* scooped out torn papers, the incriminating letter, and the hard copies of e-mails from Lyle Gold's account? Good God, how amateur could this operation possibly get? Just where the hell were all my tax dollars going?

I went home early and laced up my running shoes for the first time in weeks. Usually I spend my summer halfheartedly training for a fall marathon; if I'm serious about it, I abstain from wine. But the Gold Affair meant I would not have time to rack up the proper mileage. I needed to clear my head, though. Jack always told me it was a measure of my madness that I depend on long-distance running to do so.

Pounding along the path beside the Potomac, I reviewed the facts. Espionage indeed takes place; someone, an American, is selling secrets to Mao, one half of a diplomatic duo who each has his reasons for becoming a spy cowboy— personal advancement at the very top of the list, of course; the real spy, at some point, picks as a pretense to dispatch information the name of a journalist known to be a gadfly; a cleaning lady, paid off by (I would suspect) the State Department, turns up scraps of love letters, printed e-mails, and the *G* letter; the evidence, the dossier, is handed over to the deputy secretary of state and to Henry, because he is in military intelligence and because the information deals with Special Operations. The story leaks, the story breaks. And here we are.

Winded by mile five, I leaned over and placed my hands on my knees, trying to catch my breath.

・ ・ ・

Do any of us really look forward to seeing a former significant other? We might have our fantasies: the toad who once crushed our fragile emotions now gaping as we cruise past in our 1956 Porsche roadster, fat and balding as we sail past swathed in chic clothing accessorized with a movie star, or something along those lines. Jack once ran into the woman who broke his heart in high school. "If I'd known she was going to end up with a mustache and an extra hundred pounds, I wouldn't have been so upset back then," he told me. Basically, it is a depressing enterprise, which is why I never look back. No second chances, no platonic friendships. The past is past.

Except when it becomes our future. In spite of all the years that had gone by and all the successes, my heart beat uncontrollably fast as Jack and I entered the prison and frankly I wanted to throw up. Oh, I knew Lyle would give us the go-ahead—Demange had prepped him, as promised, and what options did he have at this point? But I was nervous nonetheless.

Jack glanced at me as we signed in. "Are you all right?" he asked. "I can do most of the talking if you want."

"That's not a bad idea," I muttered. "But behave."

Steel doors clanged behind us as we were led into the visitation room. We sat in plastic chairs, separated from the prisoner side by a plexiglass wall but connected by a phone. It was exactly like a scene from a television crime drama. And then the door opened, and Lyle, with guards on either side, rattled into the room, shackled and cuffed. The only thing missing was a ball and chain. Considering he had only been indicted, this struck me as particularly excessive; besides, where was he going to *go*? His naturally pale complexion looked ashen and he had lost a bit of weight. But it was the deadness of his eyes that struck me. This was not the man I knew.

Lyle sat down and picked up the phone.

"How are you, Lyle," Jack asked perfunctorily.

"Not great," he replied. He avoided my eyes.

"So Demange spoke to you," Jack began. "I guess he told you we'd like to help out."

"I'm not sure what you can do," Lyle said. "I have a lawyer."

"You wanted a firm like ours on your team," Jack reminded him. Lyle didn't say anything, and I saw that Jack was growing impatient. Reflexively, I grabbed the phone.

"I *know* you didn't do this, Lyle," I said, with as much conviction as I could summon in such a place.

Lyle looked at his hands. "Thanks."

I plowed on. "We are going to win this. Demange will do his job in the federal courts. We'll do our part in the court of public opinion."

Lyle fell silent for a moment, which seemed interminable since our five minutes were ticking away, and then he said, "Kate, everything I've got is paying off Demange. I don't see how I can do this too." His voice trailed off.

"Don't worry about it. Jack and I aren't looking to profit from this"—Jack kicked me in the shins—"*now*." I winced.

"I don't think you understand what you're up against," Lyle said.

"We understand better than you did," Jack said under his breath. Thankfully, Lyle could not hear him.

"It's not pretty," I admitted. "But why not let us take them on. At least a try."

Lyle regarded me bitterly. "They've made things up. That marine lieutenant, calling me a traitor! This 'evidence' they've come up with. I sent Mao a couple e-mails about interviewing him, and it's enough to land me here? And then your buddy Freddy Banks came for a visit. 'Hiya, pal, why don't you tell me what happened?' What happened? I'm not even sure what happened!"

Jack tapped my knee at the mention of Freddy Banks. It was a tremendous amount of interest for a mid-level White House aide to display.

"Lyle, we will—" I began, but Lyle was on a tear.

"Those people don't know me. They don't *want* to know me. They *hate* me. You really think you can fight *that*?"

He paused again and noticed the guards, who had moved closer. He shrugged. Our time was up.

"Go for it, Kate," he said. "I hope you're as smart as you think you are."

He shuffled out the door, and I slammed down the phone.

"Well," Jack said, "he hasn't lost any of his charm."

5

ALL ABOUT ME

Ten years ago, I got lucky. Not long after Mimi Ryan and I arrived in Washington and went our separate ways, I was renting a room in a boardinghouse (yes, those still exist), and in order to eat I used to crash receptions on Capitol Hill. Some were better than others. At a particularly note-worthy affair (well-stocked bar, enormous boiled pink shrimp, barrel-chested congressmen slandering each other sotto voce and cutting deals a notch louder), I met Freddy Banks. He sauntered up to me like the hotshot legislative assistant he was, brandished his gilt card, which certified him as a member of the speaker's staff, and asked for mine. I didn't have one, of course, and he was such a condescending jerk about it that I had fake business cards printed that very night, labeling myself a consultant. Why not? I wasn't sure what they did, but Capitol Hill seemed to be crawling with them.

I dropped one off at his office the next day; the day after that, Wonder Boy lost his job when graffiti appeared on the bathroom walls of the Capitol building, labeling him a "rapist." Freddy didn't waste any time putting my card to use; he called me that afternoon, explaining that the accusation was old, dating from his sophomore year of college, and that he had been acquitted. Someone obviously didn't buy this and had chosen the most public court of all to try the case again. Freddy Banks wanted his name back, and because he had limited resources he came to me.

I wasn't asking too many deep questions. The job market was looking bleak; I had worn out two pairs of heels and passed out three hundred obviously unread résumés. I wanted to be idealistic, a quality my family was not known for, and maybe I didn't think out all my reasons. But at the time, I decided to do it because even a nominal fee was better than what I had on the books then.

I met Maurice Barres later that same week at another cocktail reception. Maurice told me it was the black velvet dress, really, that made him come over and offer me a glass of champagne. I told him the reason I took the champagne was the shiny laminated press credential clipped to his breast pocket that identified his affiliation with *The Washington Post*. I gave a quote or two, and the next day my name, my words, and my black dress were all prominently displayed in the Style section (I might have preferred my first appearance to be in harder news, but then again any mention was helpful). I hadn't noticed the photographer there; it was sheer luck that the photo was snapped after I had set down the champagne glass. Velvet is one thing, but combined with a glass of the bubbly it is a bit too Holly Golightly for a so-called political consultant trying to rehabilitate a rumored date rapist. In any case, the *Post* appearance set everything in motion.

The next day, reporters from the *Los Angeles Times* and *USA Today* called me, wanting to know, first, if I was the Girl in the Black Dress and, second, if I was representing Freddy Banks. On day two, my defense argument—that Freddy Banks had a right to privacy (with a dollop of defamation on the side)—hit coast-to-coast newspapers. On day three, the networks called. A fifteen-second sound bite (I counted) made me legitimate. Once you're in the Rolodex of one booker, you are in them all. I droned on and on until, frankly, I bored myself, but no one seemed to notice. The only responses I ever received about anything I had said on TV were in reference to what I wore or how my hair looked. And, believe me, this counted. A political columnist actually wrote, "She's got the appearance part down. Now she's just working on the smarts." (When Maurice Barres called me for a comment, I said the columnist needed to work on his manners.)

I was on television a lot, all right. It was the key. Here, again, I was lucky. The camera caught my face at all the right angles, and with the art of television makeup and lighting, my cheekbones seemed higher and my eyes glowed with flecks of previously undiscovered gold. Merely the trick of the lens. If it is true that the camera adds ten pounds, I didn't worry much about it; as Jack once observed, I have the metabolism of eleven hamsters. But the luckiest stroke of all was building the coalition—from legislative aides to women's rights groups to libertarians and so on—that bought into the privacy angle.

When I happened to run into the Speaker of the House, brandishing his cigar in one hand and Armagnac in the other, I could say with relative authority that mere weeks before the election, with his party expected to lose seats and his own negatives rising because many Americans didn't believe he could build bipartisan support, he shouldn't miss an opportunity to score points on an issue viewed as distinctly nonpartisan. I suggested he put up a privacy bill that was broad and went beyond just graffiti—wrap it into computer privacy and appeal to young people—and build it with the opposing party. The Speaker might not have been too keen to take advice from a neophyte ("It's the damnedest thing, Miss Boothe, but everyone seems to think they can do my job better than me"); however, he was fairly desperate and he bought into it. Lightning-fast by Washington standards, a privacy act named after my client sailed through the House and Senate and into law. It had no teeth, like most hastily passed legislation, but Freddy Banks came out of the signing ceremony with a souvenir pen.

Now, as I sat waiting for Freddy in the Old Executive Office Building, a stone sphinx that squats on Pennsylvania Avenue, where Freddy worked with the other government slaves, I wondered what he had done with the pen. Many members of Congress get theirs framed. His assistant had escorted me into the splendor of the Indian Treaty Room, with its spectacular tiles and murals (the president some-times held photo opportunities there; the vivid colors show well on film). It is one of the few impressive government rooms I have ever seen. Of course, in Hollywood's version of Washington, the lighting is always exquisite—all movies depict an Oval Office dotted with a string of spotlights— and the furnishings sumptuous. This may be one reason Americans generally believe they are being scammed by their elected officials. They see the silk couches, the thick Persian carpets, the polished tables. But if they knew what those offices really look like under fluorescent bulbs, they might actually feel let down. Government offices are rarely glamorous. Even the Oval Office, which is roped off like a period room in a museum when the president isn't there, is not nearly as fabulous as one might expect. I know I was dis-appointed when I saw that the rug spread across the wood floor was *pink*—pink with pale yellow highlights. It looked a lot like the rug I have in my bedroom.

Following August Mercer's suggestion, I had called Freddy's assistant, and I was all set for twenty minutes with him and Mercer. That is a big deal in our town. But

Freddy—excuse me, Frederick—Banks had already kept me *waiting* twenty minutes. The tactic was transparent: the old I-work-at-the-White-House-and-you-don't move. As I attempted to ignore the tick of my wristwatch, I tried hard to imagine why the infamously cunning Mercer had decided to anoint Freddy as his protégé.

I heard the click of the door, and Freddy made his entrance, carrying a coffee cup in each hand. Real cups, not paper. He looked the same—unremarkable face cut like stone—although maybe a bit more flesh around the jaw, and he carried himself with a new bravado.

"August won't be able to make it," he said right away. This was the first sign that the meeting was not going to go well.

"That's all right," I said, taking the cup he offered. "It's nice to see that you've ended up working for him. Quite a step up. He's supposed to be brilliant."

"He is," Freddy said. "He knows everything that happens in this town." He looked at me sharply, and I wondered what game was being played here.

"Look, Freddy, I'm not here because I want something," I said. "I think it's great you're working for August Mercer."

"Everyone thinks it's great," Freddy replied, "and everyone always wants something."

I paused a moment, tapping my fingernails on the bone china. Familiarity must have prompted Freddy to drop the veneer of politeness that such meetings usually required.

"Mr. Mercer asked me to call," I said carefully.

Freddy crossed his legs, flashing a rib of brown socks. His pants and shoes were black. "I realize that, but I know you. You're a busy person. You don't have much time for chatting."

"With the president's go-to guy, I sure do," I said, and this at least elicited a slight smile. "Those hand-blown light fixtures in my office don't come cheap, you know."

"Yes. You've done well by me." Freddy was right.

"I hear Mimi Ryan is doing well by you now," I said, taking a sip of the coffee. It was weak. "Specifically, I hear from her that she's running some numbers for you on the Gold Affair."

"I'm not sure about that."

"She seemed to be," I said. "Why are you polling about that?"

"It's a matter of international relations, espionage, and treason," Freddy said. "There's every reason for the White House to test the waters."

"Come on." I cocked an eyebrow. "You don't poll unless you're thinking about running on it. I remember when a client asked Jack to do the numbers on various girlfriends of his, just so he could figure out who would go over best with voters. He married the winner."

Freddy drew in a deep breath. "This White House, unlike its predecessor, does not leverage human misfortune for political gain."

"How lovely," I said. "You'd be the first."

"So young, so cynical." Freddy sighed.

"It kind of reminds me of your difficulties, way back when. A lot of people are scoring a lot of political points off it."

Freddy frowned slightly. "I would hardly compare my situation with that of a traitor."

"Oh, I don't know. You got booted out of the Speaker's office pretty fast for something you said you didn't do—"

"I didn't."

"—and the Speaker got on board once he looked at the poll numbers that showed seventy percent of Americans, give or take a few, were for privacy protection. Remember what a hot topic it was back then? The public questioning the effects of e-mail, the Internet, genetic mapping. Oh, and the speeches on the House floor. All those congress-men, railing about the Bill of Rights and the anti-Americanism of privacy invasion. Went over great in the home districts."

I smiled. Freddy did not.

"Let me see," I continued, staring thoughtfully at the gilded ceiling. "You're working for an administration that hasn't even begun to pass its agenda. If you want to do that, you need the mandate of the people. Kind of a problem these days, don't you think, with those voters so ticked off with everyone in general? It would really help to fix those people on one easily marketable issue—or person, even. An evildoer type. And here, conveniently, he is. If your polling proves it."

Freddy frowned more deeply, which had the unfortunate effect of reducing his eyes to slits. If I hadn't known him for so long, I would have thought him sinister.

"And what's your interest in the Gold Affair?" he demanded. "If he's your scapegoat too, why meet with me?"

"Because I don't think he's guilty."

"He's your client," Freddy realized aloud. "Interesting." He fell into a rare silence, so I knew he was turning it over in his mind, running the odds: *Can she or can't she?*

"Interesting that your boss isn't here," I said.

"He doesn't come to lower-level meetings," Freddy said. "Come on, Kate. You know that a couple of pleasantries at lunch don't equal face time."

"Yes, but then both of us have visited Lyle Gold, haven't we," I replied smoothly. "I thought it was really intriguing that a powerful guy like yourself would make a trip to see him. If your polling shows a 'traitor' works to your advantage, you might want to make sure that the accused believes his to be a hopeless case. Maybe he won't challenge the charges much; maybe he'll even cut a deal."

Freddy flushed purple. "Bra-*vo*, Kate." He clapped his hands. "Aren't you a clever girl? But then, I always knew that, if you recall. Bad timing on your part, since the man's been indicted. He *will* be found guilty."

"You sound awfully sure of that," I said.

"I am."

"Lost causes aren't my style," I reminded him.

"Oh, there's always a first time," Freddy said. "All you have to do is pick the wrong side."

There is something about people like Freddy, who think they're the smartest kids in school but instead are simply the most scheming. It helps to have the White House with you—any White House. And obviously *this* White House wasn't about to lean my way, no matter what I said or how I said it.

"Freddy," I told him, "there are people who, whether Lyle Gold is convicted or acquitted, will devote their entire lives, their whole fortunes, to discovering the truth. And no amount of polling can compete with that."

A bit dramatic, perhaps, but hell, it was a tense moment. If I could have kicked myself, I would have. Not because of *what* I had said but because I had said it at all. I had laid it all out for him, in plain view. Never ever show all your cards. Hadn't I learned that yet? Hadn't I known it instinctively back when I took on Freddy's case? Here was the bitter part. With one flinty glare from this man—whose ass *I* had saved, mind you—I saw the vision divide sharply into known and unknown, safe and hostile. On one side of the wire everything was familiar and everyone a friend; beyond the other lay the enemy. Us *versus* them. And now, me *versus* Freddy.

It was suddenly clear that August Mercer—who, let's face it, was *making* Freddy's career—had taken an interest in the Gold Affair that was in direct opposition to mine. And Freddy, eager to further his name in Mercer's circle, was himself implicated to some degree. I had been in Italy for a while. I had missed a lot of things.

Well. So much for thinking I could smile my way through this one. Now that I had handed Freddy my cards, there was no turning back. It was a matter of hours before it hit the streets, and Jack and I needed to start spinning immediately. Not television, not yet. There were too many journalists, pollsters, and erstwhile experts already crowded under the hot lights. Those were the dangerous ones. They *needed* to appear, so they would say anything, just to beam to the moon and back again.

As soon as I stepped out of the building, I called Maurice Barres from my cell phone (John Jaures was in Paris, on an unrelated story) and rattled off my plans. "Are you crazy?" he demanded.

"Certifiably," I told him. Within two hours, Jack and I e-mailed a statement for him to use. The following day an item would appear in his daily column. We flattered ourselves—and him, for that matter—to think it would be favorable, maybe something about our bravery or our brashness in taking on the century's most hopeless case.

> Lovely **Kate Boothe** must have had a few brain cells baked in Italy, where she has spent the last five months. Boothe has returned to Washington to take on the cause of **Lyle Gold**. True love to the rescue? Boothe dated Gold at one time but now has been more closely linked to **Roberto Picchi,** aka the son of **Yang Xianxu**, the controversial ambassador from China.

"Oh, Jesus," Jack groaned when he read it. "I thought this guy was your friend."

Immediately we hunkered down, repairing to Le Sénateur to work through the first public stage of our strategy, bolstering ourselves with strong French 75s. We agreed that I would do the Sunday shows. By sheer virtue of my involvement with the case, I would automatically get booked. No one else had sided with Lyle except for Edgar Demange. He was a usual suspect; I was not.

"Wear that brown suit you got in Rome," Jack said. "Think sharp and tailored."

"And put your hair up," added Lili, who hovered over our table. "You look more serious and older with your hair pulled up."

"Make it neutral lipstick," Jack said. "No lip gloss."

"You like lip gloss," I reminded him.

"I do," he said, "but not on a girl who's trying to convince me of something over my morning coffee."

I tried calling Roberto to get his point of view. Like most Europeans, his cell phone—or *mobile*—was constantly attached to his person. Home phones are a nuisance to the on-the-go continental man. "You can always reach me," he had said when he dropped me at the airport. Which is why, when I repeatedly dialed and got an automated message in Italian saying (I think) that the customer could not be found, I wanted to throw *my* phone across the room. What if he had gotten a new number as soon as I left? He hadn't tried to contact me since that initial e-mail, and I had sent more than a few. He might have met someone else. I swallowed hard as I contemplated that one. A man like Roberto would not be without female attention.

I did what I always do with such situations: I vowed not to think about it. What was Roberto anyway, except another man? There were thousands of men in Washington. All I had to do was blink, and a suitable new candidate would pop into my line of sight. Except, I realized, I wasn't sure I wanted another candidate.

■ ■ ■

Theoretically, it was easier to kick things off with Eddie Drumont than with someone like Truman Pace. Eddie was a lightweight. I had done his show before, and to be honest I had never thought much of him. Such a smart guy, advising a president at one point, on his way to true-blue power when he got bit by the big bug: ce-le-bri-ty. Eddie, with his thinning blond hair and bland unoffensive face, bet that a tell-all book and a network contract were his ticket to a new life. He was right, to a degree. A lot of industry folks, including me, might dismiss him as a wanna-be, but he still presided over the most-watched Sunday morning political show (which isn't saying too much in the cable era).

The greenroom for the Drumont show was the best of all the Sunday programs. There was a spread of bagels, lox, bacon, eggs, home fries—which I love, slathered in ketchup—even strong coffee and freshly squeezed orange juice. I had just piled a paper plate high when who walked into the room but Mimi Ryan, sheathed in a bright orange micromini and wiggling a rose-colored toe ring in her beige strappy sandals. Where was she going, South Beach? Thank God Lili was with me.

Of course, I shouldn't have been surprised. A blonde in Washington—bleached or not—was never without the lens for long. Mimi's mother had bought a television set for each room of the house so she wouldn't miss a second of her daughter's fifteen minutes.

"Oh, Kate, how funny," Mimi said. "We're on the Eddie show together. Isn't that too much?"

Lili noisily slurped her coffee. I shrugged.

"I have to tell you"—Mimi lowered her voice, as if the room were bugged—"I think it's just really, really brave of you, defending Lyle like this. Especially since he trashed your heart and all. Tell me, Kate. Is this—you know—a female revenge tactic? You trying to get at him?"

"Gee, Mimi, I don't even know how to begin to reply to that," I said.

"Oh, sweetie, you don't have to say anything. I understand. We all do stupid things for men. What it comes down to, bottom line, is we all want that frame house and white picket fence." Mimi was just warming up. "You have to ask yourself, What's it all for, this work? What do we want? Marriage. A husband who adores us. If we're lucky, someone as connected as we are. No one blames you for that."

I stared at her, flabbergasted twice in the same conversation, which must have been a new record. Was it true, as

Native Americans claim, that a camera could steal your soul?

"Mimi," I said carefully, "I don't want to marry Lyle Gold."

"But what about Roberto Picchi?" she fired back. "He's the gold medal."

"Kind of like a senator?" Lili couldn't stop herself. It was widely known that Mimi was having a full-blown fling with a fast-rising senator. These were the sort of matters best discussed *behind* one's back, however. Even Washington has its standards. Mimi, understandably, blanched, and so did I. Because there was no going back: It was going to be war on the set.

We were slotted for the first segment of the show. This was twenty uninterrupted minutes, a rarity in television, and it could get you in trouble. Eddie had few parameters; the only thing you could count on was that every now and then he would lean over and proclaim, "I don't believe you." And he came armed with a sheaf of notes, compiled by a very able staff, and an earpiece that allowed his producers to save him when he was in a tight spot. Guests had no such advantages.

Eddie was waiting for us, barely looking up from his scribbles. "You two ready?" he asked.

"Oh, Eddie, I am," Mimi purred. A technician clipped microphones to each of us, and the cameraman gave us a three-count out of commercial.

"The Gold Affair," Eddie said, looking forebodingly at the camera. "For months, the treason case against journalist

Lyle Gold has gripped the country. Two weeks ago, Lyle Gold was indicted by a grand jury and is currently awaiting trial. With me to talk about this is Mimi Ryan, who is doing polling for the White House, and consultant Kate Boothe, who is representing Lyle Gold. Welcome, both."

Eddie smiled at Mimi. She would go first. I didn't mind; it helps to know your opponent's argument, but I pretty much guessed what she would say, anyway. And I was right, at least at first. It was the same old pitch: Lyle Gold was plainly guilty; this was of grave concern to all decent Americans, "because God only knows how many brave members of the military and intelligence communities, out there putting their lives on the line in the name of patriotism, could lose those lives because of one very bad apple." Mimi looked ever so earnest as she said this.

Next it was my turn. I would get my opening statement, and then it was on to the no-holds-barred question-and-answer session.

"Well, Eddie, it is important first to point out that Lyle Gold, in fact, has not been found guilty," I began, but before I could go on, Eddie interrupted.

"But a grand jury indicted him, which is serious stuff."

"And now comes the trial—" I said. Again, Eddie cut me off.

"Military and State Department appointees—very high-up respectable folks—have testified to his guilt, according to reports. Are you saying that all these hard-working

people somehow got together and coordinated a mass conspiracy against a man who, even circumstantially, seems to
have betrayed his country?"

This wasn't going according to any plan—not mine, and
certainly not the show's usual format. And if I had had any
doubt that I was being ambushed, Mimi immediately dis-
pelled it.

"You know, Eddie, the old adage in Washington: Always
know the agenda," she said. "I have a few concerns about
this one."

The cardinal rule for television appearances is never ever
lose your temper, even if they're shoving bamboo shoots
under your fingernails. It looks bad. So I sat quietly next to
Mimi, my hands folded on the cherry-wood table, as she
kept talking.

"I'm concerned about some people who get on TV and
use whoever they happen to be dating at the moment as a
way to have power and prestige in Washington. It under-
mines the credibility, for example, of all the women in
Washington who are working very hard on different issues
and care about serving the public in an honorable way, that
there's this impression out there that the way to get ahead
and influence people is to be dating important people."

"What do you mean?" Eddie asked.

"I mean, I am not one for gossip or poking into someone's personal life, unless that person's life happens to be of
valid concern to their professional life. I think, then, that it

is worth pointing out that Kate, who is a good friend and a good consultant, is currently dating the son of Chinese Ambassador Yang Xianxu."

Eddie turned to me. "Kate, do you think this is a valid concern?"

"If I was still dating Roberto *Picchi*, I think it might look a little strange," I conceded. "But it is an unrelated coincidence. Since this is Washington, it must be pointed out that in many ways this is a small town. Certain relationships overlap. But my involvement with the Gold Affair—"

"And with Lyle Gold himself," piped up Mimi.

"With the Gold *Affair*," I continued, "has everything to do with the fact that this is a man who has been declared guilty without a trial and may quite possibly be innocent."

"But you're not denying you were, at one time, romantically involved with Lyle Gold himself," Eddie said.

"I'm not denying that—"

"And you're not denying that you have been involved most recently with Ambassador Xianxu's son."

"We dated for nearly five months, when I lived in Italy."

"Did you live together?"

I cleared my throat. "Eddie, I don't think that delving into my private life has anything to do with the Gold Affair itself. I think—"

"I think I'd like to know if there's anyone involved with this case who you haven't been with." And Mimi laughed.

There is nothing quite like being called a slut on national television.

I smiled wide and leaned toward Eddie. "I think this is an excellent example of the poisonous atmosphere that surrounds this particular case. Slurs, innuendo, and lies are de rigueur these days. The challenge of the Gold Affair, as it stands now *before* the trial has occurred, is to sift through the evidence and not jump to conclusions, no matter how convenient or tempting that conclusion might be."

Mercifully, we cut to a commercial. Eddie yelled for a powder, and Mimi hummed as we walked off the set. I was still stunned when Lili ushered me out of the studio to soothe my wounds with Mimosas. But the fact remained: The bubble had burst, and in spectacular style. The Drumont show was live on the East Coast, and it would take exactly one day for the effect to ripple out to the rest of the media.

■　■　■

"Kate Boothe is an example of someone who has slept her way to the middle," opined the conservative editorialist for *The Wall Street Journal* during his star turn on a popular cable news show.

"Didn't she once say her greatest feat was that her broad mind and small waist hadn't switched places?" mentioned the dishy young opinion-giver, who was better known for dating the *Post* gossip columnist (and, no, I never said that; Mimi did, in an interview with the *Washington Times* four years earlier).

"With her moussed, blow-dried, pseudo-Hollywood

haircut, Kate Boothe epitomizes the worst parts of celebrity Washington and the East Coast elite," slammed the *Kansas City Star* (What was I supposed to do? Not brush my hair? And I was from the Midwest!).

I felt bruised and sore as I unlocked my door on Monday night. The day had been spent under a metaphorical desk. But if I was expecting comfort at home, I hadn't counted on the summer heat in all its steaming glory settling in two months early. My apartment seemed soaked in humidity. No greenhouse effect? Right. I flicked on my air-conditioning— God bless that technology—uncapped a beer, and plunked myself into the chair on the balcony. The latter, with its view of the Potomac, made the steep rent worth it. I took a couple of swigs, kicked off my heels, and, propping my feet on the railing, watched the fireflies dance along the shore-line below. Usually, I clicked on the television and caught the latest news.

Nobody had said it was going to be easy, or that there wouldn't be a cost. Lyle was sitting in a jail cell, for God's sake. This was just my reputation taking a beating.

· · ·

Oh, the sad old song, *It's hanging on the old barbed wire/I've seen 'em, I've seen 'em/hanging on the old barbed wire*. That would be my name, shredded—most relentlessly on the radio. Which I listened to the following morning in my office, coffee close at hand but wishing desperately for grappa. And by Tuesday the rhetoric had sharpened.

"I just wanna know one thing, Truman. Is there anyone this little trollop hasn't [*bleeeep!*]?"

Jack, ever reliable, looked over from the radio and said, "Good thing they've got the seven-second delay." He winked encouragingly.

"I'm a trollop now?" I couldn't believe it. How many synonyms did the English language have for *whore*?

"Truuuuman, I'm callin' from Omaha. I'm on my cell phone. . . ."

"Like we couldn't tell with all the static," Jack muttered.

"I think this Kate is the perfect person to defend Lyle Gold. . . ."

"There you go!" Jack exclaimed.

"A tramp defends a traitor," the caller continued. "Perfect."

Listening to the Truman Pace Show was self-flagellating, but I had to do it. Keep track of your enemies. Plenty of people were following *us* now, that was for sure. The office had been bombarded with calls from worried clients. They were concerned that our defense of Lyle Gold would reflect badly on them or that we wouldn't have time to give them the necessary attention. Jack fielded most of these callers. After all, a majority were members of Congress, and most happened to be male. They would feel more comfortable discussing my questionable indiscretions with a guy.

My mother had no such qualms. "I *told* you to be more careful about who you dated," she said. "Why couldn't you go out with a police officer or a nice lawyer?"

Oh, dear God. But I did call Maurice Barrès and read him the riot act for writing such a mean-spirited item. He begged off with the excuse of "my editor changed it." Sure, sure. I held my tongue. "Gotcha. I understand how those things work." That was double-edged, and Maurice knew it. But so long as I was everyone's favorite whipping girl, he didn't have much to worry about.

Ambassador Xianxu, who must have been growing weary of releasing such statements, said for the record that he had never met me or heard of me or was even aware of my existence. No one believed it. As for Roberto—well, he did surface, sort of. John Jaures called from Paris—he had been searching out monkeys who were trained by gangs to attack tourists—with the tidbit that he had run into Roberto at the Buddha Bar.

"I told him I was working with you," John said. "He said to tell you he'd call soon."

The words sank like stones. The Buddha Bar! Only players went there, with tall, thin blondes in skintight dresses and stilettos. (John, of course, went for research.) *So what in the hell was my so-called boyfriend doing there?*

"Kate, you did announce on national television that he was your *former* boyfriend," Jack reminded me, rather gratuitously, I thought.

My assistant, a bright-eyed refugee of the dot-bombs, rapped her knuckles on the doorjamb. "Rose delivery," she said, bringing in a half-dozen red buds. I stared at the bouquet, dumbly. "You want me to put them in a vase?" she asked.

"Please." I took the card from the tissue paper while my assistant scuttled off.

"Mr. Wonderful?" Jack asked.

Only if Roberto's sentiments had suddenly transformed into the words *Rot in hell, you traitorous bitch*. There was no signature. It had to have been sent locally; no respectable florist would have taken that kind of dictation, or so I would hope. Jack took the card from me.

"Well." He shrugged. "Red roses. Not a bad way to say it."

My assistant carefully clipped the ends and put the flowers in water. By the end of the day, they had turned black and died. I recognized the tactic. Right-to-life organizations sent these roses to pro-choice representatives every year around Valentine's Day. That was sinister. This was vaguely tacky. I wasn't sure if I could consider it a threat on my life, but when John Jaures called to check in again I mentioned it. He seemed to think it was serious.

"Be careful," he said. "Lyle Gold is stuck away in a jail cell. You're on the outside. You're going to become a target."

• • •

I got an unlisted phone number. Admittedly, the first few nights after the Drumont show were rough—I pretty much sank against my hallway wall and cried—but the game was on. Once you're in the race, what are you going to do, quit? I figured I was in for at least two more weeks of Kate Boothe, Slut Girl. And yet, after less than a week, I found I was so exhausted from worrying that I had stopped sweating it. Danny Daly was right. People were going to say what they wanted to say. How much worse could it get?

Lyle Gold knew, which is why, I like to think, he called. I was shocked when my assistant announced he was on the line. We hadn't spoken since that day in prison. He had exactly two minutes, and he didn't even take that. "I'm sorry about what they're saying about you," he said. "You may be many things, but 'easy' isn't one of them." I smiled ever so slightly, and he went on. "You have to understand how crazy all this is, Kate. Everyone's so connected, there's no way they're going to let you break in. August Mercer, over in the White House, is pals with Lieutenant Henry. And Henry's married to the daughter of that old senator, Danny Daly. Remember him?"

"Are you kidding?"

"Joseph Henry. Oldest story line there is: Poor boy makes good," Lyle said. "Scores a ride to Yale, hooks up with a former marine's daughter. Doesn't hurt that her father's also a connected politician. Sounds like a path your Jack would envy."

I ignored this last bit. I had met Daly before the grand jury testimony leaked to the newspapers, so perhaps he hadn't felt the need to look after his son-in-law. Or maybe he didn't *like* his son-in-law. That wasn't an uncommon turn of events in the world. Still, de facto, Henry was a protected man.

I thanked Lyle for calling. "It's really decent of you," I said.

"I try, sometimes," he replied, but then his voice caught and he abruptly hung up.

●　●　●

Jack ceremoniously put a bottle of antacid on his desk, which was littered with pink message slips. "We have some very panicky clients on our hands," he muttered. He cracked his knuckles. "Hey, Kate, what do you think the odds are that August Mercer is telling these guys on the Hill to drop us?"

"Pretty high," I said truthfully. "But you do realize, we're a snack to him."

Another bouquet of roses arrived. *Give it up, you bitch.* Who wrote such things? Jack tracked down the floral shop and asked me if I wanted to instruct the owner to put a stop on deliveries from my hate-filled admirer. I looked at the wilted buds. "No way," I said. I was going to beat this sucker, whoever he or she was.

●　●　●

Washington is a one-industry town, but despite this the branches of government do stay segregated. If most of your business is on Capitol Hill with the congressional members and lobbyists, you probably don't hang out much with guys from the Fed or the State Department. They have their beers at different bars. But once in a while, paths do cross.

It was Friday, blessedly, and I had decided to reward myself for surviving: a steak and a cocktail in the shadow of the venerable dome itself. The Capitol Grille proudly displayed its dry-aged wares in its windows, which might have prompted vegans to retch, but I like a good filet. I specifically toured Burgundy after Jack raved about the beef from the region's white cows. Jack had promised to meet me at the bar, so there I was, meditating with a French 75 next to the enormous jar of pineapple slices soaking in vodka, when I saw, at the opposite end, none other than Lieutenant Joseph Henry. Oh, he was a handsome one indeed, a veritable poster boy for the military, tall and broad-shouldered in his uniform, his light brown hair freshly cut and his dimpled chin particularly masculine. He was alone but waiting. He checked his watch several times.

I believe we can create our own luck. So I hopped off the stool and politely introduced myself with the smile that knew no refusal. Until Henry, who withdrew his hand at the mention of my name.

"You're the girl tangled up with Lyle Gold, right?" he asked.

"I'm the consultant representing Mr. Gold," I replied.

"I can't talk to you," he said.

I paused a moment. "I met your father-in-law a few weeks ago," I said.

"Lived to tell the tale, did you." Henry was unimpressed. In Washington, especially, he must have heard that one constantly. Ever the officer, he remained on topic. "Look: I'm meeting someone here. I can't talk to you. I can't talk to anyone."

"You *have* been talking, though," I said. "You're the point man in Military Intelligence on the Gold Affair. You saw the so-called secret dossier."

Henry looked around sharply. "I said I can't talk to you. And even if I could, I wouldn't. Now, please excuse me."

I did. No sense pushing it. After all, the man was trained to withstand torture.

6

THE CONFESSION

One week after my disastrous appearance on the Drumont show, Freddy Banks called me.

"How are you?" he asked solicitously.

"I'm fine," I replied. Yet another bouquet of blackening roses had been delivered and remained unrescued by my assistant (but she was trying, mixing various concoctions of sugar and rose food). Yet another uneasy client had threatened to take his business elsewhere. And yet another flood of mean-spirited e-mails had filled our Web site. "Just fine."

"I thought I would check up on you," Freddy said, after clearing his throat. "This being a difficult time."

Well, now, who knew Freddy could be kind? But then I thought, Wait a minute; Freddy is *not* kind.

"That's very thoughtful of you," I lied.

"Not unexpected, I hope." He cleared his throat again. "I just wanted to make sure my girl was okay."

"Your girl, eh?" I waved to Jack, who was walking through the hall with a stack of message slips in his hand. *It's Freddy*, I wrote on a note pad, and he immediately plunked himself into a chair.

"Absolutely. We go back a long way." He paused a moment.

"Yes, we do." I couldn't think of anything else to say.

Freddy paused again and then said in a low voice, "You know, there's been a . . . stir . . . at the State Department."

"Really."

"Yeah. Well, after you were on Eddie Drumont's show, the secretary of state called Mercer for a tête-à-tête. You know anything about the secretary?"

I knew, as the newspapers had been reporting, that he had reached his position by being a thoughtful and thorough man and that he was becoming concerned about the Gold Affair the closer we got to the actual trial date, which had been set for the end of the summer, less than three months away.

"A little," I said.

"He read Mercer the riot act, and no one does that around here," Freddy said. "I mean, these guys play golf together at Burning Tree. They're old Yale buddies."

Lieutenant Henry had gone to Yale too. Come to think of it, my grandfather once said if you wanted to track some of the more unsavory types in American politics, check to see who had attended Yale—the law school in particular.

"He told Mercer he needs one good admission of guilt."

"Well, he's certainly not going to get one out of Lyle," I said. "Lyle didn't do it, and he wouldn't make up a confession even if you shoved hot pokers through him. He completely believes in the validation of his honor."

"Honor? What is *that* these days?" Freddy's laugh was hollow. "The secretary of state has decided that if the moral evidence is insufficient, if the material proofs are too fragile, the solution is simple. The only thing to do is to release him. Of course, considering the bastard's already been indicted, that would mean a very painful discussion with the attorney general."

"I would pay you to let me listen in on that conversation," I said, half seriously.

"Exactly. For many reasons, it is not a conversation we expect the secretary of state to have."

"*We*?" I asked. "Is this the royal *we*?"

"You could say that it *refers* to the White House."

"And yourself?" I asked. "Are you the messenger, or did you actually witness this discussion?"

"I was in Mercer's office when he spoke with the secretary, yes."

I checked the numbers on the phone's caller identification panel. "But you're not calling from the White House now."

"No. We wouldn't be having this little chat if I was," Freddy said. "Kate, get out. Do you understand? You're a bright girl and you could do really well. Get yourself out of this one. It's not worth it. I don't want my girl going down."

I thought, Freddy is covering his bases. Interesting. More than anyone, he knows what I am capable of pulling off. I didn't want to *pick the wrong side*, isn't that what he had said? I knew full well, bottom line, Freddy looked after Freddy.

"Tell me something," I began. "Who else at the State Department is involved in the Gold Affair?"

"I'm not privy to that."

"But you see all sorts of memos," I pressed. "Whose name comes up?"

"There's an assistant secretary who the big guy keeps in the mix. Joan Picquart."

"I've heard good things about her," I said cautiously.

"The secretary seems to think well of her. He has her check out all that stuff. She's even called Mercer a couple times," Freddy said. Before I could respond, he hurriedly added, "Listen: all Mercer has to do is make a few calls, and you'll lose all your clients. You get that, don't you? Is this Gold thing really worth it?"

"That's an excellent question," I said, "and I promise to think very seriously about it."

I hung up and looked at Jack, who had been leaning intently over his knees.

"Hot pokers, Kate?" he asked.

. . .

So. Freddy had decided to be a cowboy. I knew this type, mavericks out on their own, protocol be damned. Some did it for selfish reasons (as I would wager Freddy did), but occasionally there was a white hat. I even met one once, so I *knew* it could happen. It was at a dinner in Washington. There were about a dozen guests, and I was seated next to a stout gray-haired man who, I was startled to learn, was not only a mere forty-three years old but also a famous rebel. He had been fighting, however, in unforgiving Afghanistan. Abdul Haq (not his real name—he had changed it to protect his sprawling family) had spent the first few courses of the meal picking morosely at his plate. Once he had been a rangy young man, crawling through tunnels, before a land mine blew off his right foot. He told me the story, how the mujahideen had tried to save the foot, operating without anesthesia right there in the field, digging in the hole of the skin, scooping out rocks and dirt (and he laughed when I winced).

He had come to Washington to rally support for a plan to overthrow the Taliban, by convincing some of them to switch to his side. But here was the problem: We were just getting into the war, and Haq didn't want to lead Afghanistan after the Taliban. He just wanted to live there and open a shop. So as he talked to me, in low tones and with many pauses while he searched his street English vocabulary for the right phrases, I knew that the United States wouldn't back him. Maybe another mujahid, but everyone at the table that night knew Haq would be alone in any action. I believe Haq knew too. But here was the one guy who couldn't be bought by any side, who was therefore still credible.

Three weeks after the dinner, Haq was at his house in Peshawar when he decided to cross the Pakistan border and go into Afghanistan. He had no backing from the United States, but plenty of people in that part of the world believed otherwise, which made him a marked man. The CIA told him they couldn't give him aid until he did something. So he took his nephew and a few others, some satellite phones and a couple of handguns, and plenty of cash (to bribe tribal leaders, of course), and he headed in, riding on a mule. He was sold out by those tribal leaders who swore to follow him. Instead, they delivered him to the Taliban, who skinned him, castrated him, and hanged him.

Such was one—admittedly extreme—fate of a cowboy. Even in the relatively calmer clime of Washington it could be risky, especially so in the snakepit known as the Executive Branch. What was Freddy playing? I wondered. I was staring thoughtfully at the ceiling when John Jaures rapped his knuckles on the doorjamb. "Hey there," he said, sauntering in. He was wearing the Iron City Beer T-shirt again, and he carried an enormous round wooden box of Camembert. "It's unpasteurized!" he exclaimed. "This is the stuff you like, right?" He plunked it on my desk and smiled. It was very sweet of him.

"Welcome back," I said. "But Jack is the gourmand."

"Didn't your grandfather get a guy off by arguing he'd gone crazy from eating spoilt cheese?" John reminded me.

"You're trying to give me food poisoning?" I lifted my brows.

"Just helping you out with an excuse for when people ask why you took this case," he said, sitting down. "Getting that cheese was one of the better uses of my time in Paris. Never did find those monkey gangs." He watched me twirl a pen on my desk for a few moments. "Should I talk to you later?"

I stopped. "No, no. I was just—did you ever hear of a guy named Abdul Haq?"

"Sure. I met him in Peshawar. He died."

"I think he knew he was going to die," I said. "When I talked to him, he kept saying that sometimes it felt like he had wasted his life, fighting all those years and for what."

John considered this. "He said one thing in an interview that really stuck with me: 'Afghans take a man's word most seriously, and they have long memories.' Maybe he believed he didn't have a choice. He had told his people he was going. And he was a soldier. He'd been wounded seventeen times. He still had shrapnel in his head. He was a man who tried to do the right thing."

"At least he crossed the border," I said.

"That's right," John replied. "That's what made him one of the good guys."

I smiled at John, feeling a little bit of a lift for the first time in over a week. I was even inspired enough to place a call to the State Department and ask for Joan Picquart. I didn't get her, of course, just a bored assistant, but what the hell. Even random phone calls were worth a try.

． ． ．

The next morning, I woke up at the absurd hour of six to attend a yoga class with Lili. It was power yoga, which means the room was hot enough to make me sweat a few buckets and the class lasted two hours. I had never done yoga before. It is probably not the best idea to start with the extreme version. My limbs are tight, and I have no desire to become flexible. I thought yoga might be helpful in learning how to breathe, since I felt I had forgotten this over the last week. The class was all about stretching and muscle control. Ten minutes into it, I swore to Lili that if we lived through it, I would kill her (it didn't help that our instructor, whose name was Thor and whose toenails were painted the same shade of blue as mine, finished the class by playing the "gratefulness game—what are you grateful for? I am grateful for sunsets, for the sea, for the trees"—honestly! Who has *time* for that?). So I was staggering, muscles shuddering and twitching with every step, to the car when my cell phone jangled. An "unknown" call, but I answered it anyway.

"This is Joan Picquart," said a crisp voice.

"Oh, God." Evidently, in my state of surprise, I had lost my manners. It was not unlike being called on, unprepared, in her class.

"Why don't you come over this afternoon."

It wasn't a question. She had the no-nonsense tone of

someone who was rarely refused. I took down her address and a time, and that was that.

I had never been to her house before—she was a former professor, not a friend. She lived in a rowhouse in Old Towne Alexandria, on a street lit in the evenings with flickering gas lanterns, its sidewalks broken like slabs of candy by the roots of centuries-old trees. My heels clanged on the wrought-iron steps up to the door, which opened before I could press the bell.

"Welcome." Joan certainly didn't sound inviting, however, and she looked every inch the part of a serious, sharp diplomat. What had seemed plain in the lecture hall appeared dignified now. Her prematurely gray hair was bobbed at the cheekbone, and she wore only a faint raspberry stain on her thin lips. Her house, long and narrow, was hung with proper Virginia chintz. The mistress of the place walked into a canary-yellow drawing room (I hadn't been sure until this point that such a thing still existed) and made a beeline, with a slight limp, to a bar cabinet.

"I'm having a scotch," she said. "What would you like?"

"Scotch is fine," I said, silently thanking my father for developing my taste for the stuff.

"I have it neat," she said.

"On the rocks for me," I said.

She uncapped a dusty bottle—"My grandfather gave this to me when I graduated from college, so you know it is old"—and poured two crystal tumblers. Without looking at me, intent on dropping a precise number of ice cubes into my glass, she said, "You must be wondering why I called you. I hardly need say that this stays between us."

"Of course." I took the proffered glass. She gestured at an overstuffed chair. Obediently, I sat.

"Do you ride, Kate?" she asked.

"I had a Vespa," I said, and she smiled, not unkindly.

"I meant horses."

I felt like an idiot. Chicago girls rarely indulged in equestrian classes, though, and I told her so.

"I picked it up when my father was stationed in Austria. He was in the service." She glanced at her glass. "I was riding this past weekend at a friend's house in southern Virginia, near Monticello."

"That sounds very nice," I said lamely.

"It usually is. Except this time my horse, as can happen with animals, got some kind of idea in his head and ran away with me, jumping hedges and hurtling over streams. I hung on as long as I could, but the damn beast pulled up short and threw me over him and onto a woodpile. No broken bones, but my back is wrecked. I have a slight case of whiplash and a sprained ankle. I spent the weekend in a hospital bed."

"That's terrible," I murmured. I meant it, even if I had no idea why someone as important as an assistant secretary from the State Department was telling me this.

"Yes, it was," she agreed. "I lay in that bed with one thought running through my head: What if I had died?

Plenty of people do, from horse-riding accidents. Or they suffer debilitating injuries. What if either had happened to me? Who would tell the story?"

"What story?" I asked.

She took a long drink of her scotch. "My dear Kate, you are embroiled in something beyond you—beyond me, for that matter. I like to think the reason you spoke up for Lyle Gold was because you felt you were doing something noble. If it's worth anything, I can confirm for you that it *is*."

I finished my scotch, and Joan stood up to pour for us both.

"I received a hard copy of an e-mail trail last week," she began, "from a young man who works in technical assistance for us. We are aware, naturally, that many State Department employees have personal e-mail accounts that they maintain. What many of *them* are unaware of is that even e-mail sent from personal accounts can be accessed and monitored by us. Any e-mail sent from a government computer is caught in our firewall."

"Everything can be traced?" I asked.

"To an extent. We occasionally do a little . . . house-cleaning. Precautions, you understand. Nothing that any other—ah, company does not do. During one such sweep, the tech assistant turned up messages sent from an . . . interesting . . . private account."

Joan looked at me, and I realized what she wanted me to say.

"Lyle Gold."

"Yes." She nodded. "Imagine what this young man thought. He thought, How did this guy get into our server? Or did an actual employee of the department have the same name as that bastard rotting in jail. This young man, when he read the actual e-mails, found himself looking at a string of missives straight out of the secret dossier."

"How do you know this?" I asked quickly. Joan looked at me again.

"Because I have seen the e-mails, and I have read the secret dossier."

I did not reply but focused on drinking my second glass.

"There is no Lyle Gold working at the State Department," Joan said. "I *think* the Gold e-mails were sent from someone within the federal government. Someone who had logged on to the private account."

It was my turn to stare. Actually, it's not difficult to access someone's personal e-mail account and send a message, pretending to be them. All you need is a vague idea of what that person's password might be and the system they might use. A lot of people may not give two whits about their passwords: Hey, who's going to copy my scanned vacation photos or steal my secret recipe for potato salad? But we're in a connected world now. It is naive to have a weak password (and, incidentally, the word *password* itself is among the most common). *What if Lyle Gold hadn't been as smart or as careful as I gave him credit for?* He was an easy mark, with all the enemies he had racked up in Washington and beyond, and maybe he had left himself open in cyberspace. That wasn't too difficult to do.

"Are you saying—" I began slowly, but Joan held up her hand.

"Wait a moment," she warned. "I have the hard copy. I have talked to the tech assistant. I can tell you that something is amiss with this dossier. But I cannot say that the worm turns in my department."

"It could come from anywhere," I said.

"Anywhere within the federal government," she corrected.

"But he—or she—would have to send it from *within* that specific server," I said.

"Yes."

"And it's not as if a random person, even an enterprising reporter, could sit down at a government desk and start sending e-mails," I said.

"No. That is possible," Joan said, "but not likely."

I leaned forward. "What did the secretary of state have to say about this?"

Joan frowned, though not at me. "I expressed my concerns to the secretary, and also to the deputy secretary, who had been the first to see the e-mails."

"And the cleaning lady?" I asked.

"I wouldn't know about that," Joan said firmly. "But the deputy secretary was not inclined to dismiss Gold from suspicion. In fact, he even said it would be preferable if the whole thing did not go to trial but that Gold took care of things himself."

"And how would Lyle do that?" I asked.

"In another day and age, a loaded revolver with a single bullet would be placed within a prisoner's reach, just in case he might choose to render justice to himself," Joan said.

"That's sick," I said.

"That was the way of the time," Joan replied. "The same thing still happens occasionally."

She looked at me significantly. My mouth had gone dry. What kind of people were we dealing with? My face must have betrayed my thoughts, because Joan added, "Keep in mind the lesson I taught in my course: People involved in shaping policy can, and usually do, define their responses as moral. They can feel they are doing something that is humanitarian, that is correct, that is in the long-term inter- ests not just of American security and American wealth but of their own values."

"Why are you telling me all this?" I asked.

"Because what if something had happened to me?" Joan said. "I am not going to my grave with an injustice like this occurring on my watch. I will not allow my family to live with that. Understand, however, that I am working on this in my own way. I am the one behind the closed doors. There are measures to be gained. But I do feel that you are entitled to know what I believe: Someone else has used Lyle Gold's name to hide his own treason."

"Is Lyle in danger?" I asked.

Joan looked at me sharply. "Of course he is. We all are. These are high stakes."

She handed me an envelope containing a copy of the e-mails addressed to Mao with information on troop movements, the part of the secret dossier that had been submitted to the grand jury and had been enough to indict Lyle Gold.

"This is for your information only," Joan said. "You understand, I am sure."

"Did you ever know a man named Abdul Haq?" I asked, sifting through the papers.

"Of course. He was disappointed many many times by many many people. Such is the usual way of things. But perhaps we can change the course of events this time." And with that, I was dismissed.

. . .

I called Edgar Demange to apprise him of part of what Joan had told me. "Damn pricks and their jailhouse justice," he muttered. "Those tricks happen more often than you think." And then, throbbing head and all, I made my way to the office with the e-mails. My assistant wasn't around—probably off trying to save another bunch of damned roses, I thought—but Jack was. "Come here a moment," he called out when he heard me walk in.

If Jack's apartment reflects his desire to seduce women, his office is all about making love to clients: very clubby, with black leather armchairs and a sleek stainless-steel desk he bought on the Lower East Side of Manhattan, and gray shades pulled over the windows. The perfect place to smoke a cigar (if he had smoked) and plot to take over the world (which he did routinely).

"I was at the Cosmos Club today," he said. This was a sore point between us; Jack had been asked to join but I had not. "You can come *with* him," I had been told. The club might have a stale air, but the bartender could mix a bone-dry martini. "I ran into our favorite lobbyist."

"Lewis Tap is a member?" I sank into one of the armchairs, dejected.

"*Yes*, he *is*." Jack's imitation was delectable. "And he told me the *news*: Lyle Gold has confessed."

"Confessed," I repeated.

"Confessed."

"Oh, please," I said. Wasn't that too convenient, considering Freddy's phone call a few days before?

"Well, he's allegedly confessed to his prison guard. Lewis said he heard it from a 'top State Department aide.'"

"I just met with a top State Department aide, and she didn't mention it," I snapped. "And I just spoke with Demange, and he said nothing."

"Hey, I'm not saying I believe this." Jack held up his hands.

"But if Lewis is talking about it?" I said, and Jack nodded.

"Exactly. But wait—it gets better." He held up a letter.

"Guess what this is? A letter from the IRS. We're being audited. Can you believe it? *Auditing us*. Mercer ought to find something a little more original than *that*."

Audits frighten me. My father endured a bad one when I was fifteen. He ended up with white hair and an eight-hundred-thousand-dollar bill in back taxes as a result. He also put the fear of God in me about holding on to all receipts and keeping painstakingly detailed records.

"We don't know that Mercer—" I started.

"Yes we do, Kate, yes we do!" Jack shouted. "Why else would Freddy make that call to you? Look, these guys needed a confession and they were going to get one, some-how, some way. And why not tie us up a little bit while they're at it? Amateurs! Bring it on!" And then he punch-dialed our accountant, who wasn't quite so enthusiastic.

A confession—sure, it was only an alleged confession, but why bother with accuracy? Within hours, Truman Pace got wind of the rumor. He didn't trouble himself to check the facts. He went with it as soon as he could. "Lyle Gold, the traitor, has confessed!" The minute it hit the airwaves, the "news" appeared on the Internet. The said prison guard never materialized, but it hardly seemed to matter. The story was attributed to a "senior State Department official," and that was good enough for most of the media, even if Edgar Demange kept insisting it wasn't true.

It was also good enough for Congress, which was just a couple of weeks away from its July Fourth break. Represen-tatives and senators would return home to attend a few barbecues and make some rousing speeches. They needed something to throw to their constituents. The House of Representatives decided to vote on the Gold Affair, now that there was a "confession."

．．．

A mere week later, Jack and I went to the House gallery. They weren't voting on an actual law, they were considering a *nonbinding resolution*—which has to be one of my favorite legislative terms. It means *expressing the sense of the House*—in other words, a New Age confessional wrapped in legislative language. We watched as the rigid, self-described "sea-green incorruptible" Jeffrey Kavenyac, a hardened veteran from Chicago's South Side, stood at the podium under the bright camera lights and declared, "I am completely certain of Gold's guilt."

"Ho-hum." Jack yawned.

Kavenyac went on. He had pored through documents. The Khan letter was just part of the story. He also cited Gold's confession.

"His confession?" I exclaimed, loud enough to get a finger-wagging from a Capitol Hill policeman (reactions from the cheap seats were not allowed). "It was a *rumor*, you idiot!"

"If Gold isn't guilty, the government is," Kavenyac said. "And this government and this body stand for a people that is honorable, that has the values and the character that have made this nation the bedrock of Democracy!" His fellow congressmen hooted and cheered. And that, I thought, was the sound of a burden vanishing. The House proceeded to express its sense that the government and the military, not to mention the honor of the American people, had been stained by the Gold Affair and by a man who, according to all evidence, was truly a traitor, 245–0.

Jack—even confident, optimistic Jack—lost the color in his face. The air stopped moving, and I began to choke. Tears pricked my eyes, because it seemed that this was it. *Finis*. What could we possibly do now?

．．．

It was a little soon to jump back into the fray, what with people still questioning my moral rectitude and all, but we didn't have much of a choice. I went on the blowhard shout fest that was cable's most popular nighttime political show the very next evening and took my punches—"Your father must deplore your taste in men," admonished the elderly senator from Alaska—before I got my moment.

The host listed the litany of crimes against humanity that Lyle allegedly committed (including, evidently, poor taste in clothing, since the host made reference to his "indecorous appearance in court") and demanded of me, "What do you say to that?"

"First of all, my client must be defying all stereotypes, if you don't think he dresses very well, since Lyle Gold is gay," I said. There was an audible gasp around the table as all discussion screeched to a halt—a first for that show, I guaran-tee. The old senator began shaking. The host himself was unable to stop his jaw from dropping.

"But—but you *dated* him," the host managed to stammer. Out of one eye, I saw a camera zoom in on me.

"Yes, I did, Tony, but he confessed to it." I shrugged.

"He said he was gay? To who?" the host demanded.

"I heard he told an old college friend," I said blithely.

"And where is this old college chum?" the senator inquired, in his deep voice.

"Oh, *I* don't know. He seems to have disappeared."

"That hardly appears to lend credence, then," the sena-tor announced.

"But you *did* date Lyle Gold." The host was still on that, turning various shades of purple and red.

"Of course I did. So I know for a *fact* he's not gay. But I thought I'd try to start a rumor—and wouldn't it be easy for me to do that on this show, in this town, which *thrives* on rumor?"

The host blinked and looked at the senator, who stut-tered unintelligibly for a second—a blip in television time—before I plowed on.

"I also know for a *fact* that Lyle Gold did not confess. I know for a *fact* that that rumor was started by a lobbyist in this town. A lobbyist! Who passes around envelopes of money to influence people! How shady is *that*?"

I did not know for certain that Lewis Tap himself had

started the rumor, but he had been the conduit. His penchant for gossip was no secret. I took the gamble and tried to look convincing. It's all in the delivery.

"I think it's more than shady for a man to betray his country—" began the old senator.

"Of course you do. Because this same lobbyist has given thousands to your campaign funds over the years." I smiled brightly at him. *That* part, I did know. Cut to commercial. Impeccable timing.

"That's not entirely true, young lady!" the senator shouted, as we unclipped our microphones. "Tony, I want you to say that's not entirely true when you're back on."

The host shrugged. "We're on to a new topic."

The senator was muttering under his breath, as we left the studio. "Young lady, you don't play very fair," he said.

"I'm a hired gun, Senator," I told him. "I'm not supposed to."

More roses from my admirer arrived after that. My assistant went to work, clipping the ends, changing the water every thirty minutes. Her watchfulness was effective. The roses lived.

7

THERE IS NO GOLD AFFAIR

There is a terrific bash held every year in Washington called Taste of the South. It's the younger set's version of the inaugural ball, and tickets are hard to come by. All the states blessed enough to fall south of the Mason-Dixon line sponsor tables that are loaded with regional cuisine: gator from Florida, barbecue from South Carolina, crawfish from Louisiana. Balance a plate in one hand and whatever local firewater in the other, then carefully stack on the plate one of the plastic shots lined up at the end of the table: watermelon shots from Arkansas, Jack Daniel's from Kentucky, mint juleps from Mississippi. The debauchery is dressed up with black tie and a live band. Southerners know how to throw a proper party, all right. Food, alcohol, dancing. It used to be held in the marble splendor of the National Building Museum until the year some yeehaws from Texas poured an entire keg into one of the indoor fountains. The event was banned from the museum after that. Now, it is held at the Historic Hanger at National Airport, where the cement floor is easier to wash down.

I have attended Taste of the South nearly every year. Usually, Jack and I co-host pre-ball drinks at my apartment, but this year we decided not to. We were in no position to throw a fling; it would have appeared irresponsible under the circumstances. Truth be told, I wasn't especially in the mood to zip up the little sparkly number that was my favorite hot summer dress and clip (badly) around the dance floor in my heels. With Lyle still sitting in jail, I thought it would look a bit like Nero fiddling in the flames of Rome. Serious times call for serious behavior, right?

But Jack thought we should both go. The ball was still a networking event, albeit a fun one, and an appearance would reinforce the idea that we might have been knocked around but were far from out. John decided to come too. Any excuse to wear a tuxedo, he said, and I admit I gaped when he turned up on my doorstep. Who could have guessed that spit-shower Jaures could clean up so nicely, especially after a splash of lime cologne.

"You look like a cupcake," John said when he saw me. I deserved that; the dress was a frothy shade of pink.

"Whose car are we taking, gentlemen?" I asked. Jack jangled his keys.

"Mine just got detailed," he said.

"It only seats two," I said.

"I don't have a problem with that," John replied.

"Me neither," Jack said. "We can take both cars—" But John had already jumped into the passenger seat and pulled me onto his lap.

"It's a convertible, right?" he said, when Jack raised his eyebrows. All right, so my hair was a disaster by the time we roared up, but the ride was just fine, thank you.

The band, a typical all-white-with-one-lead-singer-who-was-black Washington version of cool, had swung into its version of "Devil in a Blue Dress" when we walked into the room. John took a swig of his Dixie beer. "I can't believe what they're doing to this song," he said, staring at the band as if it were a car wreck. A bottled blonde, in a blue dress of course, had jumped onstage and was grooving on the off beat with an amused bass player. "This is a war crime, and believe me I know what I'm talking about." John threw back a shot of Jack Daniel's.

I wasn't nearly as particular about the music. My feet tapped away as I sipped my mint julep. In spite of my earlier reservations, this was just the sort of night I like. The air hung with the right amount of heat, the moon glowed bright, and barbecue wafted from just about every state table. I almost forgot myself for a moment.

"Hi there, sweetie!"

Moment ruined. Mimi Ryan wiggled silvery pink fingernails at me with one hand and clutched an enormous Hurricane with the other. Jack's eyes widened at the sight of it.

"Louisiana?" he asked.

"You know it." She giggled. Excuse in hand, Jack beat a hasty trail to the bayou table. "So what's this, Kate? Are they your bodyguards?" She nodded at Jack's vanishing frame and then back at John. "You probably need them these days!" She sipped at her cocktail and then flashed John an enormous smile.

"Did Jack tell you he and I used to be an item?" she asked him.

"Must've slipped his mind," John said.

"Oh, the one who breaks your heart always does," she said.

"Mimi, isn't it?" John said.

"*Mah*-mee," she corrected.

"Of course." John smiled broadly.

But Mimi had moved on. "Katie, sweetie, I am really really sorry about the Eddie show. I know you must be mad at me."

"Don't worry about it," I said.

"I don't worry about *that*," she said, and leaned closer. "I do worry about *you*. You have no idea the beating your reputation has taken." She regained her smile and turned back to John. "Did Kate tell you we used to be sorority sisters?"

I wanted to disappear. Imagine discussing the bygone days of Delta Zeta with a man who had worked behind the lines in Kosovo. But John smiled right back at Mimi and replied, "She never speaks of anything else." I didn't know if I should kill him or kiss him.

"Ah. Well." Mimi nipped at her cocktail again. When in doubt in Washington, drink. "You know, Kate, one of your former beaus is here tonight. He's looking pret-ty good."

My heart lodged in my throat. She couldn't possibly mean Roberto. But then I remembered he was not only my current (theoretically) but also that Mimi had never even met him.

"Didn't you used to date Reiff Prouty?" Mimi asked, cocking her head to one side.

"No," I said emphatically, somewhere between relief and disappointment.

"Oh. I thought you had. Seems like Kate's been around town, sometimes." She giggled at John. "Anyway, Reiff's been asking after you. You might want to say ciao." She winked and, after patting John on the arm, wandered off into the crowd.

"She's interesting," John observed.

Jack, who had conveniently reappeared, handed him a Hurricane and gulped at his own. "Only mildly," he said.

"Is there anyone in this town that the two of you haven't dated?" John asked. "A hunchback? A couple of midgets?"

I might have chosen to take exception to this, except that at that precise moment I thought I had glimpsed Reiff, his hand on the thin shoulder of a tousled redhead, guiding her toward Alabama. The lead singer of the band suddenly belted, "You make me wanna shout!" and it was Jack's turn to regard the stage with horror.

"Jesus God," he said. "If we all flick our lighters, will they sing 'Freebird'?"

I left the boys to complain to each other. With a quick lick to the tip of the julep cup (for courage—I heard the whispers and felt the sharp-eyed stares prick the back of my neck), I wove through the crowd, searching for Reiff. I can't explain this. He isn't the most pleasant conversationalist. But it suddenly seemed of the utmost importance to find out why he was in Washington again.

Almost a thousand people attend Taste of the South, and in the flash of sequins and swish of satin it is almost impossible to find someone intentionally. You have to collide with them. Failing that, you go to the ladies' room and hope to overhear some pointed gossip, which is what I did. I was actually feeling vaguely ill (the mint syrup, I thought) and was leaning against the inside of a stall when I heard the clatter of a cosmetics bag on the marble counter. Giggles; coos over the "dreamy" shade of frosted pink lipstick ("It's called Obscenity!"); then, after suffering through this, something interesting.

"Did you see that guy from State?"

"Reiff? Oh, yeah. He's been around awhile."

"I've never seen him."

"He's been overseas. Diplomatic corps."

"That sounds *so* romantic!"

A short barking laugh, and then, "Don't be fooled. He's such a slut."

I couldn't believe it. I couldn't imagine any woman—

much less many women—sleeping with him. Oh, he was handsome enough, but coldly so. But the bitter voice had more to add.

"I've never seen anyone do such strategic sleeping around. If you don't have a trust fund, he's not interested. The guy's got debts to pay."

"Gambling?" The softer voice laughed.

"Ha-ha. That's too proletarian. It's gone up his nose."

There was gentle murmuring, and then the door opened and closed. I stood still. Well, what do you know? Reiff had another weakness besides ambition. Of course, the two went hand in hand sometimes. I shook my head clear. A ginger ale, and I would be restored.

I was glossing my lips when I noticed an older woman, her smudge-black hair pulled back by a velvet headband, at the mirror next to me, glaring hard. I glanced at her, startled. "We women always think we can change a man," she said, in that way ladies of a certain age discuss distasteful topics. "It never works. They are the way they are, and we do better for ourselves—and for them—to leave them alone. You might want to consider why you are intent to rehabilitate a particular individual."

Well, that *was* the question of the last week, wasn't it? I am not fond of unsolicited advice. I looked straight at the woman and replied, "You might want to consider why you are intent on not having a particular individual rehabilitated."

I clicked my lipstick case shut and left with my head

high. Yes, that showed her, all right. But any bravado quickly evaporated as I walked back into the hall, over to the spot where I had left my two dates. I could hardly believe my eyes. Here was Jack, his face flushed, grabbing a lobbyist (had to be—his haircut looked expensive) by the silk lapels. A small crowd was gathering expectantly as I rushed over, hobbling in those damn heels. I couldn't hear the exact words at first, but I could see John carefully setting his drink on a table, keeping a watchful eye on the action.

"What did you say?" Jack was almost yelling. "What did you say?"

The young man—and he *was* young, probably a fresh K Street recruit, straight off Capitol Hill—tried to brush him off, but Jack stubbornly held on to his jacket. What could have been so horrible that Jack would put up such a fight?

"What did you call her?" Jack demanded. Oh, God, it was me. It had to be me. Nothing else would make Jack react like that. I pushed through the crowd, just as the kid shouted back.

"What are you, some sort of pro-Gold syndicate?" He laughed at his own wit. "Against your country—"

John stepped in. "Whoa, whoa, I hardly think we need to—"

"To what?" The kid shoved Jack away and swatted at John, all in one jerky move. "You think we shouldn't defend the United States? We should stick up for traitors instead?"

Ah, now, this was downright incendiary stuff, especially

when a sizable part of the crowd was in uniform. Several of them closed behind the young man. I swallowed hard.

"You must be with this syndicate, too!" the bright-eyed boy barked at John. "You're probably the syndicate's lawyer!"

A *lawyer*? Now, them's fightin' words. John drew himself up, with the scar tissue that threaded his left shoulder from the burning tire thrown around his neck in Haiti and the shrapnel from Jalalabad that remained in his knee, and said, in a quietly dangerous voice, "You are a coward."

Testosterone surged through the room. The kid threw back his fist to clock John, but Jack slammed into the kid's stomach before he got the chance. And then, chaos. Girls shrieking, trying to get out of the way, chairs clattering to the floor, glass breaking. I lost sight of Jack and John, washed back under a sea of polyester. Groans, grunts, more shouts, a few sounding vaguely helpful. But before I could make sense of what was happening, I felt long nails scraping my scalp as thin fingers grasped a handful of my hair and a powerful thrust sent my forehead cracking into the concrete wall.

I almost immediately bounced back upright, my sight exploding into stars. I hadn't believed in that particular cliché before, but it really happened. I was stunned. No one had ever attacked me—physically—and I started laughing hysterically (I wouldn't be much good in a bar fight). I had no idea who had smashed my face into the wall. It was complete pandemonium. Taste of the South would probably be banned now from the Historical Hanger too, I thought inanely, as I stumbled around, trying to escape the grabbing hands that tore at the air. The next thing I knew, I felt liquid splash squarely in my face and dribble down my dress. Sadly, it appeared to be a Bloody Mary (what southern table was serving *those*?). I wiped the alcohol from my eyes, smearing my mascara, and saw three young girls, probably no more than twenty-one, regarding me with perfectly distilled hatred.

. . .

The bridge of my nose was fractured, and a beautiful shiner spread across to the corners of my eyes. A few more bruises spotted my arms, but other than that and a hefty dry cleaning bill, I emerged relatively unscathed. Jack had two broken ribs, and John sported a shattered eardrum. But they were pretty happy about their wounds. The strange ways of male bonding, I suppose.

The melee made all the papers, of course, and so did that term the kid had thrown out so angrily: The Syndicate. We Goldians had a title now. Truman Pace went at us right away. Editorials appeared in the most conservative and liberal papers alike. Our corporate clients were really nervous now; the phone was ringing off the hook. My parents and my uncles and even my cousins called. They thought I should sue for damages. Who, exactly, was I going to sue? I demanded.

But in the midst of all this, a relatively encouraging note came from Lyle, the first part even qualifing as decent:

I hope my thoughts add some comfort, if possible [I didn't know Lyle had that in him—but he was also being useful]. You realize I knew Mao—I interviewed him a few times. I never had access to the kinds of files I'm accused of giving him. It was all aboveboard. I once talked to a low-level diplomat, a guy who knew a lot about China, about Mao. I even broached Mao with the communications director at the Pentagon. They keep records on this, I'm sure of it.

Disreputable words continued to be uttered by supposedly respectable people. A taxi driver refused to let me in, spitting with disgust. The audit loomed. My swollen nose made me look like a boxer. But someday it *would* all be finished. Come on, I told myself, hadn't I fought back at mile 23 of the New York City Marathon four years ago, when three Brits had boxed me in? Sagging tired, with muscles cramping so hard my legs were splattered with black-and-blue splotches, I found enough energy to aim a few well-placed jabs with my elbows *and* I went on to finish in my best time yet. So *this* wasn't so bad. Besides, I was on the right side of this one. Say it a few times—I am right, I am right—and it eases any pain. Say it a few more times, and you truly believe it.

I tried. Good God, did I try. I consider myself to have

fairly decent persuasive powers, but I was so *tired*. Maybe it was the shock of a physical attack, but trudging back to the front lines seemed beyond my capacity. I was thinking hard about this, one night about a week after Taste of the South, when I unlocked the door of my apartment after working late and fumbled for the light switch in the hall. And there, sitting in the chair on the terrace, was Roberto.

.   .   .

It was quite possible, I thought, that I was going mad. I stared at the handsomest man in the world, unused to seeing him in this setting, in my space. Roberto belonged to a different place—oh, hell, maybe even a different time. It was like looking fondly at an old photograph. He moved slowly, like a dream, from the terrace into the apartment, his eyes shining despite the bruise-dark shadows under them. I might have gasped.

"Well, Kate, there is a traitor," he said, by way of a greeting, "and it is not Lyle. You were right."

I blinked dumbly. He had just uttered the three little words most dear to me.

"Don't you have anything to say?" A faint smile flitted across his lips. "Maybe, you are glad to see me?"

"Of course." I regained my voice. But I did not step toward him. I remained rooted in the hall. Roberto noticed, but then he would. He was a writer. He was also an aristocrat, which meant, even in unsettled air, he could drape himself across the velvet armchair in an effortless imitation of nonchalance that would have fooled anyone else. I knew better, particularly when he lit a cigarette.

"This story that you are in," Roberto began, in a quiet, steady voice, "exists."

No kidding. I already knew that much from Joan Pic-quart, of course, but to hear it from Roberto was salve. I noticed, distractedly, that his hair was longer.

"The pallid little prick who worked for my father, when he wasn't screwing men *and* women—"

"Mao," I murmured. "What is his real name?"

"Does it matter?" Roberto asked, and I suppose, other than morbid curiosity, it did not. "A very ambitious sort, who met another ambitious sort from Lahore—"

"Khan."

"—who thought his country should have a seat at the exclusive table of geopolitics," Roberto continued. "If Russia could sit with the United States and China, why not Pakistan? To this end, a little light espionage couldn't hurt, and it was easily expensed."

I sat on the camel-colored sofa across from him. I don't know why I couldn't bring myself to fling my arms around him, as I felt I should. He smoked silently for a moment.

"Mao and Khan spent a great deal of time in Paris. I met a friend of yours there when I was looking into this."

That would be John, of course. "Yes, I heard," I said. "At the Buddha Bar. How was the overpriced Calvados?"

Roberto paused only slightly before replying. "Difficult to swallow."

"I'll bet." I crossed my arms.

Roberto ignored this. "Mao and Khan had their regular places around town, in the Marais. It wasn't too hard to find people who knew one or both of them. Those people aren't afraid yet to talk. There are others, diplomats, who aren't happy to answer questions but will, under certain circumstances."

As in, When the right person asks, I thought.

"The trajectory was this: Khan knew a young man who he thought might be useful. He introduced this young man to Mao. But this contact, unfortunately, produced little of consequence. He became a burden, begging for more money, never taking the precautions that Mao and Khan asked him to take. This contact sent e-mails, for instance. At least he had the acumen to use an alias."

"Lyle Gold."

Roberto stared, almost through me, it seemed, and reached over and lightly touched my face. "Your nose. It isn't too bad."

"It's healing. The swelling has gone down." I blushed.

"Yes. I read all about it." He inhaled deeply and then stubbed out the cigarette. The last time I had seen him smoke was when he had chased me to Venice and taken me to Harry's Bar, that historic American refuge. He had ordered Bellinis. It wasn't the right season for peaches, but that concoction of sweet peach puree dissolved in the bubbles of *prosecco* might as well have been nectar, or whatever those Roman gods pounded down. I had four and announced to Roberto that I wouldn't kiss him if he continued the nasty habit of smoking. He had quit on the spot.

"Kate," he said, gently now, "I want you to finish this matter. I want you to come back to Rome. You will have the solace, if you can call it that, of knowing you did the right thing. You will have the realization that you were, despite all odds, right as well."

"But if I am right," I began, "I can't go back."

"These things that are said about you, even about my father . . ." He trailed off, shaking his head.

I was quiet for a long moment. "Have you seen him?" I asked.

"Not yet." Roberto lit a second cigarette. "I don't know if I can. He wouldn't handle it well. I wouldn't handle it well."

Roberto stood up and started to walk out. I felt numb—this was not how I had envisioned reuniting with him. But then he stopped short of the door, his hand resting on the knob.

"The alias *was* Lyle Gold."

"I know."

"Then what else can I do for you." It wasn't a question. The door closed with a click behind him. He was here; he was gone. It had happened so quickly I hardly believed I had seen him. I sank into the velvet chair that Roberto had occupied.

Always have two sources—my hard-earned lesson from

journalism school. But I ached with exhaustion as I dialed Jack's number.

. . .

"Do you want to talk about it?" Jack asked, as we walked from his car into the jail. We were visiting Lyle.

"I do not." I kept my sunglasses pulled over my eyes. Jack had periodically needled me with the same question for the entire hour-long drive, which compelled me to remind him that he never liked it when I asked him if *he* wanted to talk.

"And you have no idea if he stayed or if he went back to Italy."

"I said I didn't want to talk about it."

"Well, I think it's weird. I'm sorry, Kate, but it's weird and creepy. The guy just shows up—how did he get into your apartment anyway? You gave him a key?"

"When he gave me his," I explained. We entered the vast bleakness of the prison, pulled out our identification, and signed in as visitors.

"And he'd been in Paris checking up on this. No phone call to you, no e-mail."

"Jack," I said, in a warning tone, as we were led into the same drab room where we had first met with our infamous client.

"I mean, hey, *I'd* like to go kick around Paris and do a little *research*. That's all I'm saying." Jack shrugged.

"Coffee's not as good there as it is in Rome," I said.

"Didn't know that. Excellent point." And then Jack assumed the role of the suave consultant as Lyle was led into the room. He had the same washed-out pallor as before, but now his face was creased with worry lines, the dent of disaster.

"How're they treating you, Lyle?" Jack asked companionably. Lyle did not answer, but I pressed my heel on Jack's toes to remind him of the virtue of tactfulness.

"I hear I've confessed," Lyle said finally.

"Yeah. Kate also said you were gay on national television." Jack certainly seemed to relish this revelation, not to mention Lyle's look of surprise. "Don't worry—one rumor that didn't go too far."

"Oh, good," Lyle said.

I reached for the receiver. "So, last time we were here, you mentioned a visit from Freddy Banks. What did he have to say then?"

Lyle shrugged. "It was a while ago. I don't know. Hard luck, that kind of stuff."

"A guy from the White House came all the way here to express sympathy with you," I said.

"I don't know why he was here. He said things like 'If you're not guilty you've got to keep your head' and 'An innocent man's always strong.'"

"Not too out of the ordinary," Jack said to me.

"What did you say to him?" I asked.

"What could I say? I told him I had to be cleared. He

seemed understanding enough of something like that. He said he himself wasn't in a position to clear me, but surely everyone would be fair." Lyle laughed bitterly. "Fair! He did ask me what the charges against me were based on. I told him I didn't know. He didn't seem to believe that part, but it was true. How was I supposed to know? No one told me much of anything, except I was lucky not to have been named an *enemy combatant*."

Lyle *had* gotten a break. If he had been tagged with that title, he could be held, indefinitely and without charges or representation, by the Department of Defense. Only American citizens can be deemed *enemy combatants*. The strange logic of wartime law. *Traitor* had its own benefit, in a way. At least he was entitled to due process.

Lyle looked at me with fierce intensity.

"You know how I am?" he demanded, his voice hoarse. "I write, I work, I dream. I spend most of my days in the cell. I think of who I was—what I hoped to be. I don't understand it. I sit here, and I think death wouldn't be all that bad at this point."

"No—you can't believe that!" I exclaimed, a bit too anxiously.

"Kate, how can it be now, in a place like this, with all our ideas of justice and truth, that something as fundamentally unjust as this can happen? You know, if only—whoever committed this crime—if only I had him for just five minutes—"

He was hoarse when the guards took him away. And I

furiously blinked away tears as Jack and I left. My partner said nothing until he unlocked his car. "Ironically, he may have had that guy in front of him," he observed.

"You can't really think it's Freddy," I said.

"I can't take him off the list either." And Jack turned the key in the ignition.

. . .

When I was a little girl, my father made a point to take me on a crack trip (that was what I called it then, years before freebasing gave it a double meaning; my younger uncle still asks to this day when my father is going to take his daughter on another drug tour). We went to every pile of ruins in the eastern Mediterranean. You've seen one, you've seen 'em all, to my thirteen-year-old eyes. Crumbled marble columns, eaten brown by smog or choked by weeds. The stone had split with age and abuse. Once a crack appears, it is almost impossible to preserve the whole.

So what happens when a story starts to crack?

It took just over a month from when we met him that evening in Jack's apartment, but finally, three days after we saw Lyle, John Jaures began to publish his articles on the Gold Affair. I suppose that isn't too much of a time lag, considering the amount of research required and then the scouring by editors and the newspaper's legal department. Investigative journalism isn't so much exciting as it is ponderous. All those weeks ago, John had interviewed Saeed

Khan. And now, in the first article, Khan spoke from the grave about the all-important *G* letter.

Khan knew about the letter that U.S. military intelligence had stuffed in its secret dossier. He had been called in to a particularly mortifying meeting with the Pakistani ambassador as a result. But once given a copy of the letter to examine, by way of verifying that, indeed, Mao had addressed it to him, he told John there was something wrong with it. A letter had been changed. Instead of reading, *I am asking you to my home in the morning, since* he *has brought me many things of interest,* as had been originally written, the sentence now read, *since* G *has brought me many things of interest.* Mao had never given even a hint of the spy's identity. Saeed was not at all familiar with a *G*.

I read this, and I smiled. Any reasonable person would have to conclude, then, that the letter was forged. John himself had taken to calling it the False *G* Letter. So who had done the forgery? I might find this the next logical question, but there were plenty of people who had no intention of acknowledging a problem with the letter itself. Since John had already been tagged a charter member of the syndicate, his article did not have the resonance it might otherwise have had. Still, to his distaste because he didn't like to flack his work, John had to put on his only suit and jump from talk show to TV interview, butting up against the likes of Mimi Ryan and Maurice Barres. Truman Pace was having none of it, practically calling for John's traitor-by-proxy head.

Watch what Mercer does now, I told myself. The sensational possibility that the False *G* Letter could be, indeed, false just might prompt a preemptive measure. And then, just a few days later, during a routine press briefing about special forces winnowing through Southeast Asia, the vice president was asked about the Gold Affair. He immediately snapped, "I will say right away what will be the last word in this debate: There is no Gold Affair." The White House, with its air of dignity, had taken exception to the title the beast had given its prey. And why should an affair be acknowledged, when it appeared to have been solved? The announcement came from Mercer, I decided—it had to, since he coordinated politics in the White House.

In the House of Representatives, the youngest congressman, a fresh-faced twenty-six-year-old, strode to the floor to officially (because it was on television, after all) declare himself to be "anti-Gold" in a rousing speech that must have wowed 'em in Salt Lake City: "Here, there are neither friends nor adversaries, neither partisans nor enemies of the White House. There are representatives of the country, there are Americans anxious to keep intact that which is most precious to them, that which remains in the midst of our struggles and party discords the common ground of our invincible hope—the honor of our men and women in uniform."

How can you compete against *that*? Tie a yellow ribbon around a tree trunk, buy a copy of the latest laudatory volume about World War II, shell out a few bucks for red paper flowers on Veterans Day. But for God's sake, don't take on our men and women in uniform. Unless they took part in an unseemly massacre like the one in My Lai, they were beyond reproach. And now, effectively, Lyle Gold's fate was tied to their honor.

The stakes had been oh-so-publicly raised; of course Hollywood would have to weigh in. Melvin Gluck might be a publicity-mad blowhard, but there were others. The great filmmaker Anthony France, who in his youth had virtually invented the term *blockbuster* with thrillers about alien invasions and historical epics and now busied himself with "significant" movies (in black and white, shot with handheld cameras), spoke up from his rambling estate in Southampton. He was in the process of laying out the boards for a cinematic ode to the humble yet brave soldier. Like many men his age who had been too young for Vietnam but old enough to know a neighbor boy who had perished there, Anthony France exulted in the military.

"An army is admirable!" he exclaimed rapturously to a writer from *The New York Times*. "Think of it! So many hearts united in a single thought! Such beautiful order!"

Anthony France didn't speak about the Gold Affair. Instead, he took a dim view of John Jaures. "A writer cannot be permitted to say everything, every way, in every circumstance, to every sort of person," he said.

I read this and could not believe his nerve: France, the great war expert. Who was France anyway? He dealt in fantasies. The closest he got to contact was having his makeup team artfully daub ketchup onto actors, while there John was in the trenches, *real* bullets flying past his ears. France was shooting off his mouth; he wasn't privy to the files John had seen.

"Gold is nailed and the case is buried forever!" Mimi Ryan ejaculated on a talk show later that night. Jack and I were laughing so hard at this that my assistant had to rap on the door a few minutes before waving in John. We were all working late these days.

"Can you believe it?" Jack asked.

"It's what we've been waiting for!" John exclaimed. "For the first time, I'm sure we're going to beat these guys. Kavenyac talks, so he'll be beaten. Don't you see? Kavenyac has named the documents—officially, named them on the House floor—and we know they are false! They feel false, they smell false, they are forgeries, and other people will believe it. I'm going to prove it. We'll have them by the throat."

Jack shook his head at this display of macho optimism. I went for a walk. Washington in early July could be considered, by some people, to be sultry. I consider it wretched. My hair flattened and my linen skirt clung to my legs. Well, it *was* a drained swamp. I sighed in the prickly heat and watched as other K Street consultants and lobbyists, some of whom I had known for nearly ten years, hurried past. Some nodded perfunctorily; others ignored me. Here, I thought, was the essential problem: I needed to sell them my side.

A basic contemporary strategic tenet: Whoever most effectively stakes out the high ground of "values" wins. The problem was that this territory to date had been ceded to the anti-Goldians (read: everybody). No wonder, then, the public had its collective back up against the concept that someone had forged the *G* letter to frame a man they had already processed as a traitor. People don't like to be told they are wrong.

The question I could not answer yet was how to position *us* on the right side of good, where I knew we were. Then again, I was no different from anyone else; we all want to think, *I am a good person for believing what I believe.*

I walked to Georgetown and back again—a long stroll, all right—and over to Le Sénateur. It was closed for a special event, which was winding down. Lili took me into the kitchen and poured us each a glass of Sancerre.

"My feet!" She groaned. "Did you see the sous chef? He's a cutie."

Lili and I will never be in competition for the same man. She prefers them broad-shouldered and beefy. She brushed a stray lock behind her ear and took a sip of the wine.

"All right. You haven't asked my advice, but I guess this is my one shot to give it," Lili said. "Forget the media for now. Follow the money."

"What money?" I asked, unsure of what she meant.

"You've got two main problems: media, yeah-yeah, we all know how that's going; but there's a lot of money floating around this. Think about these *guys*—the deputy secretary at State, August Mercer, some of the lobbyists they come in here with. All the people you keep hitting up against have serious money. I think you should tap into that first."

"There's always a lot of money around this town," I said.

"Right. It's a factor. Think about it. When people want reservations at eight on a Saturday night or prefer a certain table, what do they do? Give me a couple folded bills, maybe theater tickets."

"Yes, yes. Money buys access. Old story."

"And how often have you heard of someone using it *well*?" Lili asked.

I knew of a few, one in particular, a trader with a shock of white hair and a neat gray mustache, who spent over a hundred thousand dollars a month to press the case of the Afghans in the corridors of Washington. He had nothing to gain. He was that rare idealistic individual with money who did not want a population to starve once again. Most people don't have his restraint.

"I knew a guy in college," Lili continued, "who used to say he didn't want to be a millionaire by the age of thirty. That was just rich, he said; he wanted to be *big* rich. You know, have an IPO that nets you several hundred million on paper. Remember when that used to happen? But think about the type of person who *gets* to be big rich." She tilted her glass toward me. "Once you're big rich, if you have those financial resources, you can avoid all the pitfalls that other people can't."

"Like a miscarriage of justice," I murmured.

"Those with money often have the power," Lili said.

"The haves versus the have-nots."

"And they'll do whatever they have to in order to keep it."

I considered this. Just as the beast rarely attacks one of its own, the old boys' network protects its interests.

"Think about it," Lili said, and I did.

. . .

The media, reliably, followed John Jaures's lead. Reporters hate to be wrong, but they despise being beat out on a story even more. I knew a few were poking around, talking to people about the False *G* Letter. I heard from two of them—clever sorts who file for wire services—that they found sources who verified the letter had been doctored.

"So when do I see the story?" I asked.

"You won't," one replied. "If I write it, I'll get my White House credential revoked."

"I'm not writing it," said the other. "Next thing I'll be called anti-American, and I might lose my job. My editor just fired our political columnist for writing *unpatriotic* pieces."

"John Jaures hasn't been fired," I pointed out.

"I'm not working for *USA Today*, am I? I can't get away

with everything. Besides, I've got a kid starting college. I can't risk it."

And so the beast balked.

The False *G* Letter was false. Fat lot of good that did me, I grumbled to myself. Even those who believed it didn't want to. But how difficult could it be to identify the forger? The most likely candidate would be someone who actually held the letter in his hands. Someone who was also in the old boys' network here, or at least on its fringes, maybe even making a bid for full-fledged membership.

Who was under tremendous pressure to come up with some "hard" evidence against Lyle.

Who knew a trial was coming fast and that circumstantial evidence might not be enough.

Who might have felt, especially if he truly believed Lyle to be guilty, that a little padding wouldn't be wrong, not in these dicey times.

The good lieutenant Joseph Henry. I sighed and had another glass of sancerre. Abdul Haq crossed the border. Compared to that, it wasn't so difficult to cross the old boys themselves. I just needed to do it with a better vehicle than a mule.

8

SUCH A GOOD-LOOKING YOUNG MAN

The power corridor runs from Washington, D.C., to New York City, although New Yorkers might reverse the order. The elements that make the country tick—politics, finance, media—are often found on any train or shuttle flight. Once I sat behind Henry Kissinger (who buried his face in a gossipy newspaper), and another time an oh-so-debonair television anchorman gallantly hoisted my suitcase into the plastic cupboard above my seat. This is why, when Lili suggested a weekend break, Jack consented. I padded the trip a bit, to justify the first-class seat on the high-speed train (the civilized way to travel). There was a launch party for a magazine. Usually, these were tiresome prospects, but the new editor was a playboy hipster, so it was sure to draw the mediati, even on a Friday night during the summer. I was vaguely acquainted with the woman who coordinated the festivities, and she put me on the list, as they say. I might have become a social pariah in Washington, but New York was a much bigger town.

Lili had gone up a few days earlier for the annual gourmet food show. So I boarded alone, feeling faded and dried to paper-thin as I kicked off my shoes and flexed my toes. I had a stack of morning newspapers at my side to plow through, a cup of coffee on my tray table to rejuvenate me. There was an intriguing headline in *The New York Times*: GOLD AFFAIR BECOMING DEPARTMENT MILLSTONE. A few paragraphs prattled on about the deepening involvement of State and Defense. I already knew most of this, so I was skipping past the front section to examine the restaurant reviews when my cell phone rang.

"You looking at the *Times*?"

I was listening to the gravelly voice of Reiff Prouty. I tried not to drop the phone (how had he gotten my number, and did he chew coffee grounds to achieve that particular effect?).

"Hi, stranger," I said—gaily, I hoped. The fine art of expecting the unexpected.

"Hi, yourself. I've been a bad boy—in D.C. for a while and I'm only getting around to calling you now."

"That's all right," I replied. "A lot of people aren't talking to me."

"Yes, but I've got ulterior motives. You still owe me a drink. Besides, I'm going to be in Washington for some time." A triumphant pause. "I'm working very closely with the deputy secretary of state."

"That's great," I said. So Reiff had a sponsor now.

"There's an anonymous source quoted all over the *Times*. Did you see? Saying the State Department is withholding evidence about Gold. It's not true. We've followed all the rules. Everything's in order."

"That's . . . good," I said.

"Frankly, Kate, you know what I think?"

"Can't imagine." I opened a little packet of cream for the coffee.

"This is coming out of the White House."

I swirled a plastic spoon, gently turning the black liquid brown. "What part of it: the e-mails, the treason, the leaks?"

"You think the e-mails originated in the White House? So do I!" Reiff jumped fast. No wonder, I thought, that he remained an *aspiring* diplomat.

"I didn't say that," I replied carefully. "But it's an interesting theory."

"It's more than theory," Reiff said. "August Mercer runs the place, we all know that. Mercer doesn't know dick about international affairs. Why does he care about this scandal? There've been plenty of them since those guys got into the White House. That's point one. Let me give you two more: No one who has as much influence as Mercer does likes a strong State Department—that's competition for the president's ear, and Mercer is always looking to score points with the big man."

"I was under the impression that the deputy secretary and Mercer are old buddies," I said.

"You know how this town is. There's always a turf war when it comes to influencing the president."

Indeed. "So you think it's Mercer who sent the e-mails? Who posed as Lyle Gold?" This was going from ridiculous to delusional.

"I remain firmly in the camp of the deputy secretary, and therefore I believe the traitor truly is Lyle Gold." Reiff parroted the official party line. "But it appears someone is trying to make the State Department look bad. Not Mercer himself, of course. He's too smart. But he might have hinted to an eager beaver who works for him, someone who wanted to look good for his boss."

Freddy Banks. I held the spoon in midair. Reiff certainly knew of my link to Freddy. He had grilled me about my Banks strategy on that long-ago afternoon at the Hay-Adams.

"Think about it," Reiff continued. "Freddy wants to get ahead; he works for a powerful guy. Nothing like a few key leaks and rumors to help things along. Kate, I'm just trying to help."

Ah, random acts of kindness. I thanked Reiff and hung up, just as the train lurched out of the station. I took a deep swallow of coffee. Follow the rules: Information is spooned agenda. *Why* is *who* telling me *what*? It was too early for me to ponder that with a clear mind. I would need at least three cups, or perhaps caffeine injected directly into my veins.

The conductor walked through the aisle, punching tickets. He nodded at a man two rows in front of me: "Mr. Director." That was enough to get a girl out of her seat on the power express; a recognizable director could only mean a significant player. I headed toward the ladies' room for an inconspicuous glance. There in a dark navy suit sat the head of the Federal Bureau of Investigation himself, next to the chairman of transportation safety. Perhaps they were checking on train security. On the way back to my seat, I flashed a smile at the gentlemen and said, "Mr. Director, Mr. Chairman." They barely gave me a cursory look, but as I turned, I could see that the FBI director had figured out who I was. No secret in Washington anymore, I suppose, but how damn fascinating that he immediately shrank back into the upholstery. That was the move of a man who did not want to talk. I made a note to call Lili: Let's see if his wife got that coveted dinner reservation *now*.

■   ■   ■

Each time I went to the University Club (and I did not go often), I might as well have been on safari. Its wood-paneled walls, well-stocked library, and cribbage tournaments seem out of another era (which, of course, the venerable club is); average age: dead. Lili waved from a table, her stack of silver bracelets clicking their own greeting. There was an older couple with her, very upper crust: the woman with a surgery-pinched face and nubby suit, the gentleman with a yellowed comb-over and tasseled loafers. Genevieve and

Emilio Strauss were the primary investors in the restaurant in Washington. They had no children and adored Lili. I was the designated friend, so they smiled at me. A bottle of white Côtes-du-Rhône glistened in a silver chiller until the matron shot our waiter a hard look. He scuttled over to serve it.

"You poor, poor dear," Genevieve clucked, squeezing my hand in hers. "Darling Lili has told us everything."

Darling Lili shot me a look: *Play along, honey, because these folks sign my check.*

They had read all about the Gold Affair. It was, they believed, flat-out embarrassing. "We are the laughingstock of the world," Genevieve said.

"Of Europe," Emilio corrected.

"Well, that is the world," Genevieve snapped. "You should hear the things they're saying. The French can't get over it. The great democracy, crippled by a rotten journalist. And you know how sanctimonious the French can be. As if they've never had a scandal. Their foreign minister was just found guilty of embezzlement."

"You are not a real politician in France unless you've been found guilty of a white-collar crime," Emilio said. "You ladies know what I mean." He nodded at Lili and me and, for lack of a better response, we both nodded back.

His wife had drained her glass of wine and tapped her fingers impatiently until the waiter refilled it. "And what about the Germans? They're saying *we're* anti-Semitic. The Germans! Can you believe that?"

Emilio ordered a second bottle of wine. "The way people are behaving. I don't know what is going to come out of all this, but I am certain that I shall see justification—and more than justification—for all that I think of human stupidity."

Genevieve was having none of her husband's pontificating. "Please," she said. "I am sick of this entire subject. One troublesome man has ruined just about every dinner party I've been to, a man whose mother grew up in a trailer park. Did you know that, Lili? She did. In a trailer park in Florida."

"No, I didn't know—" Lili started.

"I thought Lyle Gold was from the Upper West Side of New York," I interjected.

"He grew up there—he went to public school, you know; he didn't get into Dalton—but only because his father had a rent-controlled apartment. His mother is trailer park. We all knew that. You can bribe that type with a bucket of fried chicken." The silver-haired matron laughed at her own joke. "The apple doesn't fall far from the tree, I suppose. But I can't really blame her son for trying to climb up a bit, with that fancy house and car."

"There are bad apples in every crop," Emilio said. "Look at the Prouty boy."

"Yes, yes." Genevieve nodded, picking at her *boeuf en gelée*.

Lili paused, her spoon above her plate, and glanced at me. "Reiff Prouty?" she asked.

"We know his parents," Genevieve said. "Lovely, lovely people."

"Does he come into the restaurant?" Emilio asked.

"Kate knows him," Lili said.

I ran down the list. "Tall, dark, handsome, State Department."

"That's him," Genevieve said. "His mother and father are going out of their minds. We saw them in Nice. Such a good-looking young man. I don't understand what went wrong."

"It's called *cocaine*, Gennie," Emilio said.

"He's been in and out of rehab," Genevieve told us, "and he spends all his money on drugs. His mother even said he's stolen some of her jewelry to pay for his habit."

"You shouldn't be talking about this," Emilio cautioned.

"Well, it's all true," Genevieve said. "He'll never rise far now, even with August looking out for him."

"August Mercer?" I asked.

"Long, long, *longtime* family friend," Genevieve said. "He's at the White House."

"He nearly runs it," Emilio corrected.

"I think the president runs it, dear," Genevieve said, with a tinkly laugh.

"By appearances only," Emilio said.

I glanced sideways at Lili, who shrugged as slightly as she could.

Genevieve tripped on breezily. "It doesn't really matter, I

suppose. Jules can just ring up August, and I'm sure his son will be fine."

"That is where you would be wrong," said Emilio, as he dug into his lobster. "Mercer wants nothing more to do with him."

"But that can't be. I spoke to Claire last week. Jules and August sounded as close as can be." Genevieve seemed to have forgotten Lili and I were there with this bit of intrigue.

"Mercer stuck his neck out for the boy, and look what happened. He's been a failure his entire career, and now he's blowing his salary up his nose to boot. That's a significant handicap, my dear. Mercer isn't going to protect him, no matter how much Jules donates this next election round." Emilio doused his lobster with butter sauce.

"Well, I don't understand. We do have *standards*. I just don't understand." Genevieve turned to me. "More wine, Kate?"

Emilio glared at his wife. "What? You don't understand that the most powerful man in the country gave the Prouty kid a break and that he fouled up from the beginning? You should understand that Mercer's in the worst possible position. He's the one who spoke up for Jules's kid; it isn't Prouty's name on the line where it counts, it's Mercer's."

"Of course I understand. It's like when we sponsor someone to join the club here. If the rest of the members don't like them, it's our name that is besmirched." Genevieve sat back, satisfied.

"Something like that." Emilio gave up.

Genevieve brightened. "Do you girls want to try some dessert now?"

. . .

We hurtled down the stone steps of the club and headed east.

"What was *that*?" I shouted, loud enough for a pair of tourists in pink sweatshirts to stop and stare.

"I don't know!" Lili exclaimed. "Oh, God, Kate . . ." Her voice trailed off.

We walked silently down Madison Avenue, past the glittering plate-glass store windows, and stepped carefully over potholes that pockmarked the streets. The magazine party was downtown, but even if we planned to catch a cab, walking a couple of blocks seemed in order.

"Is it Reiff?" I asked, a little taken aback. "Do you think Reiff is the real traitor?"

"Oh, Kate, I can't say for sure." Lili deftly avoided a garbage bag. "But he's definitely on the insider track, if that tells you anything."

It told me quite a lot, actually. So Reiff's father knew Mercer. And Reiff was a member of the club, ticked off at the system, with connections that would cover for him (because their fortunes were tied to his), who had an additional reason—a drug habit—to seek payouts from other sources. And then there was all the interest in China. It *had* to be Reiff. He was the one that made sense—and even if Mercer was not on to Reiff, treason happened on his watch. Mercer could convince himself that an undesirable like a journalist had done the crime. He might even conclude that the events swirling around Reiff were just so much *chatter*, as administration types like to call rumors of espionage.

Then again, there was Freddy to consider. Also ambitious, and not one who could stand another major scandal. Mercer had hired him. He was not likely to believe in either one's guilt, because to do so meant to doubt his own judgment.

"Don't call Jack yet," Lili cautioned. "All of this is only gossip."

Oh, yes, and I was better than that. Hadn't I staked out the higher ground?

■ ■ ■

The new glossy had shelled out big bucks for the party. Debauchery and abandon hadn't come my way in a long time. Here was a grand opportunity, though, spread out in an eleven-thousand-square-foot apartment that rented for twenty grand a night. We stepped off the elevator onto a *lawn*. With *trees*. In downtown *New York*. The brick stairs to the left led to a wooden deck that shimmered with a swimming pool. The winding steel staircase leading to the next level opened onto a meditation garden. This was *big* rich.

It wasn't my crowd. A lot of leather, piercings, tattoos,

bloodred lips, and fabulous shoes (so you knew these were the well-to-do, despite the artistic trappings). I knew no one except Lili—my friend who had done the organizing had come down with a terrible case of food poisoning, or so said her assistant, who was barking orders into a headset as she stomped around, armed with a guest list. The party, lush with several full bars, featured a band noted for its working-class roots. God bless capitalism, the great equalizer.

Lili wandered off, engaged in a detailed conversation with the caterer. I felt ridiculous standing in the enormous main room on a concrete floor and holding a lime-green martini, an inane color for a cocktail. But not nearly as ridiculous as the band's guitarist, evidently. In between sets, he had pressed himself away from the crowd and as close to the wall as possible, clutching a shot of tequila and a beer. I recognized him from the posters displayed near the bars. He had the requisite long dark hair, pulled back neatly, but no scruffy five-o'-clock shadow for this guy. A clipped, exquisitely maintained goatee around a full mouth, which I was staring at, quite rudely, when he nodded at me.

"How's it going?" Perfunctory stuff. He didn't seem like he really wanted to know. Which is perhaps why I replied, "Pretty lousy, thanks."

"You're welcome," he said. "I hope things start to improve for you."

I winked and sipped the martini, a patented move meant to seem cosmopolitan, if the rim of the glass hadn't tipped just far enough from my lip to dribble green liquid down my blouse. Slick. I started to dab the vodka with the sliver of a cocktail napkin and only succeeded in spilling more of the glass down my wrist. The guitarist took pity on me and handed me his napkin.

"I can never drink those either," he said. "That's why I stick with the tried-and-true." He held up his beer and tequila.

I thanked him and introduced myself. That was how I met Charlie Peguy, the half-American, half-Pakistani son of immigrants who followed his soul into music instead of medical school, as his parents had wished.

"Who do you consult for?" Charlie asked.

"Lots of people, but these days mostly Lyle Gold." Why try to hide it? I thought. He would only find out from someone eventually. Better to face his opinion now, in person.

"Who's Lyle Gold?" he asked.

I stared at him. "You're kidding me."

"I'm not. Who is he?"

I summed up neatly. "He's the guy locked up in jail right now, accused of treason he didn't commit."

Charlie Peguy squinted. "Not one of those terrorist guys."

"No. One of those American guys."

The musician looked thoughtful. "I've been in a recording studio a lot lately. But I think I've heard about him."

"A journalist, accused of selling military secrets to the Chinese," I prompted.

"But that doesn't make any sense. Why would a *journalist* do that?" Charlie asked.

"They say he was desperate to get ahead," I told him, realizing rapidly that I had a captive. "He was from the wrong side of the tracks, though, an outsider, up against the ultimate insiders of power."

A look of disgust washed over Charlie Peguy's face. "Typical. If you're a member of the proletariat, like me, you don't count."

"I would hardly call either of you members of the proletariat," I said.

"Yeah, but I'm not their type either, right? I dropped out of college. I play guitar for punker-dunker kids for a living. Come on, if it wasn't Lyle Gold, it could've been me, right? And who's going to protect me?"

"Well—"

But Charlie was getting worked up now. "One thing I keep telling myself, watching these guys making new rules; I keep telling myself, There's some sense to this; different times call for a different way of doing things, right? But that doesn't mean I don't get creeped out by it. And I've got to wonder, like when I hear about people like this guy you're talking about, who's figuring out all the new rules?"

It was nice to have a reminder of something we Washingtonians lose sight of: A dose of suspicion is common and inherently American.

"There are a lot of good, smart people who write and

pass our laws," I said, feeling the need to defend the other half of my client base.

"Sure, sure." Charlie nodded, putting his beer and shot glass on a table so he might gesture more effectively. "But there're always a lot of people who look out for themselves. You know? Like that shitty little homophobe homo, the lawyer guy?"

None of this was jogging my memory. I stared at him, perplexed, until Charlie, his face a grimace of frustration, burst out, "Come on, you've definitely seen the movies about him! The guy who was the lawyer for McCarthy, you know, the one with the Communist hearings?"

"Roy Cohn," I said. "Skinny, bitter, bad complexion."

Charlie delightedly pointed his finger at my nose. "That's him! You know, after all that crap about going after Communists, all those people who jumped out of windows and stuff, Roy Cohn hung out at Studio 54! Like, the Valhalla of vice!" He shook his head. "No one ever called him on anything, and all those lives destroyed. Roy Cohn. He was protected, all right."

"It's called the old boys network, Charlie," I said, taking a sip of my cocktail. "It's been around forever."

"That doesn't mean what those guys are doing now is right," Charlie said. He picked up the tequila and shot it back. "Man, what I'd give to be the one this time who asks, 'Sir, have you no decency?'"

I smiled a little, and why not. This guy played guitar and

wrote songs for one of the most promising bands in the nation. He had an audience. "Well, it was good to meet you." I handed him a card.

He looked at it. "Are you coming to the show tomorrow night?"

"I think I'm heading back to Washington," I said, because after dinner with the Strausses my plans had changed. A relaxing weekend in New York would have to wait; I had work to do, Reiff and Freddy to contact. "Maybe I'll catch you next time." And I left him to grapple with the debutantes who prowled the room.

I caught the high-speed train back to Washington the next morning; Lili decided to stay in New York for a muscadet tasting. I was walking through the gilded splendor of Union Station, dragging my suitcase behind me, when a young man in a ragged sweater came up to me. "Kate Boothe?" he asked.

I paused a moment before replying, "Yes."

"This is for you." He stuck his hand in his pocket, and for a flash I thought he was going to whip out a knife or a gun. But no, what he handed me was a summons. I was being called to a grand jury.

9

THEY SHALL NOT PASS

The Boothes descended on Washington. My parents arrived at my apartment with suitcases, my uncles checked in to a suite in one of the swanky downtown hotels. The cavalry had arrived.

My uncles informed me Freddy Banks had alleged that I attempted to bribe him so that my client, Lyle Gold, would be exonerated. Was there anything I could have said, they wanted to know, that might have set him off?

Freddy, there are people who, whether Lyle Gold is convicted or acquitted, will devote their entire lives, their whole fortunes, to discovering the truth. And no amount of polling can compete with that.

I closed my eyes, disgusted, because he couldn't honestly have interpreted that as a bribe. Our Freddy certainly had turned out to be a snake. In a way, it was brilliant. Put the focus on me and score some points with the boss. My suspicions about his role in the affair must have somehow made it back to him. He wanted to make a preemptive strike before I had a chance to speculate in public.

. . .

I wanted to go on the stand. It was the only way to fight back.

My older uncle, steady and methodical Sig (as in Sigfried, a name to which my grandmother had attached some romance but which made his brothers buckle with laughter even now), thought this was insane. They had already cut a deal with the prosecutors. Give a statement, enter it into the record, walk out. You didn't betray the integrity of a deal with the grand jury, which wasn't even *my* grand jury. It was a "continuing investigation."

Uncle Sig said he had never done anything of the sort, and he wasn't about to start now, with his *niece*, of all people. My grandfather would roll over in his grave, and God only knew what my parents would do—"Probably sue my ass," he snorted. He noted, rather unkindly, I thought, that his three daughters, all lawyers, had agreed with his strategy. But Will, the youngest of the three brothers and a con-firmed bachelor, examined me closely. "You think you're going to change that kid's mind?" he demanded. "You know Kate when she looks like that."

"But why?" Sig fairly wailed. "There's no need. They don't want her. They're after Gold. We've cut an immunity deal. We're set."

"They're messing with her, you know that," Will said.

"I don't want the deal," I interrupted. "The grand jury won't do anything to me."

Both uncles paused, their cognac glasses dangling from loose fingers. This had to rank among the longest nights of work ever spent in their hotel suite. I had waited until now to unleash my argument on them, because I knew how hard it would be resisted.

"Kate, honey, you don't know what these people will do," Sig said gently. "And if I go to the government and tell them the deal is off, well, I just don't know. In all my years, I've never encountered this sort of thing before. You are very clearly not the fish they want to fry. That is just about the only thing in our favor."

"But I have to testify," I insisted. "Really. This is important. I need to get on that stand and tell everything."

"I don't understand." Sig threw back the rest of his drink, but Will thoughtfully pursed his lips.

"I'm innocent, for one thing," I said.

"We don't doubt that," Sig said.

"So let me play it," I said.

Will leaned forward. He was the leanest of the brothers, with a long face and long fingers. He was a hell of a long-distance runner, actually. He once qualified for the Olympic Trials in the marathon. And he liked risks.

"Let her do it, Sig," he said. "She'll play them."

Sig stared at his brother. His eyes were bloodshot as he regarded Will incredulously. "Are you out of your mind?" he demanded.

"Not tonight," Will replied.

"No one testifies before a grand jury after the deal's been cut," Sig repeated. "Don't you two get it? Are both of you idiots?"

But Will was fired up. "She can do it. You know she can. Put the kid on the stand. She'll charm 'em out of their seats. She's not going to take the fall for anything. They know she's innocent. The feds know she's innocent. Let her play *them*. They won't be expecting her on the stand—"

"That's what I'm afraid of," muttered Sig.

But Will continued. "They won't know what to do. And by the time the feds figure it out, she'll have beaten them."

"We're supposed to be protecting her," Sig said, with weighted responsibility. "Robert and Vera will have our hides if we don't."

I leaned forward. "But this will help the most," I said. "With the deal, I don't help my client. If I testify, I have a shot at it."

Sig looked at his brother, then at me, and back to his brother. He sighed. "I want it in writing that this wasn't my idea."

"I'll do you one better," said Will. "I'll bet you a thousand bucks she pulls it off."

■ ■ ■

The moment I finished testifying, I knew I had. I could see it in the jury's eyes. I smiled at the men and women, sitting so attentively in their wooden chairs, and stepped off the stand. Oh, I told them everything. The False *G* Letter and my suspicions about it; the conversation with the Strausses; even nonsensical things—but sure to tug at emotions—like when I drank *prosecco* with Roberto an age ago in Rome. Why not spill it all (I left out a few details, like, for instance, sobbing in my hallway, which seemed too private and embarrassing). The point was to appear to be the auxiliary person that I really was—*I* hadn't committed the treason, after all.

And when I left my chair, there was a moment of silence, almost of stupor, as if all the listeners in that chamber were beginning to suspect the terrible noise that this case was going to cause. My uncles looked up almost simultaneously from their yellow note pads, and I walked over to them. I was finished. It had only taken two days, even with all the questions and interruptions. I felt exhilarated, ready to jump off the cliff again. So as I sat down between my uncles, I leaned back and said, very very quietly, "Leak this."

They exchanged glances. Sig whispered out of the side of his mouth, "Are you kidding?"

"Leak it," I repeated.

"Kate, we can't—" Sig began, but Will hissed at him.

"You already owe me for the testimony. You want to owe me for this too?"

I wanted everything out in public now, word for word. Leaking a transcript was easy. Explaining why to my uncle Sig was not. He wouldn't get it. But if the transcript was out there, I knew it would be the most significant step forward to revealing the truth behind the Gold Affair. Let it all hang out.

My parents were waiting in the cold marble hall of the courthouse. "You did a very good job, Katherine," my mother said, putting a protective arm around me. She looked nice in her lemon-colored lace blouse and long brown skirt. Every inch the midwest mother, sensible heels and all.

"I was a little nervous," I murmured.

"It didn't show," my father said stoutly. He was playing it tough in his dark gray suit. The two of them, such talented lawyers in their own right, must have been sitting outside the room in agony the whole time. Bribery! What a crock! Get the kid out of the way, right, and take care of other business? It had to be an unnerving experience for them. I was their only child. I decided I needed to go home to Chicago for an extended visit when things had calmed down a bit.

Jack was still holding my raincoat, which I had handed to him as we walked into the courthouse. "You want this?" he asked. "It's kind of wet outside."

"No coat." I waved it off. "It's also humid."

"At least fix your hair," my mother said, handing me a comb. "It looks straggly."

I obliged—it was useless to protest—and my mother pushed a few stray strands into place.

"There," she said. "Perfect." She steadied herself to walk with us through the doors out into the cloudy, damp day.

My uncles led the way. They were, after all, the lawyers. Sig would make the first terse statement, and then I would make mine. I had told my uncles that I had only a few words to say. They would have liked to read my statement in advance, but I reassured them that I had faced many cameras before. My parents walked beside me, my mother briefly linking her arm through mine. Poor Daddy, I thought, stealing a glimpse at his pale drawn face; this wasn't doing much to help his nervous stomach. Behind us walked Jack, his brow knotted with worry but his blue eyes hard and his suit, of course, impeccable. Lili had ducked into the crowd, which was mostly press, gathered in a close cluster near the podium that had been set up for all official statement-making.

The camera shutters clicked like cicadas mating as we drew near, flashbulbs popping and fuzzy gray boom mikes lowering and waving as if this were a parade instead of a press conference. It struck me, as we neared the podium, how strange that term was: *press conference*. The press didn't confer; a conference meant watery coffee and U-shaped tables and speakers droning on and on. And a conference was never pressed (otherwise they would last no more than an hour—ha!). The same genius who came up with that term also probably invented *think tank*. Useless, empty, stupid words.

Sig cleared his throat in a manly way and launched into a summation of the defense. I didn't listen. Come on, there had even been scattered applause from the grand jury as I stepped off the stand. How did we think this would turn out? My uncle Sig finished. There were shouts at my parents, who merely receded further. I stepped up to the microphones, black, silver, furry lumps. Reporters, sweat rings bleeding into their suit jackets, shouting and jumping, hoping to produce some emission of sound—maybe, dare they hope, an audible quote?—that they could rush onto the air even as it was uttered. Does an orgasm even come close? Not according to any of the reporters I know. And then a voice cut through the din: *What do you think of the military tribunal?*

I leaned in to the microphone. "Pardon me?" My uncles dove for the podium, trying to intercept my response, but I cut them off with an impatient wave.

"The military tribunal, Kate!" a reporter shouted. "It found Lyle Gold guilty today."

What the hell was this guy talking about? I whipped around, from one uncle to the other, but each stared fixedly at his shoes. I cocked an eyebrow. So they were right: The government was after a bigger fish; I was merely the distraction. My beloved uncles hadn't bothered to fill me in. Then again, judging from the confusion contorting their faces, perhaps they hadn't known either.

That was how a *secret* military tribunal was supposed to

work, after all. The civilian world wasn't quite sure of all the rules, as cameras and reporters were not permitted to observe. Much of what we knew had been gleaned from a fictional television drama with which the Pentagon had worked closely. We knew, for instance, that the court could conceal evidence in the name of national security, and that it could find a defendant guilty even if a third of the officers disagreed with the verdict. All things considered, it was fortunate that the tribunal hadn't seen fit to execute Lyle on the same day. A tribunal! As a "traitor," Lyle was supposed to have an actual civilian trial. He wasn't a "terrorist"; he didn't *actually* fall under the executive order issued by the president. But details, details. Oh, the Justice Department had repeatedly assured the public that such a procedure would never, ever be brought to bear on an American, and the public had accepted this as truth.

"I was not aware of the tribunal," I began, and I could hear my uncle Sig groan behind me, "but then, that's been the natural course of things, hasn't it?"

Careful, sweetheart, there are twenty cameras out there, plasma TV, every color brighter, and all flaws visible.

"Well, the tribunals began for good reasons. We are in a race to shut down terrorist operations. There are no established parameters. In the beginning, at least, we needed speed, and we needed to be able to move against these cells covertly. Therefore, we needed secrecy.

"I often hear politicians—my clients—say we are fighting

for our survival. One congressman told me recently, 'Balance is the key; we may go too far and then have to go back.' But he was willing to take that chance. My question, then, is: Have we finally gone too far? Following the tribunal rules, the secret dossier on Lyle Gold will remain, largely, a secret. But those of us who have seen parts of it—some of us, anyway—have serious concerns about its legitimacy.

"Those of you who haven't seen it should wonder: What if a secret dossier is compiled about *you*? Is that going too far? What recourse would you have? Because now Lyle Gold doesn't necessarily get a civilian review. He doesn't necessarily get an appeal. He does possibly, according to the tribunal rules, get death.

"I began my career by saving the reputation of a young legislative aide whose name appeared on a bathroom wall, accusing him of a rape of which he had been acquitted. This aide, in whose name a privacy law was passed, now works in the White House. The truth, however you define it, usually rises to the fore.

"There is evidence—suppressed by the federal government, I might add—which proves that much of what convicted Gold actually originated *within* the federal government. *Within*. How did a mere journalist get access like that? What are we to believe? I would ask August Mercer, over in the White House: What are we to believe? Because, there *is* a traitor, all right. He still moves among us. Mercer knows this, the State Department knows this, the

Pentagon knows this—but those powers-that-be would rather occupy our time and theirs with bribery charges and innuendo. Again, I ask: Have we finally gone too far?"

There was only the briefest moment of silence. My uncles attempted, Sig most unsuccessfully, to mask their horror. My parents looked grim. Jack grinned like mad. And when the press recovered and started shouting a barrage of questions, it was Jack who seized me by the shoulder and guided me away from the unblinking cameras and the courthouse steps, into the shiny black car. It was only after the car door closed that I realized my hands were shaking.

■ ■ ■

Again, I ask: Have we finally gone too far? Oh, God, had I been for real? I poured myself another glass of bourbon (leaving out the mint syrup; it was sticking to my stomach) and watched the endless replays from my supine position on the couch, wincing every time that line came up. What had I been thinking? Well, that *was* the question batted about by pundits.

Ugh. My little outburst was great fodder for the twenty-four-hour cable channels, hence the clump of photographers and reporters camped outside the door of my apartment building, elbowing and jostling and kicking for a sound bite. Oh, I don't mean to be harsh on the beasties. Many work doggedly in their blind alleys. A few are even vaguely noble. But most of them would pour acid down the throats of their loved ones if they thought it would earn them an edge or, better yet, an award.

The bureau chief for one top albeit aging cable network, a weasel-faced man who might have done a bang-up job if he hadn't appointed himself an anchor, was typical. From the moment I returned to my apartment, he had been calling relentlessly, prefacing all his messages with references to our "relationship" (which consisted of occasional run-ins at cocktail parties), pleading for an exclusive interview. "It's time to cover your ass, Kate," he said. "You need to think about yourself. You have my word that we'll hold the interview until you're ready."

His word! I knew full well that snake of a man would immediately air any interview I gave, just for a one-day bump in the ratings, and, believe me, he would sleep soundly the same night.

Before, even if my name and reputation had been through the grinder and I had made the usual talk-show rounds, the audience had been limited to the Washington-and-New York set. For much of the country, I had not registered. Now—well, pretty much every grandmother in Kenosha had caught a glimpse of my courthouse-steps speech. And by now, the leaked testimony had made its way into the hands of a few well-placed reporters. Let *me* convince you of this truth.

Here's some truth: *Girls* don't often deliver spontaneous remarks tinged with politics, even in this post-feminist era.

Because *girls* aren't regarded with the same seriousness as their male counterparts. *Girls* with unplucked eyebrows and ungainly jawlines give speeches that aren't listened to; *girls* with glossy lips and trim suits give speeches that are dismissed. And *girls* who flaunt the rules are castigated. I knew this. It was literally my business to know such things. But for whatever insane reason—truth, justice, the American way (Ha! I thought, and took a big swig of bourbon)—I had imagined I might be the one to pull it off.

Truman Pace was—surprise, surprise—calling for my head on a platter. "What could this little lollipop know about going too far?" he demanded of his listeners. Maurice Barres, obviously horrified to find himself in the least enviable of positions ("possibly sympathetic"), immediately took to the talk-show circuit. "Kate Boothe is less convinced of Gold's innocence than of the general guilt," he said. "She acquits this traitor only in order to condemn society." He was on his twentieth appearance of the day, milking it for all it was worth. I felt sick, watching him; sick not just in my gut but in my heart because at one point I had trusted him.

I lifted my glass again, and my mother, who was studying the contents of my refrigerator, pursed her lips.

"Robert," my mother said, "your daughter is turning into an *alcoholic*." The ace lawyer reverted to maternal type as far as I was concerned.

My father looked critically at the glass in my hand. "What are you doing?"

I stared at him, uncertain for a moment. Then he added, "People who drink scotch can't drink bourbon."

"Why not?" I asked.

"They just don't. It's the taste."

My mother clucked her tongue disapprovingly. "This is the advice you're giving your daughter?"

"For God's sake, Vera, I took the girl to Scotland for her graduation present. You'd think she'd have learned something."

My father had other things on his mind. There had been death threats, of course (oh, and the *National Enquirer* had called Lili). This matter *had* gone too far, and no one was going to hurt his little girl. It was time to call in the troops. An old army buddy was a mucky-muck at the Federal Bureau of Investigation, and my father determinedly punched the phone number.

"Why not just call one of Johnny Russo's pals?" I muttered.

"Because they're all dead or irrelevant," my father answered. "Hi, there, Bill. . . ."

The clattering of pans shattered in my ears. My mother was cooking tonight. ("Can't Jack come by?" my father had asked plaintively; my parents adore Jack; he had stopped off for the last three nights, whipping up concoctions or unveiling a particularly aromatic cheese.) My head rang, and I thought of the little blue pills that Lili had slipped me, concealed discreetly in a white envelope. She said they would kill the pain with drowsiness. This was a fine idea: sleep and sleep, and maybe the whole thing would have blown over by the time I woke up again. And then I could go back. I had a career, I had a handsome boyfriend.

Except the handsome boyfriend was back in Rome. He would be dogged a bit; a few photos would be snapped. But I was sure to see him gracing the cover of a society magazine before long. Roberto was protected by his bloodlines and an ocean. Hell, I had overshot, right? My chest tightened so painfully at this that I swallowed the rest of the bourbon. The knot would loosen soon enough.

I wandered into my hallway. Grapevines climbed the walls, a passable effort at a personal vineyard that I had painted one winter weekend, when snowdrifts shut down the city. I wanted to sit there on the hardwood floor, hug my knees to my chest, and cry. But I couldn't, not as long as my parents were around. They couldn't know. They were already so upset, and they thought they were helping, braving a fold-out couch and stepping gracefully past the press.

The blue pills. I shook the envelope out of a book Jack had given me a few years ago, a history of the world in the last century, which, I thought as I tossed two pills into my mouth, I really should get around to reading. I curled up on my bed, on the embroidered spread I had found in Château-Thierry, when Lili and I were young and bright and champagne went with everything. . . .

My mother stood in the doorway. "The phone's for you," she said, and she looked at me in that knowing way of a mother who realizes something isn't quite right with her child. Groaning—because this meant I was in for a lecture later—I reached for the receiver.

"Kate? This is Joan," announced a brisk voice, and I jumped straight out of my fog. Joan Picquart—oh, my God, my testimony! It was all over the place, with reporters making their fact-checking calls. My father reported that Uncle Sig had run through his ulcer medication, trying to deal with furious federal prosecutors. Of course this had implications for Joan.

"Oh," I stammered. "Oh—I, well—"

"I want you to come to my house tonight," she said.

"How? The press sees everything. They're outside my door. I'll never get there without being spotted."

"You're a clever sort," Joan shot back. "Find a way."

. . .

The fictional Rhode Island Group called a press conference; its members apparently had new information about further crimes committed by Lyle Gold. By the time I ducked into the backseat of Lili's car and pulled a scratchy woolen blanket over myself, no cameras were around to record it. The media might be a bit sore when they found out it was all a ruse, but what the hell. Jack and I had sprung for a platter of assorted fruits and cheeses.

"How long do these pills last?" I asked, muffled by the blanket.

"It helps if you don't wash them down with a few shots,"

Lili said. Ever the solicitous hostess, she had brought along a thermos of strong coffee, which was dribbling down my chin and onto my shirt as I desperately drank several cups. This was Joan Picquart I was meeting with—I simply could not present a pathetic figure.

The press brigade outside Joan's door was nowhere to be seen, no doubt en route to the Rhode Island Group conference, but still I rolled out of the backseat and dashed up the wrought-iron steps to the door, which immediately opened. Lili winked the headlights.

"You pulled it off, I see." Joan shut the door firmly. "I'm afraid I don't have *prosecco*."

I drew a breath at the pointed reference to the testimony but said, "I'll take bourbon." One more couldn't hurt, and now that I was in her presence, I needed a boost of confidence.

"Yes, well. As you know, I prefer scotch." There was no note of humor in this as she took crystal glasses from the cabinet.

"I like scotch," I said, my voice rising slightly, to my embarrassment. I cleared my throat. "My father says this is impossible. People who drink scotch can't drink bourbon."

"Your father is right," Joan said, handing me a glass. "But you'll learn, presumably." She waved her hand at the overstuffed chair, and once again I sat.

"I like scotch," I repeated. "I drank it the first time I was here. I like—" A sharp look from her silenced me.

"So," Joan said. "I heard your speech, of course." She

paused, and it seemed to me ages before she spoke her next words. "I liked it."

My heart leaped. "You did?"

"More than I did the testimony, shall we say. A reporter read a good portion of *that* to me over the phone. But the speech I thought was interesting. You've caused quite a stir with both."

She was quiet. I felt I should say something. This was what Joan Picquart wanted; it was an elementary tactic, and I fell for it. But how could I not, with the last honest person bearing down on me with that steady stare. I *liked* her, and I wanted her to like me.

"I didn't mean to put you in a bad position—" I began, but Joan cut me off.

"Oh, but you have," she said. "I was working on this from the inside, where delicate situations involving the welfare of the nation are best resolved."

"But you told me—"

"I told you information in confidence. I imparted this to you in the unlikely case that something should happen to me and I was unable to complete the task. I thought I had made this clear."

I was quiet, a flush steadily burning up my neck.

"You have brought it all out into the open. It remains in the open. You understand that, right? The entire situation is different. Now it plays out in front of the world. There is nothing that certain entities like less."

"You're talking about Mercer," I said.

"I'm talking about everyone intimately involved in this case," Joan replied sharply. "There are those who preferred to work this out behind the scenes. Quietly, quickly, without cameras or microphones. Now they can't do that."

"If you'll beg my pardon," I began in my best manners voice, "it seems to me that you weren't working it out all that well behind the scenes to begin with."

Joan smiled briefly. "You might be right. But the rules have changed. I think you should be aware of that."

Joan leaned over and poured a splash more into my glass.

"Let me tell you a story," she said. "During the First World War, Ataturk, before he was called that, stood in the trenches with his men. We forget about trench warfare now. We forget about any history before Hitler, it seems. But those trenches—well, I'm getting carried away, but it was a terrible place to be. These deep pits on all sides, with mud, rats, and things worse than nightmares. You went in knowing that, chances were, you weren't coming back out. American generals sent their boys in with flasks of whiskey. Makes sense to me. The British gave their boys pots of tea. The Brits were shelling the hell out of the Turks, coming closer and closer to where Ataturk was standing. A lot of men would have ducked. Certainly most of his officers turned and fled. Ataturk refused to move. While his men watched, he lit a cigarette. He stayed with them. And, miraculously, the shelling stopped."

"Who's Ataturk?" I asked, and she shook her head.

"What does everyone else teach you these days?" she asked. "I suppose it doesn't matter whether or not you know who he was, as long as you understand what he did and why he did it."

She pulled open a drawer of the delicately carved secretary at her side and drew out a sheet of paper. "This, my dear, is a copy of a memo I wrote." She handed it to me. "Read it. Go ahead."

It was dated three weeks earlier and addressed to the secretary of state. It read, in part:

> A number of indications of which I will speak to you on your return from the Middle East show me that the moment is near when those who are convinced that a mistake has been made are going to do their utmost to prove it and to cause a huge scandal. I believe I can take the necessary steps to allow the initiative to come from us. I should add that these people do not appear to have the same information we do, and that it appears to me that their undertaking will create an awful mess that, nevertheless, will not lead to clarification. This will be an annoying and useless crisis, one that is possible to avoid by rendering justice *in time*.

I looked at her steadily. "You went out on a limb here."

"Perhaps. But I do like to think that I have a higher allegiance to the department and to the national interest than to myself. My record is clean. I like my job and am not particularly ambitious to rise any higher. My loyalty to the secretary, and to my country for that matter, remains unwavering and unquestionable. But"—she shifted in her chair—"I also felt a need to untangle this affair before this syndicate of yours forced the truth into the media."

She sat back and paused for a long moment. "Your instincts were right—although reckless. Now you will see that there is a note clipped to the top of the photocopy."

Sure enough, a tiny square on the upper right-hand side, with an outline of a paper clip running through it. *It is a case we cannot reopen. Say nothing.*

"Who wrote that?" I asked.

"Look carefully at who was copied."

One name: August Mercer.

"I do not expect to see this released to the media," Joan said. "Think of it as *your* smoking gun. Use it only if they have taken me out and are about to do the same to you. These boys don't play fair. If you think it was tough up until now—well, you haven't seen anything yet. And after you finish that"—she nodded toward my glass—"stop drinking. You can't afford to have your mind softened up. When this is over, go on a bender, whatever you want. But not until then. What you do and what you say affect more people than just yourself. And, frankly, Kate, now that you've dragged this into the open, you'd better not fold."

"Light a cigarette," I said weakly.

"Not literally." Joan smiled and led me to the door.

10

FIVE FEET FORWARD, SIX FEET BACK

Relentless, marching their prose and hyperbole across newspapers and television, the anti-Goldians had no intention of abandoning the cause. Tonight on the typical talk show: Some Random Guy Who Was in Lyle Gold's Third Grade Class! Or, Let's Debate the Merit of Kate Boothe, Starring a Former Sorority Sister, a Former Neighbor, and a Former Lover! With the latter, I didn't know if it was worse that such a thing aired or that my parents watched it *in my apartment*. My mother's mouth pressed thinner and tighter until her lips disappeared altogether. For three more days, it went on like this. I couldn't bear to go to the office. The pack was waiting outside.

I pulled apart *The Wall Street Journal* over my morning yogurt. I shook the front section open. Ah, there was a distinctly unflattering woodcut of me and the denouncement that I was a "civilian accomplice" and "the soul of all this agitation." Wow. The soul of agitation! I sipped my coffee and considered this. Once, one of our congressional clients had been inconsolable over a letter he had received from a resident of his district following a particularly controversial vote: "She says I'm worse than Hitler! Worse than *Hitler*?"

"Sticks and stones," my mother said, reading over my shoulder.

Oh, there was a flash of hope. An unnamed source from the Pentagon told *The New York Times*: "We must avoid all erroneous maneuvers and above all initiatives which might be irreversible." I wondered how much longer the cowards would hold out on me. *Go on the record, you bastards*, I thought. I was in a fine mood when I finally checked my e-mail. I hadn't glanced at it in three days, an unprecedented amount of time during a business period, even for me. There was quite a backlog to sort through. One in particular, I wished I had read sooner:

> Kate—I've been told by many well-informed people that you are actively involved in trying to substitute me for Gold. In the face of such a monstrous accusation, and in spite of proof that has been given to me, I hesitate to believe that a young woman of your intelligence would try to substitute *one of your friends* for the wretch who has been proven to have committed the crime.

Well. The missive had come from Reiff Prouty's account, but with all the false e-mails floating around, I was a bit suspicious. There was one way to find out, and it wasn't hard to track down his phone number. He sounded incredibly alert, but in a sleep-deprived way, and startled to hear my voice.

"Quite an e-mail for a girl to wake up to," I said to him.

"What are you talking about?" he asked.

"Who's saying that I'm saying you're the guilty bastard?" I kept my voice even.

"I think—I think—wait—" he stammered, and then he chuckled. "Why don't we start over."

"All right. Last I checked, you were the one making accusations. Remember the one about Freddy Banks being the traitor?"

"Yes, I did call you about that, but you know better than most people that there are a lot of rumors around town. I can't help hearing what I hear. I've even heard it said you once were accepted to astronaut training school and turned it down."

"I—" I lost my train of thought. *Astronaut training school?*

"Some former secretary from your old consulting company is saying it," Reiff told me.

"What the hell would I do in space, diagram sentences?"

"She's also saying you don't wear underwear."

"Oh. Well, that one's true." I knew I could disarm him there, and I did. He chuckled. "Reiff, come on, what's up here?"

"Maybe you should tell me," he said. "You're the one

with the client who's in trouble. And it looks like you're in trouble too. The grand jury, the boyfriend missing in action. What happened to Roberto Picchi anyway? He was your trump card."

I did not care for the edge that had crept into Reiff's voice. "How exactly do you figure that?"

"Someone with your feminine wiles, you could've convinced him to run and ask Daddy. Then you would have known for sure. You blew it there, Kate."

"Thank you for the observation," I said.

"Listen to me, my dear old friend. There are a lot of people—powerful people—who are really pissed at you." Reiff sounded quite insistent, even indignant. "Did you have to *name* Mercer the other day?"

"All I said was—"

"You'd better back off of this fantasy you're pursuing, that's all I'm saying. Lyle Gold is the traitor, and he's going down. That's the official version of things. Some backhanded moves might be made by some people, but they know what they're doing, Kate. They've been in the game longer. They've got a big stake in it."

There was no point in continuing the discussion. I thanked Reiff for his time and hung up.

■ ■ ■

The exchange with Reiff did accomplish one significant thing: It made me creep back to the office. All right, so now the syndicate defense of the Gold Affair had burst out of the beltway. That *had* been my goal. So I put on a white blouse and gray pants and went out to meet the world. The photographers outside my door were so startled to see me they were a little slow on the draw. I decided to wait for them to get their shots. No sense teasing the beast. Feeding works better.

I stopped at my favorite coffeehouse and bought espressos for Jack and me. And when I walked past a newsstand, I broke into a broad smile at Mimi Ryan, who was vamping from the glossy cover of a political magazine: BELTWAY BABE: FIGHTING FOR JUSTICE. At least someone was having a zesty time with this. I moved on to the cover of a New York tabloid (yes, we get those in Washington). It was Charlie Peguy, his nose streaming blood and his eyes swollen, sagging against the ropes of a boxing ring. I threw down a quarter and ripped open the pages.

SRO K.O.!
ROCKER ROCKED IN REC FIGHT

It was supposed to be a friendly sparring match between club members at the Chelsea Piers: guitarist Charlie Peguy of the rock band Kitchener's Wood *versus* real estate lawyer Felix Saussier. But things turned ugly when Peguy was overheard before the match defending the traitor Lyle Gold.

"Anti-American," Saussier said. "That's what I could call him that could be printed in a newspaper. When I heard him, I knew I had to teach him the kind of lesson that we taught bin Laden."

Regular sparring matches do not allow blows to the head or the face, according to club rules. Saussier pummeled the rocker for "at least ten minutes," observers said, until the instructor stepped in.

Peguy was taken to an area hospital for treatment for a concussion. A Kitchener's Wood concert scheduled for later tonight has been canceled. The fitness club had no comment.

Charlie left me a message later that day. "I looked into his eyes, and I saw the Enemy." He told me he was writing a song from his hospital bed. It wasn't because of me or even because of Lyle Gold. It was because some "silver-spoon jerk," as Charlie put it, had smacked him around.

■ ■ ■

That night, almost a week after my testimony, my father sighed and stepped out onto the balcony. "Kate, come on out here. I want to talk to you." He shut the screen door behind him.

Oh, God, I thought, on top of everything else, I'm finally going to get the sex talk. I dragged my feet. My father was tapping a cigarette out of a red carton. He was supposed to have quit three years ago, after undergoing open-heart surgery. Now I felt even worse. I had driven him back to smoking.

He glanced at me and smiled faintly. "You gave me worry lines on my face," he said. "This"—he waved the cigarette—"comes from your mother. She's painted the whole damn house the color peach. Makes me want to sell the thing."

I smiled back at him and leaned against the railing. It had rained earlier that day, and sticky clouds of steam curled up from the hot pavement below. My father puffed thoughtfully. He had always been the go-to guy in my life. My mother could shout and stamp her feet in a fruitless attempt to make me do something, like clean my bedroom, but all my father had to do was look at me and say, "Kate, I'm disappointed," and I was reduced to tears. My father had been the one member of the family not to choke at my failure to attend law school. Instead, he had consumed cigarettes, one after the other until he had gone through a pack, and then had said, "All right, then, Kate."

Now, I could see only the shadow of his face in the moonlight and the burning glow of the tip of the cigarette.

"I hate you smoking," I said to him.

"Well, I hate you drinking bourbon," he replied. "And I hate you being involved in this situation. This is bad, kiddo. This is beyond what I've ever seen."

There was one of those interminable silences that he had always been fond of, in the courtroom and out, then he continued. "Your uncle Sig told me tonight that you're going to be just fine, at least as far as the government goes. They weren't after you, as he had guessed. They're not happy with the leaking of your testimony, but they can't trace it to you. So they're going to drop the charges. They know they'll never get an indictment."

The threat of an indictment had never been in doubt. I had always known I would win on that count.

"They are going to go after you in different ways," my father said finally. "I don't know what I can do to help you. I've turned this over and over and wracked my brain, but I can't figure out the magic combination that will protect you."

His face looked so drawn and pained that I immediately started with "Dad, you don't—" But he cut me off.

"Oh, Kate, I know I don't have to," he said, and took a long drag. "When you spoke on the courthouse steps, and when you gave your testimony, I knew what you were doing. Kiddo, not even your grandfather, at his best, had the moxie to try something like that. You almost pulled it off—you came damn close. But you know that no one outside of—what are they calling you, the syndicate?—was ready yet to hear it. I watched you, though. You *can* change people's minds on this one."

"Do you really think so?" I asked.

"Of course I do," my father immediately replied. "You know what you need to do? You need to make people feel good about believing in your argument. I happen to think this is a special skill of yours. I listen to you. Even when I don't agree, I *want* to. Now, of course, I believe you got this from *me*, but your mother might disagree."

"I want to win," I said suddenly.

"I know you do. Which is why your mother and I are getting out of your hair. You've got enough work without us around."

"Will you stop smoking then?" I asked.

"When this is over, I'm sure I will," my father replied.

"Ataturk lit a cigarette," I said, almost dreamily.

My father drew on his with gusto. "For heaven's sake, don't follow his example. You'll be in a trench for years."

·　·　·

I knew Kitchener's Wood was playing London at the beginning of September. It was supposed to be the first show of their European tour, according to an e-mail sent to me by Charlie Peguy. He added, "We're trying out some new stuff." I did not pay much attention. I wasn't going to be anywhere near the Astoria. I wasn't going to hear the refrain of Charlie's song "Goodbye to All That," which went, in part:

> *They say money doesn't make a man*
> *unless you're an aristocrat or diplomat or democrat*
> *Then lock away the innocent guy*
> *Who's counting?*
> *It's not junoon*
> *Goodbye to all that.*

I heard the crowd loved it, especially the driving, angry beat. I also heard British officials were less pleased. Within twenty-four hours, Charlie was arrested on charges of "inciting religious hatred," a crime, according to the country's antiterrorism legislation.

"Who do we know in the House of Lords?" Jack drummed his fingers on his desk as the news crossed over our cable networks.

The situation was complicated. According to British law, Charlie could be held indefinitely and without trial (not unlike our classification of *enemy combatant*, which also has no standard of review). What damned Charlie Peguy was the use of the word *junoon*. The British claimed that this Urdu word for *crazy* was most likely an appeal for jihad to fervent Muslims everywhere.

Now, naturally Charlie would know the meaning of *junoon*; his mother was from Pakistan. But since it was frequently used in the context of passion, as in for a girl or a boy, and since Charlie technically was Catholic—his father's side—how the usage could be construed as anything other than a song lyric was beyond me. But you can always spin anything. With this song, Charlie Peguy had become a problem. He needed to be dealt with.

"I love wartime law," Jack muttered as he tried, vainly, to work through our client list. No one wanted to touch this ("In England you're guilty until proven innocent," said one of our congressmen. How is that different, I wanted to ask, from what our attorney general is trying to do?).

Amazingly, Charlie managed to place a call to the office.

"We've got our lawyers trying to work on this," he said, "but it's not easy. I look like their version of a terrorist."

"Don't worry," I said. "This will become a free-speech issue. You watch."

He laughed bitterly. "I don't think so. You're being way too optimistic. There aren't too many mavericks in the artistic community. They're worried about their paychecks. You watch. They'll fold."

And to my horror, they did. I always liked to believe the creative types of the world weren't afraid to say something different. But very few were not beholden, somehow, to a corporate conglomerate for their fortunes. It didn't pay to upset the big boys. Besides, it wasn't as if Kitchener's Wood was a huge group; aside from a few plumb gigs, they mostly played the up-and-coming venues. Charlie's band was dropped by its label.

Then, the letter arrived at my apartment. I recognized the thick cream stock, the same that Roberto had used to write to me right after we first went out in Venice, cajoling me to join him in Rome: *Your lips, your eyes, your smile are in my mind; you are always in my mind, and so it seems to me I am close to you; one thing is certain—something has changed in me. And, whatever happens, I want you to know that you will be always, for ever, in my thoughts and in my heart.* Tell me, who would ever write me letters like that again?

I poured myself a glass of *prosecco* before I opened the envelope.

Dolcissima Kate,

I met with my father. It wasn't too bad. I am his son. He acknowledges me; he acknowledges my mother. This is not why I met with him. I wanted to know—I had to know, for you.

I have learned who it was who passed information. Not long ago, Reiff Prouty showed up at the embassy for an unplanned meeting.

My father is not going to admit any of this to anyone other than me. Presumably, the ambassador knows his son will report this back to you. I am certain that you will use this information discreetly.

Your Vespa is still here.
Take care of yourself.

I smiled at this last part. Roberto had thought I was crazy when I went out and bought myself a seafoam-green Vespa. I suddenly realized that I hadn't left much behind other than the Vespa. When I packed my bags, I told myself it was only a temporary move. I was fully expecting to return. Or at least, this was the surface of my plan. Scratch a bit deeper, and it certainly didn't appear that I was returning. Roberto wasn't stupid or shallow. He must have known before I did.

Turning the envelope, I saw that the postmark was Washington, D.C. He had come back and had not told me. I poured another glass of *prosecco*, berating myself. Oh, I was not such a good person. I liked to think that I was noble, that I was strong. But I was selfish and single-minded. How else did I explain what I had done to the one person I had ever loved? He treated me far, far better than I deserved.

■ ■ ■

It was time to act as the savvy consultant I pretended to be. I turned the letter over. It was fine for my own confirmation, but my proactive defense in the affair had stumbled. Less than a week after my grand jury testimony, I might as well have been sinking in mud. I needed a well-known name, a respectable name, a figure untouched by party or ideological affiliation, to serve as the next mouthpiece. I needed someone—and quite definitely a legislator, because those *were* the folks who moved the action—who was known for his or her strong convictions, preferably and specifically dealing with truth and honor. Who the hell had the guts to speak their mind just a year away from an election? I had to lace up my running shoes and slog through seven miles along the Potomac, turning the question inside out in my mind, until the name came to me: Augie Scheurer-Kestner.

Hadn't I once heard the venerable senator comment more than once, "We are in a difficult time and therefore we might be inclined to look for easy solutions. That would be our downfall." Arguably, Scheurer-Kestner was the most venerated man in politics. He had managed, in a long career, to elevate himself above mere party maneuvering. He was a *thinker*, people liked to say. He had a well-known love for the institution he served (he was the author of a fifteen-volume history of the Senate). And he never hesitated to take a stance on a subject he believed in, even if it was unpopular, like criticizing single parents or even questioning the validity of missile defense ("Looks like my grandson's video games!" he had jabbed at the secretary of defense during one memorable hearing). *My* senator, I might add, whom I had admired from afar as his tall frame bent slowly with age, his hair practically gone but his white beard tidily framing thin cheeks.

Scheurer-Kestner had been politely uninterested in the affair at the start; once I reached the office, I dug up an article in which he was quoted as saying, "The information I have received leads me to believe in his guilt." But in subsequent interviews I read, he gradually became puzzled by Gold's crime and piqued by the case. He was my man, all right.

I also happened to know his chief of staff. As luck would have it, she was the only one of Jack's former girlfriends I actually liked. So I rang her from my cell phone and asked how her boss's mood was these days. "He's seventy-eight," she said, after sucking her teeth for a moment. "He's going to do whatever he believes in."

Just what I wanted to hear. I would put together a special packet to send, via my trusted assistant, over to the Senate Office Building for Scheurer-Kestner's reading pleasure. I told the chief of staff as much, and she promised to give it to him. "We girls have to stick together," she said. I knew what that meant, so I promised that Lili would squeeze her in for an eight-in-the-evening table-for-four on Saturday, complete with the Treatment (champagne, extra courses, digestives). Lili would gnaw her fingernails at the gymnastics she would have to perform, with only two days' notice. I would have to properly compensate her, no question.

I have to admit, for the first time in a long while, I felt the faintest stirring of hope. Augie Scheurer-Kestner was the perfect man to rally to the cause. After all, words were the weapons of choice here. All I had to do was turn to the pile of newspapers beside me. For instance: "I am indifferent to the Gold case," a prominent author told *The New York Times*. "If Gold is innocent, so much the worse for him. There have been famous victims of judicial error. When one discovers one of them, it serves no purpose to make a lot of noise about it, because anybody can make a mistake."

Or everybody can make one. I knew Americans would join the two camps—for or against Gold—as if God would judge them on how wisely they had chosen. If there were something to make everyone feel good about being against Gold, I had to give everyone some reason to feel good about being *for* Gold.

■ ■ ■

What I gave Augie Scheurer-Kestner, of course, was a copy of Roberto's letter. It was a betrayal of a confidence, but a safe one, I felt. Scheurer-Kestner was the sort of man whom

Roberto respected. And the senator would not reveal his source, I was willing to wager. It would merely serve as a confirmation of preexisting suspicion. Also, copies of the e-mails, courtesy of Joan Picquart, and the missive I had received from Reiff.

The information package, duly passed by the hand of the chief of staff, successfully pushed the button of conscience. The good senator called me shortly after he had received it.

"It seems to me," he began in his stentorian voice, "that there is someone—this Joan Picquart—who ought to sense more forcefully the immense moral responsibility that she is wedded to. It is impossible to admit that an honest person keeps in her possession so terrible a secret and leaves an unfortunate to languish in prison."

"I hardly think it is fair to say that," I replied. "The assistant secretary has been working behind the scenes. There are others, higher up, who know just as much, if not more, and they have done nothing."

"What are you suggesting? What can I possibly do with information I cannot reference?"

"You are a man of unimpeachable integrity," I said. "People listen to your arguments."

"And how am I supposed to argue this, Miss Boothe? I should rely on my reputation?" he asked, half seriously.

"Who else has one?" I returned.

Three days and sleepless nights later, he delivered. Jack swaggered into my office, slapped a copy of *The Washington*

Post on my desk, and said, "Well, how 'bout that? Augie Scheurer-Kestner's written a letter to the editor. Wonder who put that bug in his ear?"

Dear Sir,

I am dumbstruck by the situation known as the Gold Affair.

At the time of his conviction, everyone, including military judges and functionaries of the government, was convinced of his guilt. Today, we have reason to believe that the opposite is the case. Some doubt; others, and an assistant secretary of state is among them, recognize the situation for what it is: Gold is innocent.

Not only is it known in the State Department that Gold is innocent, but among the top levels of our government, the identity of the true culprit, the criminal, is known also.

I call upon these men and women, who have sworn to uphold the Constitution of our great nation, to do their duty and to make right a situation that mocks what we stand for.

"Oh my God," I said.

"Nice work, babycakes," Jack said. "Now watch him hang."

■ ■ ■

The letter certainly jolted the chattering class back into action. One of the more roundly mocked, although avidly attended, dinner tables in the city belonged to a beautiful woman, a member of the intelligensia, who had married into money and politics. She aspired to host a great salon, but these do not exist in a one-industry town; every conversation revolves around politics. In a moment of excellent timing, however, the night that Scheurer-Kestner's letter ran in the newspaper just happened to be the night of one of the socialite's dinner parties. I have no idea exactly what was said. I heard about the slamming of fists on the table, about the House majority leader (who, I always thought, was famously nearsighted) beaning the secretary of agriculture with a roll, and about the bottle of 1986 Château Margaux spilled in its entirety when the secretary retaliated by leaping around the table and striking the majority leader twice on the back of the neck with his hand. The hostess finally got the noted soiree she had always longed for; her husband, a congressman, would only say dryly to the media, "For the first time at our table, there was talk neither of policy nor of philosophy."

Not surprisingly, Scheurer-Kestner's chief of staff declined to meet with me when I called the following day. "What's done is done," she sighed.

Truman Pace called her boss "a doddering fool." The press caught August Mercer outside of the downtown steak restaurant that he now haunted after being seated near the kitchen one too many times in Lili's establishment, and he was ready with the sound bite: "We are disappointed that the senator chooses to end his career taking a traitor's side."

End his career? Well, there were no guarantees he would run for reelection, although the Senate did sometimes seem like a retirement home for millionaires.

Those old boys weren't too happy with their colleague. "But, damn it all, when one goes by the name of Scheuer-Kestner, one isn't a Goldian! The gentleman has always before had the highest sense of moral responsibility," groused an equally senior senator, Duke Guermantes, who could hardly believe such an established figure would sign up with the syndicate.

To Scheuer-Kestner's credit, he did not fold. He lumbered from his office to the Senate chamber each day, repeating his standard answer to the beasties that trailed him: "There should be a revision, but at least they should try the boy again, this time in public, if they're so sure of his guilt."

Only days later, outside Lili's restaurant, carrying a gift-wrapped bottle, I told reporters, "There are those who can justify their actions in withholding the truth through lying to themselves about the reality of the situation. It is a very sophisticated defense mechanism to trump the sense of individual responsibility." For the first time in weeks, I smiled.

THE RATS:
Traitor gathers allies!

God love those tabloid headlines. And God save the beast.

"Katie! Katie! What do you believe?"

"Is the senator senile?"

"Is Charlie Peguy a terrorist?"

"What do you believe?"

I counted the cameras stalking my office: one, two, four. No, I was determined to wait for six. What did I believe? Oh, they didn't *really* want to know. I could have dished it out. Mostly, though, I believed—I knew—that I did not want to be a coward. To fold now would be embarrassing.

I was at my desk, throwing away the lurid tabloids, when Joan Picquart called.

"Interesting reference to me in the senator's letter. Thank you very much, but when I want credit for destroying my career, I might seek it out myself. What do you think?"

"Oh, come on, professor," I snapped back. "Irrefutably, we all know the damn traitor is Reiff. Let's *go*."

"The only thing going is your business," she retorted. "You don't understand your enemy. Didn't I teach you anything? You are now up against Mercer directly. Best of luck."

"But this isn't even about treason anymore," I protested. "This is about a falsely accused guy, sitting unfairly in jail, and the cover-up that's been going on."

"You will never work in diplomacy, you know that," Joan said. "Look, you've struck at Mercer. You know the rule. You better make sure it's a hit that knocks him down and out or else."

I knew, all right. The old adage: If you go after someone

in politics, go hard and go for the kill, because if he does manage to survive he will inevitably rise above you. But then, I thought, wouldn't this same rule apply in the reverse? If Mercer was going after me, he would hedge that a bright young thing wouldn't have a shot at a second coming. In this town, those were long odds. Still, Mercer undoubtedly was not losing sleep. I was a girl; he was a man. He had all the power at his disposal. I had myself. He was going after my name, though. What the hell, I thought, I'll go after his.

11

JOHN HANCOCK WOULD HAVE DONE IT

I knew a defense lobbyist from around town, Joe Morgan. We used to haunt a few of the same bars, although he preferred whiskey to wine. He also had a ropey scar across his throat that he did not seem inclined to discuss, nor did I particularly want to press him on it. Defense lobbyists usually did time in the military beforehand, and Joe Morgan had done his in Special Ops.

It was easy to find my old friend, a process of elimination. By the third bar I found him, nursing a highball and pulling apart a bloody steak.

"Miss Katie Boothe, in the flesh." Morgan barely glanced my way, but he smiled. "Haven't seen you in a while."

"How's business?" I asked, leaning against the slab of chipped marble.

"The members are back from the August recess. They've got to pass the defense budget by September thirtieth. It'll never happen. Same old stuff. Pull up a seat." He waved his knife at a vacant stool. "You've been busy lately, I see."

"Busy getting pounded," I said, and Morgan laughed heartily.

"Oh, you sure have! But you've given as good as you've got, I'd say. What're you drinking tonight? Hey, Mike! Mike, you know who this is?" he called out to the wan-looking bartender. "This is Kate Boothe, the poor kid out there standing up for Lyle Gold. Give her whatever she wants. She needs it." He guffawed again.

"Sparkling water," I said, and Joe Morgan really laughed then.

"Must be going worse than I thought," he said.

"You've run across August Mercer a few times," I said. "What's he like?"

Morgan snorted. "A prick. All you need to know about that guy is he's on a power trip. He answers to no one but the president. With him and his crowd, it's easy: You're either with them or you're against them. That's all there is to it."

"What's his relationship with the defense secretary?"

"He doesn't seem to give it much thought," Morgan said. "The defense secretary knows him—they all go way back. But there's a turf war going. Whoever can get an edge. You know how it goes."

Morgan glanced at me.

"Mercer feels invincible now, and maybe he is. But say someone put a chink in the armor. Everyone has a weak point. If someone found his and exploited it, there're enough people in this town who wouldn't mind seeing him go down. Won't be a lot of tears shed for that guy—*if* it happens. Chances aren't good, Kate. He's the king right now, and it's good to be king."

■ ■ ■

This is probably why we were hemorrhaging clients left and right—literally (we prided ourselves in middle-of-the-road ideology, not party affiliation). We wouldn't even make payroll if we didn't forgo our salaries for the month, a sad state considering we had only two assistants. And we had the audit in the offing. I sat in my office, the sunlight faintly peering through wooden slats. The television, glowing blue, was tuned in to the floor of the House. Idly, I remembered the time, a few years ago, when a sweet legislative aide brought me there in the out-of-session hours and convinced the guards to let me sit in the speaker's chair. Engulfed in leather—what a way to view the room.

I glanced up at the television in time to catch one of our congressional clients, a handsome young cad from Tennessee, bellowing from the floor of the House in his best dramatic voice, "Now is the time for vigilance! Our very nation is on trial, standing at the judgment bar! Our course of action is the course of democracy, a democracy threatened by this traitor among us and those who support him!"

And I suddenly remembered that the congressman

wanted to run for the Senate, and that the incumbent senator had just that day opted not to seek reelection. A timely
call from the White House, no doubt.

. . .

They waved the newspapers in my face as I was coming into
the office the next morning. The black-and-white-and-red
headlines were from New York tabloids, of course, hence
the particular sangfroid:

GOLD KINKY SEX!
Ex-Lover's New Bombshell!

"Kate! Kate! Did he tie you up too?"

"Did you see the pile of neckties under his bed?"

"Are you also into bondage?"

The media cluster, a one-celled organism, moved toward
me as I tried to walk up the steps. I sighed and regained my
game face.

"Ladies and gentlemen, I wish I had salacious details to
give you, but I don't," I said, and I tried again to step
around them.

"Would you call Gold 'kinky'?"

One, two, four, six. Well, then. I wanted Lyle Gold to get
a revision. According to the rules of the tribunal, he wasn't
automatically allowed one. It was time to start steering
things in a different direction. I breathed deep.

"I would say that whenever consultants take on a client, we usually know a *little* more than we want to about the people we represent—it's called 'preemptive opposition research.' And therefore I can say with some degree of certainty that I was unaware of any knotted ties other than the ones Mr. Gold occasionally wore around his neck."

The amoeba oozed again, blocking my way.

"But did you sleep with him?"

"Are you still sleeping with Xianxu's son?"

Careful, now, I thought, don't lose your temper. Control. Smile.

"At the rate I'm going, I may never have another boyfriend."

This elicited laughter.

"Come on," I continued. "What you're really saying, in not so few words, is, We don't like Lyle Gold. Well, so what? You don't have to like him. I don't have to like him.

"We have been asked, in the last few years, to believe in one overarching concern: You are either with us or you are against us. Simple as that. In fact, a whole system has been built around the concept. All that has to happen is for one person—a librarian, a coworker, a family member—to tell authorities that you are engaged in suspicious activities—a book you bought or an Internet site you checked out—and you can be taken into custody, declared an *enemy combatant* by the federal government, and that's it. You will not be charged with a crime; you will not have access to counsel;

but you are subject to interrogation for the duration of the 'war.' That doesn't happen to foreigners. That is the procedure for Americans. An actual terrorist like Timothy McVeigh was afforded greater protection.

"You might think, Oh, that could never happen to me. These laws, these courts, don't affect me because I have nothing to hide. But someone like Lyle Gold had nothing to hide either. Have you seen any of the evidence in this secret dossier? You have only heard innuendo. Is that enough? According to men like August Mercer, it is. But men like August Mercer do not believe in limiting principle. They think nothing of rolling over our civil liberties in pursuit of freedom. They say, You are with us or you are against us. And if you question their disregard for American values, they dismiss you as a traitor.

"Because remember what Lyle Gold did do: He did question some of their actions. They must not have liked that very much.

"But that was his job—to ask questions. How that translated into an act of treason terrifies me. Because, ladies and gentlemen, there but for the grace of God go *you and me*."

And the one cell became two.

. . .

Next step. I spent the afternoon calling a few reporters across the country to poll how comfortable they really were with one of their own languishing in jail without a real trial and with the real traitor still at large. Only a few hung up on me. The nice young man I once met who filed for the *Los Angeles Times* yelled at me. But the alternative press, bless 'em, listened with interest. The alternative press, usually owned by a family and staffed with freshly minted college graduates or professional gadflies, historically has more moxie than the establishment. *Old-boys network*, I whispered.

The Chicago paper came through, publishing a screed by one Bernie Lazard.

JUDICIAL ERROR: THE TRUTH ABOUT THE GOLD CASE. I might not have paid it close attention, since it did not reveal anything I didn't already know, but it quoted, at length, a Harvard professor named Lucien Herr. Quite the respected legal academic, as it turned out. I called on the only professor I knew, and Joan had plenty to say. "No one lays out an argument like him," she said. "He perceives the truth so completely that he can communicate it without effort."

Thank God, then, that Herr was on our side. Thoughtfully, I forwarded the Lazard essay to a few television bookers I knew. And, sure enough two days later, Herr surfaced on the Eddie Drumont show. "It seems that matters of state are outweighing a question of justice," he opined to a flummoxed Eddie. "To men who want to stay in office, the nature of justice is not so clear." Eddie, outclassed and outwitted (which, I suppose, the dead fern in Edgar Demange's office could do to Eddie), looked desperately toward the unblinking eye until his producer, mercifully, cut to commercial. But it was Bernie Lazard who caused the biggest stir, the son of a South Side butcher who put himself through school by joining the army. With his buzz-cut hair and blue oxford shirt, Lazard defied the public image of the suave media elite usually served up on the pundit circuit.

It was not without a small sense of glee that I greeted the familiar face gracing cable networks everywhere by the end of the week. August Mercer's voice was calm and his expression implacable, but just below his left eye, the skin twitched as he told the press who gathered outside his office, "The East Coast elite is coming after the heartland of America and the values and character we hold so dear." You could almost hear the giant sucking sound of Middle America inhaling. Lines like this were almost invariably winners— you know, *Damn the fancy city boys!*—except that most of the East Coast elite was clearly on Mercer's side. And Middle America—you know, the folks out in Nebraska who had looked at me askance—were left completely confused, because Mercer went after a working-class guy like Bernie Lazard and blamed it on the elite, or called him elite, or something like that. No matter how it was viewed, Mercer looked bad. He must have known. Mimi Ryan was doing the flash polling for him.

·   ·   ·

It was a wonderful week.

"The world needs to know: If you come into this land,

you must respect its people," explained the conservative activist who had run for president twice.

"Justice does not come down from heaven," said a solemn Lucien Herr. "It must be conquered."

"We are in real moral danger here, people!" ranted Truman Pace. "The syndicate is gathering! It's everywhere!"

"This is great stuff, great stuff." Jack was flipping from one channel to the next. "All Gold, all the time. Is anyone pitching this to Melvin Gluck as a feature film?"

. . .

I called up Scheurer-Kestner's chief of staff and suggested she make a phone call of her own. "You've seen the information," I told her. "You might want to drop Reiff Prouty's name with a couple of reporters who you trust."

"I don't trust any reporters right now," she said.

I was not deterred. "What about one of your local guys? Surely someone in Springfield would love to hear something before the dailies in Chicago."

Later that day, she did ring up the editor of the *Springfield Press*. And the following morning the name of Reiff Prouty appeared on the front page of that small midwest newspaper. By noon, the article had been picked up by the wire services, which began running with it. At two o'clock, I received a phone call from *The New York Times*.

"We have always maintained that Lyle Gold did not commit the espionage he is accused of," I said carefully.

"There would appear to be many people in Washington with a vested interest in seeing that someone like Lyle Gold is accused rather than a diplomat like Reiff Prouty." I told the same journalist, off the record, about Prouty's relationship with August Mercer, and wasn't that *fascinating*?

"Gosh, and you know, if it does end up that Reiff Prouty did it and not Lyle Gold, your paper is way behind the curve," I added. "John Jaures has been all over this story, investigating it for months now. Oh, well. At least you might be able to beat *The Washington Post*."

I like to think that *The New York Times* cannot be spun but that appealing to its competitive sense is what works. Whatever the case, three investigative journalists were promptly assigned to the story. The only reason I knew about it was because John Jaures called. "I used to have it all to myself!" he exclaimed. "I don't know if I'm mad that I don't anymore, or if I'm glad because it no longer looks like I'm crazy."

Spilling out onto the soft gray pages of the fat Sunday edition: Reiff Prouty, the young diplomat with the unfortunate drug habit . . . needed money . . . thwarted ambition . . . whispers of treason. The mentions were slight—remember, investigative journalism takes awhile—so this was easy to ignore for men like August Mercer. But then, the following Monday, very very inside and very very quietly, another story trickled out of the embassy mansions along Massachusetts Avenue and down to little people like the gnatty Lewis Tap.

He had traded his seersucker suit for a three-piece pin-stripe, topped off with a cravat (who, please, wore one of those outside of London?) when he sidled up to my table at Le Sénateur, where I was waiting for Jack. "*So*," he cooed, "your one-time future father-in-law has had enough, I hear."

"Dare I ask?" I looked up at him expectantly. Lewis winked and sat in the chair meant for Jack.

"Oh, Kate, it's *marvelous*. I don't know when I've heard such a thing. The ambassador is *very* good friends with Douglas *Dawson*, the *British* ambassador. The story *I* heard, and I even wrote it down on a piece of paper—where is it? Ah!—Xianxu told Dawson that, and I quote, 'It is no longer a *question* of saving a man and getting the *real* culprit con-victed but a question of defending our *honor* and at the same time giving this *Mercer* a lesson, putting him in his place.' Hmm. Now what do you make of *that*?"

A gleeful grin wrapped itself around Lewis's face. A hor-rifying sight, the red lips pulled over chalky white cheeks. I thanked Lewis for his story. He was a little put off by the lack of a dramatic reaction, but I was saving that for Jack. Between the British ambassador and Lewis Tap, the story would make the diplomatic rounds by the end of the cock-tail hour.

■　■　■

Well, of course there wasn't much for the United States attorney general to do by the end of the week. The sour-faced man, who still had not managed to ban all alcohol on airline flights but had quietly edited chunks of the Constitution, called in Reiff Prouty to have a chat with a grand jury. We might not even have known about it but for the excellent sources cultivated by John Jaures, because the whole thing was executed with secrecy worthy of Special Operations itself. Whisked in, whisked out, Reiff had rattled off his tale before I even heard he was sitting in a courtroom.

"It's not good news," John said, calling me from the courthouse steps. I could barely hear him with an early fall wind blowing interference. "It doesn't look like anything's going to happen."

I looked indignantly at the receiver. "How could *nothing* happen?"

"For one thing, the attorney general is an old school buddy of Mercer's."

"Of course," I conceded. Well, when one angle fails, turn to another. "Anyone else around? Anyone getting pictures of them coming out of the court?"

"There's a few," John said, "but that's no good either."

"What do you mean?"

"You'll know when you see the shots."

Which I did that night on television. There was the good-looking young man in his nicely cut suit, just the right shade of dark blue to set off his fair complexion. Reiff looked straight into the cameras and coolly said, "I am not a traitor." His teeth sparkled white. I knew, then, he wasn't going anywhere but up.

Lili actually overheard a group of lobbyists, sitting at the bar of Le Sénateur, clink cognac glasses together and cheer, "Long live Prouty!" While the rest of the country might have wondered what, exactly, had transpired, most of Washington swooped like vultures on two voices who had spoken against Reiff.

Joan Picquart had done so quietly, but her name was out there nonetheless, mostly due to me. The secretary of state (it was suggested) decided to dispatch his trusted aide Picquart to wade through the oil issues of São Tomé. There was one flight a week from Lisbon to the island nation in the Gulf of Guinea, on the equator. Conveniently, then, Joan would be on the other side of the world, far from prying reporters or persistent consultants. In a moment of generosity, Joan called me. She considered herself lucky, she said; the secretary could have asked for her resignation. I felt horrible.

Things happen quickly behind the scenes—scores are settled, and certainly in his long long career, Senator Augie Scheurer-Kestner had racked up a few enemies who had been waiting for an opportunity to knock him down a few notches. He was of the same political party as August Mercer, but that did not save the senator from losing his chairmanship.

Someone's power, at least, remained undiminished.

Extreme highs require extreme lows, I suppose, but did it all have to happen so quickly? One week after I was sure I had turned things around, the syndicate had officially lost not just the battle but also the war. *They shall not pass*—well, they did. Despite Joan's advice, I opened a bottle of scotch and drank, with enthusiasm, two glasses. I thought I would feel reasonably bolstered to face another day. Instead, I sat on my balcony, the stereo radio wailing from inside, and felt the stirrings of a throbbing headache. I touched my temples, half closing my eyes. And then I heard the vacant voice on the radio announce, "Here's the latest from Kitchener's Wood; it's topping the charts here while lead guitarist Charlie Peguy remains jailed in London." The unmistakable opening chords of "Goodbye to All That" poured out.

. . .

It started with the kids—the shoved-aside punker-dunker kids, as Charlie called them, who felt ignored and irrelevant and who didn't like one of their heroes winding up in a foreign prison. They bought the record. They downloaded it from the Internet. There was even talk of organizing protests, which would have kept it a grass-roots movement, except that the song became a hit. The kids didn't lose interest in Charlie Peguy, even though their counterculture protest fantasies had been swept aside by the wave of lawyers and important types who suddenly landed in London. If anything, the kids became more interested in what Charlie Peguy had to say.

I did some research. Even on the campus of my alma mater, a private university just outside of Chicago and so competitive that the students studied on Saturday nights, there were students walking around with FREE CHARLIE!

T-shirts. In other parts of the country, there were rallies and Kitchener's Wood marathons on college radio stations. The issue of free speech, if not the Gold Affair itself, had finally taken hold of the students. The fact that the alternative newspapers had already gotten involved bolstered Charlie Peguy's claim to the title of antiestablishment bard.

"If it's number one in the United States, how long can they keep him in prison?" I asked one of our remaining congressional clients.

"If it's number one, his record company will get him out somehow," she replied.

. . .

"We all know what this is about," Charlie said, after the British released him, jostling through the crush of reporters that awaited him outside the jail. "I fit a part, right? I've got 'crazy' hair and I write 'crazy' words in songs, so lock me up! Yeah, I'm a threat. I'm a threat to exposing hypocrisy! I'm a threat to the bullshit artists—can I say that on TV?— who care only about protecting their money and their power! That's what's going on here, man, and not just here but in the United States, where they're telling us, 'Trust our law, trust our justice.' Screw that! All my time, all my energy from now on, is about taking down these pricks who have set up an innocent guy. I hear they're shouting 'Long Live Prouty' in bars in the States. First thing I'm going to do is go to my dive bar in LA, buy a beer, and shout 'Long Live Gold'!"

"Oh my God," murmured Lili when she heard this, because she had swung by the office to share the moment. "They'll kill him!"

"Are you kidding?" Jack laughed. "They'll make more T-shirts."

Neither happened, although when Charlie reached Los Angeles, there was a fantastic photograph of him lifting a beer to Lyle Gold, as promised, surrounded by a crowd of like-minded fans.

. . .

I am not one to gloat. Especially not with nasty little letters and messages still coming in, not with skittish former clients still scuttling out of my path, my mentor in exile, and my most infamous client languishing in a jail cell. But I will concede that it was difficult to contain my excitement when I opened a brown envelope, postmarked Charleston, the next morning. Someone's lips had slipped. A cast-off girl-friend of Reiff's, as it turned out. *You didn't get this from me,* she had scrawled across the top. Poor dear. Her dreams of being a diplomat's wife dashed when Reiff took up with her best friend. Kind of tacky, actually, and especially unfortu-nate for Reiff that after he had discarded the friend as well, the girls had patched things up and thought it a fine idea to send me a few letters from their former paramour. Do not mess with southern women.

Even if the letters had not been signed, it would not have been tough to guess the author's identity:

If I were told that I would die tomorrow as a double agent ruining the lives of those jerks who don't think I'm good enough to serve in their shitty diplomatic corps, I'd be perfectly happy.

Bingo! This certainly proved Reiff was disgruntled and, perhaps, had *intent*. But then I saw the best part of all, a hard copy of an e-mail sent from Reiff to one of the girls. It was a lovely apology for missing drinks the previous evening due to *extenuating circumstances, you know, my job*. The e-mail had been sent from the address of Lgold@hotmail.com.

My first reaction wasn't a triumphant punch into the air but "What an idiot!" Here I had considered Mao to be one of the messiest spies in the history of espionage. Well, so many lovers to contact, so little time; perhaps Reiff could be forgiven for trying to cut a few corners, but what a one to slip on! The entire Gold Affair as a lesson in what not to do was soon to be taught in intelligence briefings around the world.

But, now, with whom to share the wealth? I thoughtfully examined my right shoe, dangling from the tip of my toes. Forget the authorities. It would probably wind up in the hands of the U.S. attorney general and disappear forever. Someone from the media. Not John Jaures; we needed someone with no ties to the syndicate. Not television, because it wouldn't play on tape, not the way I wanted. This required respectability. The story had to be the star. Two possibilities: *The New York Times* or *The Washington Post*. Well, I was mad at the *Post*, what with Maurice Barres turning Kate Boothe–bashing into a second career, and the *Times* did have that hardworking special investigation team on the story. The *Times* would get it.

And did it ever! Front page, above the fold. I asked my assistant to have it framed. Play that Peguy song again. Jack snapped his fingers and whistled as I passed by his office.

The State Department and the White House immediately denounced the story as a forgery by the syndicate ("And is anyone really surprised that *The New York Times* has joined that side?" queried August Mercer, in a rare appearance on the Truman Pace Show). I listened to Pace stumbling through yet another bout of malice and smiled. Babble away, old man. Maurice Barres went on a television show and denounced me as "a logician of the absolute."

"Kate Boothe is one of those people who believes in absolute truth and will twist a situation to fit her logic," Barres explained.

I consider myself to be a smart young lady, and I have no idea what that meant, but I kind of liked it. The girl who nearly flunked college calculus deemed a logician. I was moving up in the world.

All this cheered me up considerably. In fact, I found the energy to pull on my running shoes. No marathon for me this year—I asked my younger uncle, When did I have time to train?—but I could at least sweat out some of the stress. A few fallen leaves rustled across the path along the Potomac. I clamped on headphones to shut out the world. I had pounded out maybe a mile before the umpteenth playing of the Kitchener's Wood song rang in my ears.

Goodbye to thought, goodbye to words
Don't tell me you haven't heard
They're keeping a list and checking it twice
They'll wipe you out if you aren't their kind of nice.

That was for sure, I thought. Poor Augie Scheurer-Kestner, kicked out of his chairmanship because he didn't follow the rules. The last time he attempted to deliver a speech about the Gold Affair, he had been hooted down by several of his colleagues, in particular by a fellow party member from Mississippi. (Perhaps it was jealousy: Scheurer-Kestner had been a football player in college; the gentleman from Ole Miss had been a cheerleader.) When—not if—public perception began finally to turn, I could only imagine how many of those jeering lawmakers would suddenly switch sides and begin effusively praising Lyle Gold. That was how the cycle always worked. The farther I ran, the angrier I became. Because those people certainly did not know what courage was; Scheurer-Kestner and those like him stuck their necks out but would never get any credit for taking an early stance. Of course, Scheurer-Kestner and Edgar Demange and John Jaures did not necessarily predicate their position upon a need for recognition, but it would have been a nice bonus. Most people adore acknowledgment.

My mind was moving faster than my feet. What would happen when time thoroughly vindicated us? Six months, a year down the line in our ad hoc world, beasties and pols, citizens and stars would be attempting to rewrite their roles. *Oh, yes, I was with the syndicate the whole way.* Spinning a legacy. What we needed was a list of everyone who now stood with the syndicate, and who stood against us. One that counted for public record, laid the divisions bare. Let the anti-Goldians like August Mercer, men who claimed to love their country above all else, see clearly what was happening. Let the weaker types get forced into the debate. I wanted everyone in the muck *together*.

And then I stopped, just a mile from Mount Vernon. No one else was on the path, so no one heard my gasping laughter. Of course—I wrapped my arms around myself—of course, a letter! This whole thing had started with letters. Maybe another one, a well-placed one, thick with impressive signatures, could help end it.

■ ■ ■

"An open letter?" Jack asked. "Who's going to write it?"

"You are," I told him. I had run to his apartment, which was only a mile from mine.

"Who's going to beg for all the signatures? It's not

persuasive without signatures. And we need a lot of very important types."

"I know," I replied. "I'll go after them."

Jack took the night to draw up the letter for a revision and called it AN OPEN PROTEST FOR THE RIGHTS OF MAN. Okay, so it didn't have a gender-neutral title, and I knew feminists might groan at this, but its intention—a call for a reexamination of the entire affair—could not have been clearer. So I took it.

Senator Augie Scheurer-Kestner was the first to sign. I brought it to him, ushered through the door of his office, which was littered with a politician's memories: an autographed photograph of Barry Goldwater, a football signed by the 1987 Chicago Bears, a stuffed glass-eyed stag. Silently, the senator scrawled his sprawling name.

My father knew a former assistant U.S. attorney general, James Thierry, who did not hesitate to affix his signature in blue. And then, because it counted to have three major names at the top, I went after the one that I really wanted. For that, I flew to New York, to attend an event hosted by the Save Venice Foundation (an organization that does exactly what it sounds like). It was a lecture on Tintoretto. It was there that I spotted Amy de Caillavet, the sleek blond mistress of the great filmmaker Anthony France. Regardless of how I brushed off his dilettante forays into political matters, his signature would go a long way toward lining up other influential names, including Melvin Gluck. I might despise Gluck, but I needed him on my side.

"Madame de Caillavet," I said, addressing her in the language she was known to prefer, and when she glanced coolly my way, I told her about the letter.

"But Miss Boothe, you are going to set us at loggerheads with Mr. Gluck!"

"I hope to have his signature too," I said.

She frowned slightly. "Who has signed so far?"

I listed Scheurer-Kestner, which failed to impress her.

"Oh, him. He doesn't count, that goes without saying. This sort of thing is his bread and butter." She turned back to smooth out her program, which she had folded into a fan.

"Well, Thierry has signed," I said, brandishing my trophy, who just happened to be a de Caillavet acquaintance. She raised her delicate eyebrows.

"Ah, good, excellent." She was satisfied. She promised France would sign the petition. And he did. I took it to his penthouse myself. He got out of bed for the occasion, padding in his slippers with a head cold, and said, "Show it to me. I'll sign. I'll sign anything. I am disgusted."

•   •   •

Lucien Herr signed, of course, but it was difficult to persuade many other professors, who worried that they might lose their jobs as a result. Even those who had tenure were not safe these days—there were organizations, one of them enthusiastically endorsed by the gimlet-eyed wife of the vice president, that kept lists of professors who were considered "unpatriotic." The painter Estivalet signed (to the consternation of her great friend and peer, Eddie Gass, who didn't speak to her again for months). The streetwise filmmaking team of John and Warren Thompson signed. The scientist DuClaw, who had won a Nobel for his work mapping the human genome, signed immediately. "If we were afraid of revision in the laboratory, truth would never be reached except by accident," he said. "That is not very scientific." And when his colleague Louys, who had shared in the Nobel glory, refused to sign, DuClaw used his influence to have him removed as chair of biology. The famed literary editor Leo Daudet signed and, at a formal dinner, threw a chocolate pudding in the face of his publisher, who had not. On and on the stories went. Everyone knew about the letter, it seemed, and it hadn't even been printed yet.

I felt much better after four days of this, well enough to go to Le Sénateur for an actual dinner. Since our finances had become crimped, I had been restricting myself to one drink and an appetizer. Jack said we deserved dinner.

"Wouldn't it be great if you got Truman Pace to sign?" Jack asked, half jokingly, as we dug into our steak tartare.

"I'm good, but I'm not that good—or that stupid," I said. I would have gone on, but my cell phone jangled, far too loudly for such a posh place. I would hear about it from Lili later, and other diners shot me annoyed glares over their cheeses and soufflés. I muffled my voice as I answered. A clipped shrill voice demanded, "Why the hell haven't you asked me to sign this fucking letter of yours yet?"

I blinked several times. "Uh—well, I—" and then I regained my composure. "Who is this?"

"Melvin Gluck." And he roared with laughter. I stared at Jack, who shrugged. Gluck was yammering so loudly that Jack could hear everything.

"Well, Mr. Gluck, I was planning to do exactly that when I thought I had enough to persuade you," I said.

"You weren't going to come and persuade me yourself?" he asked. "I've heard a lot about your abilities in that department."

"Pardon me?"

"How many of these guys have you fucked?"

"All of them."

"Even the women?"

"Especially the women."

Gluck laughed even harder, that strange Hollywood humor. "You believe in this?" he asked.

"With all my patriotism, my intelligence, and my heart," I replied dramatically, and Gluck fairly screamed in delight.

"Great! Wonderful! I'm on board! Anthony told me all about it, and I'm with him. Besides, I own more Estivalet than I do Gass, so, count me in." Then, mercifully, he hung up.

Who signed; who didn't? By the end of the second week, I had one hundred and four signatures of some of the nation's leading lights. Scraping into my savings account, I paid for the first full-page ad, which ran in *The New York*

Times. By the end of September, we ran the letter again, this time in five smaller newspapers across the nation and with three thousand signatures. We ended it at that. The number was significant, and the names were recognizable. And now, every television booker and all the twenty-four-hour cable stations owed me big-time, because I had just handed them the tool with which to perpetuate the debate.

Would either Roosevelt have signed? Nixon? Lincoln? Washington himself? It was delicious to watch Mimi and Maurice and the like sputtering through historical arguments, something for which they, like most TV whores, were woefully unprepared. Lennon? Cobain? Sinatra? That took care of the music networks.

"Well," I said on the Eddie Drumont show, "John Hancock would have done it."

I exhaled with relief as I drove away from Drumont's television studio that morning. Sure, there were still glares and whispers directed my way by strangers and acquaintances alike, but these rolled off me now. I carried myself straight, which I thought made me look taller, and ignored the hisses like so much white noise. No sense starting to care now.

The road from downtown Washington to Old Towne Alexandria, where I was meeting Lili for brunch, stretched along a particularly picturesque route, with the Potomac on one side and swaths of trees on the other. Such a lovely bit of parkway; how ironic that it had a higher rate of road rage incidents than any other in the country. The persistent traffic jams had something to do with this. I was so firmly lodged in one—even on a Sunday morning—that it would take me thirty minutes to go seven miles. No matter. *Nothing* was going to bother me. I cranked up the radio and leaned back in my seat. Out of half-closed eyes I thought I saw a face staring at me. I glanced to the left and, sure enough, a face loomed, obscured by tinted windows but recognizable nonetheless. Lieutenant Joseph Henry regarded me as he might an enemy soldier. Which, in a way, I was. The cars ahead of us weren't moving. We were stuck next to each other. Like the good officer he was, Henry didn't break his stare. Like the good consultant I was, I flashed a smile and waved. He shook his head and turned away.

12

THE FALSE HENRY

I could not shake Henry from my mind. I started to see him everywhere—his name dropped into articles, his face across crowded bars. It wasn't him, of course, it was me. Jack has called me high-strung before. If you believe in that sort of thing, you could chalk it up to my being a late November baby. However, I think it is just another term for *obsessive*.

I fixated because I knew the cog had become the linchpin, and I needed that linchpin. I couldn't prove in a court of law that Henry had been behind the falsified letter, but I knew, based upon John Jaures's work and my own belief in Henry's character, that if he was responsible for one forgery, casually inserting a *G* where there had been none, he could excuse another—in the name of a greater cause, of course. Because we do want to believe we are good people.

I confided my hunch to John. "I know, I know," he agreed. "There's something there, I can feel it. He's not the easiest guy to get at, though. I'm not going to start getting breaks until the people around him with a lot more to lose believe they're about to lose it."

There were some who were gaining. Charlie Peguy seemed to relish his new role. He told a music magazine, "Whoever is designated must march; whoever is called must respond. That is the deal. That's what is required of heroic lives." Heroic lives?

Lili found this highly amusing. "The spiritual side of rock stars," she shouted, when we stood backstage at a Kitchener's Wood show. They were playing to a sold-out house at the Black Cat. Well, the words might have been excessive on Charlie's part, but he had a hit record that he had earned. And were those *congressmen* I saw in the audience, jumping up and down alongside leather-clad teenagers? It wouldn't have been the first time lawmakers mingled with the masses at a concert—one well-known incident had the chairman of the finance committee storming the stage at a Grateful Dead show and subsequently landing in the slammer. But that was benign compared to an appearance at a Kitchener's Wood show, celebrating a song that their colleagues across the Atlantic had deemed proof of terrorist sympathies. Come to think of it, I could have sworn I spied Mimi Ryan, flicking her blond locks in the front row.

■ ■ ■

My partner took off his blue jacket and loosened his bright orange tie as he walked through the office door two days later. It was nearly three o'clock, but Jack usually ended his lunches late.

"I just had the most enlightening conversation with Duke Guermantes at the Capitol Grille," he said.

The good senator from Alabama had approached Jack to ask him what new bits he had heard about the scandal. "They're *asking* us for information now," Jack said gleefully. "The doubting has really started."

"Only because Guermantes is starting to regret not getting his name on the open letter," I pointed out.

If it was true that the tide had turned in our favor, it was also clear that we still had a long way to go. Henry, Henry, Henry. I tapped my pencil on my desk throughout the afternoon. Ambitious but not clever. He had to have left another track besides the False *G* Letter. I called John Jaures again. "There's got to be a *there* there," I insisted.

"I'm working on it, I'm working on it," he grumbled. He was on deadline for a series his editors hoped to run shortly and was therefore tense. He was also disappearing often and not returning calls or e-mails. Every time he disappeared into the ether, I made sure to let Jack know.

"Kate, it's not as if Maurice would have been a better choice," my partner reminded me.

. . .

Friday. An unseasonable heat wave soaked the city in a layer of dank air. The miserable summer would never end, I thought. My crisp white shirt drooped; I picked at a stray black thread from my skirt as I sat in my office, waiting. For what, I don't know: an idea, a moment, a life.

At around three o'clock, deliverance arrived. John Jaures walked through the door, carrying a six-pack of Iron City beer and a brown envelope. He paused in the doorway of my office. "Ask and ye shall receive." He tossed the envelope onto my desk and then popped open the top of a can. "I'll get Jack," he said.

Inside the envelope was a letter. The cross-ruled paper was identical to that used by the unfortunate Saeed Khan. So was the blue pencil. The penmanship, too, seemed to match.

My dear friend,

I have read that a deputy is going to ask a question about Gold. If they ask for any new explanations, I will say that I never had relations with this man.

That's understood. If anybody asks you, say just that, for nobody must ever know what happened with him.

Khan

I was rereading the letter as John returned with Jack in tow.

"The greeting and the signature are authentic," John said. "The rest is not."

"How do you know?" Jack asked, taking the letter from my hands.

"Because it's not a very good forgery," John replied. "Khan's English wasn't that perfect. I talked to him. I know. And look: The lines on the graph of the paper are blue; the lines on the greeting and signature are mauve, and the graph squares aren't even the same size." He shook his head. "You'd think they would've tried a little harder. Forgery is an art form."

"Where did you get this?" I asked.

"When are you going to quit asking me questions like that?" John smiled.

Reporters and their sources. Well, when it came to unwrapping the secret dossier, any connections would of course be zealously guarded. I cocked my head to one side.

"Come on," I cajoled. "Don't front."

John paused for only a moment. "Military intelligence. Someone—ah, close to Lieutenant Joseph Henry."

"Well, what do you know." Jack reached over for a can of beer.

I turned the envelope over in my hands. "This looks original," I said. "It's even got a postmark."

"It *is* original," John said. "The forged letter was placed in it."

"What was there to begin with?" I asked.

"Who knows? Probably another love letter. There were quite a few of those, you know."

I marveled at the audacity. Such an exquisitely bad job. How had anyone believed this even for a moment?

"Mercer bought it," John said, leaning back in his chair. "It was a new addition to the secret dossier. Assembled, by the way, by Henry and the deputy secretary of state. It satisfied Mercer, evidently. And my editor bought *that*. I've written all about it. A follow-up to my initial story about the False *G* Letter. Now I can say other parts of the secret dossier appear to have been forged."

"But by who?" I asked. "I think Henry, but what does anyone else believe?"

"Convenient made-to-order evidence," Jack murmured.

"I'll bet I get someone to point the finger Henry's way, once they know this article is coming," John said.

We fell silent. Thirty seconds ticked by. Then another.

"Does Joan Picquart know about this," I asked, "if it's new to the dossier?"

"Not unless she still talks to the secretary," John replied. "Aside from him and the deputy secretary, I don't know who else there saw it."

"Joan's still in São Tomé," I said.

"Then you'll have to call the secretary himself if you want a reaction," Jack said. "He might even be grateful for a heads-up."

"Certainly," I replied. "I am sure there is nothing else that the secretary of state, a busy busy man, has to do other than take *my* phone call."

Because Jack laughed, and because John was sitting across from me with that challenging look in his eyes, I picked up the phone and made the call. Of course, I got no farther than the secretary's secretary, who took a message. I hung up and gave Jack a smug smile. *Told you so!*

Ten minutes later, my assistant rapped on the doorjamb of my office. "Kate, the—um, secretary of state is on the line for you."

Jack coughed.

"Miss Boothe." The even, methodical cadence instantly melted my confidence.

"I have seen the Saeed Khan letter," I told him, trying to steady my voice. "Not the one merely referencing a *G* but the one specifically naming Gold."

"Yes," he said guardedly.

"I am assuming you have seen it," I continued. "It's a little . . . strange."

"Well, Miss Boothe, I would have to say I am not enthusiastic about the letter," the secretary said.

"Why?" I asked.

"I am aware that we are living in suspicious times," the secretary replied. "I am not enthusiastic. This paper has a bad smell about it."

"Did you express your concerns to the White House?" I asked.

"You know better than to ask me that," the secretary replied, "but should you speak with him, you might ask the lieutenant what he has heard."

"Lieutenant Henry," I said.

"Yes. Good day, Miss Boothe."

A man who reaches the position of chief diplomat does not bother with idle words. Despite my surprise at what passed for candor in this town, I almost smiled. Forget about the False *G* Letter. If this new, entirely doctored document—the False Henry, as John was calling it for symbiotic purposes—exploded, there was the unappealing prospect of three divisive trials: Gold, Henry, and Prouty all investigated by yet another grand jury. The secretary knew this. No wonder he wasn't "enthusiastic." Of course he would want someone unconnected to him to convey a message to Henry: *You're on your own, pal.*

. . .

Locating the lieutenant wasn't the task it might have been in any other city. Washington is old-school enough that I could narrow the search down to three or four establishments. Fortunately for me, he happened to be in a place sprawling enough to get lost in the crowd but divided into booths so as to allow intimate conversation. And it wasn't far from my office.

Henry was tucked into a high-backed wooden booth, his hands around a bottle of Belgian lager. "Expensive taste," I observed, as I slid into the seat across from him. He looked up, startled and not at all pleased.

"What are you doing here?" he demanded.

"It's a bar," I said, shrugging.

Henry visibly gritted his teeth. "I don't care to be seen in your company."

"Oh. Well, that's too bad, because I have something you might be interested in."

"You have nothing."

I looked at him a full moment, studying the face of the man I was about to destroy. His eyes were clear, his chin clean-shaven, his cheeks tanned. I drew a deep breath, reminding myself that this was, in fact, a man who had done worse than I was about to do. And then I slid over a copy of the sheet of cross-ruled paper.

"How do you explain this?" I asked.

"I don't have to explain anything to you," Henry said levelly, not even glancing at the paper.

"No," I agreed, "but your superiors will want to know. This artwork of yours will be running soon in newspapers."

Henry stared, then let out a short, bitter laugh. "My artwork? Oh, this is rich. Nice try."

"All right. Let me use a more retro term. You fabricated it. You forged this letter," I continued with resolve. "Which is worse—though not by much—than your first foray, when you added a *G* to the love letter to finger Lyle Gold."

"I don't have to talk to you," Henry said. "I want you to go."

I cocked an eyebrow. "That's no way to treat a girl who's trying to give you a tip."

"Either you leave now, or I'll—"

"Look, lieutenant, this is *already* out there. Your superiors know about it. The public will know about it soon enough. John Jaures has already written a series of articles about it which start running this week." I was hazarding a guess here, but if the secretary of state had deigned to speak to me, surely he had done the same with his counterpart at the defense department.

"I didn't." Henry was livid. "I swear to you that I didn't invent anything."

"You invented—"

"I swear I didn't! I only—"

"You aren't telling the truth," I said. "Not telling the truth to me is one thing. Not telling your ranking officers, well . . ." He was starting to break. I could see by the way his fingers nervously danced up and down the neck of the bottle. I leaned toward him, adding gently, "The doctored love letter was just the tip of the iceberg. This letter"—and I held it up—"you concocted the *entire* thing. You used other documents as a model. Not bad. Some nice touches. The special paper, the blue pencil."

Henry avoided the letter as if it were coated with poison.

"Who put the idea in your head?" I asked softly.

Henry blinked.

"Lieutenant, please."

"The woman brought me the information," he said in a low voice. "I met her off campus, at Christ Church, in Olde Town."

"The cleaning lady?" I asked. I had assumed she was paid by the state department, but I guess I had underestimated Henry's ambition.

"Yes." He looked at his hands. "I got the information first, and then I gave it to the deputy secretary of state."

It was my turn to gape. "But why him?" I asked.

"I knew him from Yale."

Always Yale.

"And August Mercer?"

"He got everything when we were sure we had the traitor. And we knew there was a traitor. My COs were worried." He said this in a fierce whisper. "I wanted to calm them, to make their minds rest easy. I said to myself, Let's just add a sentence; if we had one more piece of evidence! No one else knew anything about it."

"Mercer didn't?"

"No," he replied vehemently.

I pressed my lips together and then asked, "But why Lyle Gold? Why was he the guy?"

Henry examined me with a hint of impatience. "Because he *is* the guy," he said. "He's the one who dug up those stories on my men. He was the one who, just weeks before I got my information, was constantly bothering the State Department about whether or not the secretary of state was fighting with the defense secretary. In a time of war! It couldn't be anyone else."

And I sat back, illuminated. Of course. Reiff Prouty, sending off his treacherous e-mails, slapping on Lyle Gold's name because he was the most likely suspect. And, simply, it fit.

The lieutenant blinked again, furiously this time. I swallowed. It was not pleasant to watch a man cry. Henry stabbed the table with the tip of his forefinger.

"I acted solely in the interests of my country," he said forcefully.

Me too, I thought, and I walked out of the bar.

. . .

The newspaper's executives were suffering a bout of nerves, but John Jaures's articles edged closer to publication. A few days later, the fact-checkers began making their phone calls to authorities. Then the Pentagon began to bleed.

By the weekend, the lieutenant was arrested. This I heard from my old friend Joe Morgan. "My buddies were the ones who went to get him," he told me, through the crackle of his car phone. "Henry kept saying, 'What do they want? What do they want? It makes you crazy.' And he kept talking about his wife and his little boy, what to do."

I felt the color drain from my face. I hadn't known about the kid. "What happens to him now?"

"The military takes care of him."

"With a tribunal?" I asked.

"Maybe."

"Let me ask you something," I began. "I once heard a story about an old method of jailhouse justice."

"The loaded revolver, placed near the inmate?" Morgan

asked. He laughed, but bitterly this time. "Doesn't get much more old school than that."

"But surely—"

"Katie, tread carefully now. This is when it gets sticky," warned the man who had been in Special Operations. "You look both ways."

Sticky! How much worse could it get, for God's sake? I had been threatened with an audit, hauled before a grand jury, eviscerated by the media, and had my virtue assaulted. An innocent man was still in jail. *Now* it was supposed to get *sticky?*

I stormed down the hall toward Jack's office, kicked the door open, and when he started in surprise I said quietly, "The cover-up comes down to Mercer. Maybe he didn't initiate it, but he sure as hell pushed it along. He threw everything he had at an innocent man—and at those defending him—despite the fact the evidence was flimsy, all because digging out the truth would have exposed something he didn't want to see. He calls himself a man of morals, of honor. I don't think so."

It was always so much less frightening to Jack if I shouted.

• • •

Friday. My assistant was practically drowning in a wash of pink message slips, but she managed to fish out a brown envelope and hand it to me. "I think you'll want to see this first," she said pointedly.

Inside were photocopies of two letters, both addressed to the president. One was from the chairman of the Joint Chiefs of Staff, a veteran of two official wars and three "skirmishes." It read, in part:

> I have acquired proof that my trust in Lieutenant Henry was unjustified. That trust was absolute and led me to the mistake of believing a document to be genuine which was not. Given the situation, I must ask you to relieve me of my duties.

I swallowed hard and turned my attention to the second letter. This one was from the secretary of defense:

> I have lost confidence in my subordinates as well as those others in your administration who caused me to deal in forgeries. It is not possible to wield command with the knowledge I now possess, of an innocent man falsely charged during my watch. I have the honor to request that you order my retirement; upon your refusal, I respectfully request that you accept my resignation.

I turned the envelope over to check for a return address, but there was none. It had to have been hand-delivered. There was only one place both letters could have been sent: the White House. No member of the military would betray his superiors to someone like me, a private-sector consultant. Only a political animal, someone more interested in self-preservation than anything else, would do that. I sat back in my chair. Who best fit that description? Only one person who knew me, I thought, and dialed the number.

"Is this my apology?" I asked Freddy, when he answered.

Freddy laughed. "Exactly. Why simply telephone when you can send love letters?"

Oh, sure, love letters sealed with the spit of Narcissus. Freddy hadn't done it for me, of course; it was all about him.

"Mercer intercepted them," Freddy said. "They were too incriminating to give to the president right away."

"Are they actually going to hit the president's desk?" I asked.

"At some point." Freddy was vague. "All this stuff goes through Mercer to begin with."

"So whenever Mercer feels like it."

"He's got some time, let's put it that way. And maybe the president won't ever find out that Mercer held them back."

"But the letters are dated," I said.

"You doubt Mercer's powers of persuasion? You think he's not going to try to talk these men out of their decision, try to save some face? The president, he's the kind of guy who might not mind being out of the loop for these kinds of details—he likes to delegate, remember. If Mercer works his magic and the press, as usual, stays in the dark, and in the meantime the president never had to lose sleep over it?"

The cynicism of it all. "But you don't believe that, do you?"

"Just checking out all the angles, Kate. You know what I mean."

Freddy was switching sides. The chink in Mercer's armor must be visible then. I looked at the letters for a long moment.

"There's going to be a revision of the military tribunal, isn't there?" I realized aloud.

Freddy paused before replying. "Let's just say that it's definitely less respectable among the top military brass to remain opposed to it at this point."

"But Mercer is."

"Is he ever. It's a measure of his power to stop it," Freddy said. "You know that old saying, 'Absolute power corrupts absolutely'?"

"Machiavelli," I said.

"Yes. Well, don't you think absolute power *reveals*?" ·

How do you use power when you answer to no one? Except Mercer's hand *could* be forced now, whether or not he realized it.

And so it came down to this: Who could turn the screw first, Mercer or me?

13

MEN OF HONOR

Scenarios clicked through my mind like the family vacation slide shows my father used to subject us to. Forget the media; reporters were useless in this case. Oh, they would get the information eventually, but not from me. John Jaures's articles would start running soon. And the letter signers were no help. Melvin Gluck made for a marvelous gadfly, but I needed action. The fine men and women tramping through the halls of the Capitol—what would they do other than make speeches on the floor in front of the cameras or stage a posturing press conference? Worse yet, they might do nothing at all.

I stared at the silent phone. While I was fretting away, Mercer was burning up the phone lines. I could only hope for a lot of overloaded circuits . . . like Lili's reservation line, which was always jammed.

Lili could help me! Suddenly I remembered who desperately wanted a Saturday night reservation.

I reached Lili on her private line. I begged. I wheedled. I groveled. She had only two questions: How the hell was she going to just ring up one of the most unreachable men in the city out of the blue, and how was she going to free up a table on such short notice?

"Call his wife," I suggested. "She'd love an eight o'clock table tonight."

"Oh, sure, I would too, since it's a *Saturday*," Lili snapped.

"It's not as if she hasn't hounded you for one before," I reminded her.

"Let me see, let me see." Lili paged through her Very Important Person reservation book. "What do you know? You're right. I have their home number."

What a surprise. Lili had everyone's number.

"She may already have plans," Lili pointed out.

"She'll cancel. Tell her it's a special tasting menu. Truffles or something."

"We *did* just get the white truffles," Lili said thoughtfully.

And who, tell me, can resist the allure of a white truffle? Certainly not the wife of the FBI director. She was thrilled when Lili called with the good news and said *absolutely* reserve a table; even her overworked husband would make time for *this*.

Lili placed them in a corner, set apart from the rest of the room by a potted palm. Perfect. I waited until they cut into one of the five desserts that Lili had sent out. Sated by the previous six courses and two bottles of burgundy, they drowsily lifted dainty demitasse cups to their lips.

"Good evening, Mr. Director!" I said brightly. The poor man coughed espresso onto his tie. I turned to his wife. "I'm Kate Boothe, ma'am."

"Oh," she said. "So nice to meet you." She had a drawl, so it sounded as if she actually meant it.

"Georgia?" I guessed, and she glanced at her husband, who was turning red.

"Why, yes. Marietta."

"I love Marietta. I love the coffee at Cormier, off the square in—"

"In that wonderful old square!" the director's wife exclaimed. "I have a cousin who goes every day. Do you know the town well?"

"A little. All those antiques stores." I smiled, thanking my luck for once having a client there who swore by Cormier coffee, which the owners roasted in-house.

"Oh, yes! The antiques stores are among the best!" she exclaimed. "Would you like to join us?" Her husband shot her a look, but southern etiquette prevailed.

"Thank you, but only for a few minutes." A waiter rushed over with a chair. "I've actually got a stack of things to get through tonight."

"I'll bet you do," the director said. He asked the waiter for a scotch, a double.

"So I guess the last time I saw you was on the train to New York City," I said pleasantly.

"I don't recall," he said.

"I'm sure," I replied. "You seemed to be very busy. I wonder"—I turned to his wife—"if you can ever get your husband to take a vacation!"

She laughed, but the director blanched. The bureau had been criticized for management problems, and Senator Duke Guermantes had been threatening to haul in the director for a hearing regarding, in particular, the money set aside for the bureau's computer system, which had been in disarray for over ten years. There were whispers that the computer funds, for a long time, had been used instead to make up for shortfalls in other areas, like the travel budget. There were suspicions that the director might have used some for his own personal travel.

"All right," the director said. "I'll bite." He folded his napkin.

"I thought you might like to have something," I said. I handed him an envelope containing the resignation letters. The director opened it and slowly scanned them.

"The president doesn't know these exist," I added quietly.

"I see," the director said, looking up at me.

"I figured you would." After all, why not score a few points with the commander in chief? It was known that August Mercer wanted one of his own buddies in the appointed spot of director.

"How do you have them?" he asked.

"A White House source, who was a little concerned when they were not passed on immediately to the president."

"Why didn't this individual pass them along?" the director asked.

"That isn't his job," I replied. "And he would like to keep the one he's got."

"And you're giving them to me instead of one of your media buddies," the director observed archly.

"I hardly think they've been charitable to me," I returned.

The director pursed his lips. "You had better hope that my phone calls to these two gentlemen do not result in any awkward moments."

"You had better call them soon." I stood up. "I think we understand each other."

He nodded as I shook his hand, and then I left. But not before arranging to have Lili send over cordials, just to end their evening on the right note.

■ ■ ■

This is what I know about such men: They are ruled by ego. The FBI director, a man not beholden to Mercer but who had had his own struggles with him, needed an edge. I had given it to him.

And then Mercer beat me by exactly two hours. He was meeting with the chairman of the Joint Chiefs of Staff at the latter's home in Arlington when the FBI director placed his call. The chairman was not one bit pleased that someone *other than the president* had his letter of resignation. That placed a sacrosanct matter into public play, which was not the way such business was done. A betrayal had occurred, and the chairman had in front of him the man who had done it. He wasn't pleased at all. I was told you could hear him yelling at Mercer from three blocks away.

I made the call to John Jaures. "You might want to take a drive out to McLean."

"Who lives in McLean?" John asked.

"The secretary of defense," I said. For that, naturally, was the FBI director's next call. If John conveniently turned up in the neighborhood, the aforementioned might feel compelled to make some sort of statement. After chatting with the president. Who, I would wager, would not be at all happy to find himself out of the loop on *this* one.

I also called the quite reasonable chief of staff to Duke Guermantes and apprised her of the situation. After all, the man did chair the Judiciary Committee. He might want a heads-up. The chief of staff thanked me profusely. Guermantes would appreciate knowing in advance about the resignation letters, she said; it certainly cast a new light on the Gold situation.

The director of the FBI would look like the hero—and he would want the spotlight to himself. No need to worry about his revealing me as his source. But he wasn't likely to forget who had helped him along. Best of all, Mercer wouldn't know to whom he owed his impending ruin. Because the clock, finally, had begun to tick.

* * *

The first article in John Jaures's series, entitled "The Proofs," ran the next day. The article offered an in-depth blow-by-blow account of the Mao–Khan correspondence, the e-mail trail from the State Department, and the False Henry Letter. The star, of course, was Lieutenant Joseph Henry himself.

John's articles would have been the talk of the media even without the news of the resignations from the Pentagon that never made it to the president's desk. As it was, the series prodded Truman Pace into near hysterics. *They're trying to destroy the country! Our boys in blue are at risk!* Shuffling through a stack of notes in my office, I half listened as Pace opened up the lines. It took me a moment to recognize the first caller's voice.

"You know what your problem is, Pace? You don't know when you've been beat. You were on the wrong side, and you can't admit it."

I dropped the note cards. "Jack!" I shouted. "Get in here! Melvin Gluck is on Truman Pace's show!"

"I'm on the side of justice! The traitor was found. The traitor was convicted—"

"In a secret trial with concealed evidence!"

"He was convicted, and you Hollywood wackos can't stand that."

"Hey, there's plenty of evidence that this guy Reiff Prouty did it, and your boys in blue lied."

"Only an unpatriotic son of a bitch could say—"

"Look here, I'm in California, surrounded by goddamn tofu eaters, and I'm hearing about nothing but this bastard Henry. His own bosses are saying—"

"Mister and missus America aren't going to be surprised that you cocksucking Hollywood shitheads believe—"

"*What?* Look here, you fucking fuck, all I'm trying to fucking do is bring this fucking country together."

It flew so fast that the censors, who usually work with a seven-second delay so they can bleep out expletives, couldn't keep up. "These guys are true masters," marveled Jack. Truman Pace's producer eventually hung up on Melvin Gluck, but that wasn't the end of his involvement. John told us that Gluck had actually bought the screen rights to his articles. Screen rights! Who would do the sound track, Kitchener's Wood?

. . .

I urged Edgar Demange to press for a revision of the military tribunal. But it seemed Demange had lost his nerve. "Mercer is still there," he said, sitting in our office. "Mercer is still there."

"Mercer is going," I snapped.

"He's not gone yet." Demange was unswayed. "Listen, young lady, I might be old but I'm not foolish. I don't want to get into something I might regret if the timing is not precisely right."

"What else do you need?" I asked. "What else could you possibly need?"

The immediacy of twenty-four-hour news. Jack walked into my office and clicked on the television. Backdrop: the splendid white-brick home of August Mercer. Topic: Lyle Gold, and the many many reasons to suspect him of treason. Live audience: the beast, smelling blood.

Mercer said, almost inaudibly, "I no longer have a reason to keep silent. I must fulfill what I consider to be my duty. Earlier this year, the diplomatic situation was perilous. If there was any haste in dealing with Mr. Gold, this must be understood in the context of Chinese complicity at the highest level.

"I have not arrived at my age without having learned a great deal about human error. I am an honest man and the son of an honest man. If the slightest doubt had touched my mind, I would have been the first to admit to you and to Mr. Gold that I was honestly mistaken."

"That's what you ought to say!" Edgar Demange exclaimed.

But, of course, "the slightest doubt" had never touched Mercer's mind. You could see it in his eyes. *It wasn't one of my boys who committed the treason; it was Gold; it had to be Gold; and the only reason I am condescending to speak to you now is because Gold has managed to wriggle out of this most serious crime due to a ridiculous campaign by his wrongheaded supporters, and because my boss, the president, has insisted I say something. No matter—you will all pay someday.*

I hardly think I am putting words in Mercer's mouth. Never had he doubted Lyle Gold's complete and total guilt. People who believe in moral absolutes can convince themselves of anything. He might have realized that Reiff Prouty, whom he helped because of an allegiance to an old campaign-contributing friend, had with his mediocre talents and bad habits become a liability and therefore some spinning was necessary, but Mercer did not believe a junior member of his own club would sell himself and his country for a price. It was easy; there was tenuous evidence and then the more substantial evidence, albeit forged, that Henry had produced. In fact, as I clicked off the television set, I realized that Mercer still believed Gold was guilty, and he would surround himself with people who agreed. There was no sense in wasting verbs and participles trying to convince him otherwise.

"Is he fired, then?" Demange asked.

"Looks like it," Jack replied. "Edgar, you have no idea how much I wish I could bill you for this."

"It's not over yet," Demange grumbled, as he gathered his crumpled coat. "A revision hasn't happened. Still might not happen." He didn't shut the door on his way out.

The phone calls came fast and furious then. Freddy told me that the Pentagon brass stormed to the White House for a meeting in the Oval Office. The president may have owed Mercer his residency there, and he may have prided himself on reciprocating loyalty, but this was legacy material. Mercer was out. Interestingly, Mercer's trusted aide, Freddy

Banks, remained solidly in. No one suspected that he would have been privy to resignation letters, and it isn't easy to find devoted staffers.

Joan Picquart called from São Tomé: *You got Mercer!* The cool, tightly wrought diplomat was wavering between laughing hysterically and crying. "Don't deny it! I know this came from you!"

"I hope *he* doesn't," I said.

"He won't for a while. Nicely done, Boothe. I must confess I now regret giving you a C."

I told her that grade had probably kept me out of law school. No hard feelings.

Maurice Barres called for a comment. I told him to stuff it.

And that should have been that. Only it wasn't. The tabloid headlines, bleeding red, greeted me the next morning on my way into the office: Lieutenant Joseph Henry had committed suicide. It happened the previous evening, right around the time I was arguing with Demange. In his cell, alone, his throat slashed with a razor. He had been dead for more than two hours when the guards found him. I spilled my cup of coffee onto a stack of newspapers, ruining several copies. Apologizing to the cursing clerk, I plunked down a handful of change and stumbled away.

Jack was waiting for me in my office. "This isn't anything we did," he said. "It's not our fault."

Of course not. We didn't make him forge anything. We

didn't convince him that this was the right thing to do. Others were responsible for that, including Henry himself. Delusion is grand, after all. The newspapers all reported his last conversation with his wife: "He told me he was absolutely innocent, and the world would know a little later. He told me the letter in question, his letter, is a copy, and is in no way—absolutely no way—a forgery. He told me I knew in whose interests he had acted. And I do! I do! In the interests of his country!" And then she broke down in tears.

The dutiful widow, Daly's daughter. And Henry left a son. I reminded myself again: Jack was right. We hadn't caused any of this. I would bet that the men who had weren't giving his death a second thought. For if a mistake had to be admitted, there must be a new scapegoat, and that role was filled by the lieutenant, who had thought he was doing his duty all along.

"Kate." My assistant hesitated in the doorway. I looked up at her wearily. "Danny Daly is on the phone for you."

My heart sank, but I picked up the line. His voice caught as he asked me to come to his office. He wasn't in Rome anymore, he explained, so the journey wouldn't be so arduous.

Even though the address he gave me was only a block away from mine, the walk took me fifteen minutes. The office was elegant, of course, with what we call I-love-me walls, framed photographs of Danny meeting this president and that monarch, a visual record of his long service to his country. His desk seemed too large, or maybe Daly had shrunk since the last time I saw him. His clothes hung a bit loosely, and his cheeks weren't quite so ruddy. He kindly waved for me to sit, and then he sighed.

"I often think upon our conversation in Rome," he said.

"I do too," I replied truthfully.

"I believed then, as I do now, that what happened to Lyle Gold would haunt us. It isn't over, per se. We may simply have reached the limits of our capacity, and therefore an end must come." Daly sighed again and pulled a cigarette from a gold case on his desk. "Allow an old soldier a moment. My senses are charred now. I don't take the cigarette out of my mouth when I write *deceased* over another name in my life."

I respected Daly eminently. I might not have agreed with his politics, but this was a man who had lived what he preached. Still, I had to wonder, what was the point? What did he want from me now? Of course Daly noticed my mind wandering. He was a veteran politician, after all.

I decided for once to be forthcoming. "I know Joseph Henry was your son-in-law," I began. "I am terribly—"

Daly fixed his gaze on me as smoke curled into the air. "We are all terribly *something*, now, aren't we? My son-in-law was terribly the soldier. He spoke to my daughter on the phone. He told her nothing. I think you know that much. He must have felt *terribly* disgraced, to some degree even betrayed." His thick eyebrows twitched. "And I am *terribly* sure that razor was left for him." He settled back into his chair. "If you understand me."

I didn't particularly want to, just as I hadn't wanted to fathom the causes behind poor hapless Saeed Khan's tumble from a subway platform all those months ago. It was too dirty.

"Last man standing, Miss Boothe. We are engaged in a war. Lest you forget, I'm a military man. I know the system has its ways." Daly crushed out the barely lit cigarette and folded his spotted hands on his stomach. "I don't think this so-called scandal has effected any permanent changes in the character, customs, and habits of the people. Mine is not to reason why. I am too old. I cannot do it. But hear this: I can conclude that I am not sure I knew Joseph Henry. I cannot say, for certain, I knew what made this man."

It was the end of my audience. I would never see him again. Danny Daly had looked into the twilight and wondered about this footnote to his legacy. He had called me in because he knew that I would stick around long enough to secure the version he preferred, even if it did not improve the status of his suddenly widowed daughter or the fatherless state of his grandson. I walked toward the door. In my wake, I heard Daly murmuring, "The Sinister Spirit sneered: 'It had to be!'/And again the Spirit of Pity whispered, 'Why?'"

You may ask, Why, now, did the attention not turn to Reiff Prouty? We all knew who the real spy was and *where* he was, sitting in his Georgetown condo, awaiting his next posting. Well, others had to fall first. Reiff might never pay, actually. Lyle Gold remained in solitary while Demange stepped up his efforts for a revision. No matter what happened, I realized, as I tuned into August Mercer's press conference, it seemed Reiff might always remain on the sidelines, as long as there were those who steadfastly refused even to consider the possibility of his role.

And then there was Mimi Ryan advancing the theory of Joseph Henry's "patriotic forgery": Everyone knew Gold was guilty; the requirements of the justice system had become so lopsided in favor of criminals it had become rapidly evident to those in the know that the traitor would most likely walk. And so some evidence had simply been massaged. Not a bad spin, I thought. From this view, Lieutenant Henry was a figure of virtue, a martyr for a just cause. So for a certain segment of society, despite all evidence to the contrary, he became a hero. Mimi opined, in a voice that trembled with emotion, "We were not able to give the lieutenant the great funeral he deserved. But his son should know that his father, in life as in death, marched forward. His unhappy forgery will be counted among his greatest acts of heroism."

14

GOODBYE TO ALL THAT

It snowed right before Halloween. Just a dusting, but in the greenhouse age even that is rare. Shopkeepers swept away the thin white blanket almost immediately, but not before it wiped us clean.

Three days later, on a quiet Friday evening when even twenty-four-hour news networks were a bit slow on the uptake, the Gold decision was finally revised. Edgar Demange called to deliver the news, heaving the sigh of an old and tired man, relieved of an immense burden.

"I can't tell you how glad I am that those boys finally came around," he said. "I didn't think I would survive. If my heart didn't get me, some yahoo with a gun would have." He yammered on about boxes and packing and Lyle's release date, but I barely heard him. I sat in my chair, and I closed my eyes.

"This does reaffirm my faith in our government, though," Demange was saying.

My eyes flew open. "What?" I gasped. "How can you say that, after all that's happened?"

"They didn't have to give in," Demange said. "They could've kept this going and going. But some smart boys figured out a better course."

I fell silent. We are odd, we Americans—eager to punish and repress, quick to get carried away in the name of freedom, capable of shooting an innocent one day and being shot for the sake of an innocent the next. The lies, the bizarre logic, the insufferable self-righteousness that infected so many—it was hard to forget, harder still to forgive. But maybe there was something to this belief of Demange's in the basic decency of democratic government.

"What did Lyle say when you told him?" I asked.

Demange chuckled. "Lyle? Oh, Lyle said something about knowing all along that his honor and his innocence would prevail."

I laughed too. Oh, hell, what did I expect, a thank-you note?

He did thank me, though. He called the very next day from his apartment to say the one thing I had not expected. "You are a smart girl, Kate," he told me. It is with relief that I add I did not burst into tears until after I had hung up the phone.

Really, it would have been so much more satisfying to

have a grand public retrial, a new verdict, or even a pardon. But following the peculiarities of political logic, the affair had been deemed to be better handled by a few well-placed phone calls. It was, quite simply, a revision of the process. To a degree, Lyle still desired a more formal acknowledgment of justice. He issued a statement to the press: "The Government of the United States has given me my liberty. Liberty is nothing without honor. From this day forward, I shall continue to seek amends for the shocking judicial wrong of which I am still the victim."

Some people, like Maurice Barres and Mimi Ryan, interpreted this as a promise to sue the government for millions in civil court. "Typical greed!" exclaimed Mimi. But that was not Lyle's plan. He told me he did not have the strength for another lawsuit. "I will clear my name, bit by bit, in public," he said.

The secretary of state told the media, "The incident is closed."

Maurice Barres proclaimed that what was at stake was the house of our fathers, our land, our dead. I thought that was nice. I would agree—from the opposite side of the table, of course. But I am sure, since Maurice is an intelligent man—and a pragmatic one—that someday he will revisit all the evidence. He will have plenty of time. The affair will be around for a while. There are those who won't want to let it go.

I was listening to the radio when Truman Pace proposed

a monument to Lieutenant Henry in order to respect "the heritage of the defenders of the country." Pace said it would stand for a "love of order, respect for work, devotion to country, demands for security, rejection of foreigners, and anxiety in the face of a changing world."

So the rewriting had begun. Reiff Prouty becomes a dashing double agent. August Mercer only performed his patriotic duty. The good Lieutenant Henry? Just an overzealous aide serving the most noble of ends. And the Gold Affair itself, in virtuous America, nothing more than an insignificant historical footnote, chalked up to the carelessness of a Chinese diplomat, a coincidental resemblance in handwriting, and the shortcomings and ambitions of the wrong kind of people.

There were always going to be those who believed, as Mercer did, in Lyle's guilt in spite of the evidence. Equally, there were always going to be those who pointed to Reiff Prouty as the real traitor who, by virtue of his connections and a certain amount of media fatigue, evaded judgment day.

Mimi Ryan fell into the first camp. She sat in a bar near the Capitol, night after night, drinking and grousing when she wasn't making the television rounds, I heard. BELTWAY BABE: FIGHTING FOR JUSTICE. I hoped she framed that magazine cover. Her compatriot Mercer was done, but only in the White House. He would be courted by lobbying firms, which collect the discarded and disgraced at bargain prices, because even they have hefty Rolodexes.

Joan Picquart, who was back in-house at the State Department, had one further interaction with Lyle Gold. With uncharacteristic camaraderie, she sent him a note: *What remains to be done is no more than a formality, for you have been vindicated as no one else ever has been before—by the entire world.* This was, for her, warm.

■ ■ ■

And me? Oh, well.

I had never been so tired in my life. My body simply collapsed. I nearly coughed up a lung, hacking helplessly, bedridden with a fever and an aching throat. My lips broke out in blisters and my gums were covered with canker sores. I lost ten pounds, since the only thing I could consume was protein shakes. My mother demanded I return home, but I didn't have the strength to board a plane. Instead, I curled up under my down comforter, with my globe lamp glowing warmly while I read, finally, *War and Peace*. John had dropped off a copy on his way overseas after he heard I had always wanted to get around to it. His new posting was a kick; after the Gold Affair, our John was assigned to the newspaper's Beijing bureau. "Hey, I can hang out with the Xianxus!" He laughed. It was true that Roberto's father had returned to China. His replacement, a quiet man with no handsome son or ghost of a former wife or stain of scandal, had already settled in Washington.

It took a few weeks, but I did get better. I dreamed of

green grass, freshly cut, that sharp smell of a new season. I drank ginger tea. I bathed in steaming-hot water sprinkled with special red salts that a tarot-card reader swore would help: "Your chakras are bleached," she said. Slowly I crawled back into the office. Business hummed along. We would do well in the next election cycle. Checks were clearing, bills were paid, the audit was settled with no penalty. But it all felt flat. I sat at my desk, twirling pencils until my eyes blurred.

No one came up to me in parking lots for my autograph or even to slap a high-five or say "Way to go!" There were no congratulatory back pats. Now that it seemed to have been settled, the Gold Affair wasn't something that the country wanted to remember, let alone celebrate. It would have been terribly gratifying to me if some stranger had commented on my bravery or something. But then again, Lyle had really *suffered*, and no one was proposing compensation for him or doling out compliments for his courage. Nor did he expect much. He simply wanted to restore his name and go on. He returned to his paper, although as an editor now. It was a more sedentary life, but appropriately out of the limelight that he had never sought.

I thought a lot about Lieutenant Henry, whose grave at Arlington (a controversial burial, opposed by many at the Pentagon) was regularly encircled with red, white, and blue candles and flowers from visiting admirers. No one except Jack and John knew about my meeting with him, so no accusations were ever thrown my way. Jack was right, of course; we had not forced him to fabricate evidence. But we were—actually, I was—the bearer of terrible news for him, which might have been a factor in his end, and I had to live with that.

What mattered, as John pointed out the week before he was to leave for China, was that "we kept trying, even when we knew we would more than likely get mowed down. We still came out fighting. Someday, someone might remember that."

Or, perhaps not. Melvin Gluck, for one, had decided to make a movie about the affair. Anthony France would direct. The lead character would be Edgar Demange, the courageous lawyer who fought against the odds to save the honor of an innocent man. Please! There was no Jaures character, no Vanzetti, no Boothe. Actually, I was more than a bit put off by this. What about *my* story? I had given up the man I loved; wasn't *that* compelling? Film-worthy? My father took a dim view of the whole business. "You're lucky *not* to be in it," he said. "That would make people more jealous than they already are. You don't need to be a lightning rod. Take it easy, kiddo. Come home."

Lili bought me a case of *prosecco*, "For that bender Joan Picquart proposed," she said. My uncles suggested I move to another city, perhaps lose myself in the concrete anonymity of New York. But I didn't want to lose myself. Jack had been right about the boost for our business. Our phones were ringing and ringing.

I just didn't feel . . . well. In an exercise in masochism, I tapped Roberto's name into an Internet search and learned that he had been spotted in various places with an unnamed blonde. My scalp pricked with—with what? With sadness? With pride? I turned off the computer. It didn't really matter much, anyway.

November bled into December. On an especially drab day, cold enough to chap the cheeks but not enough to snow, I walked into my office, flicked on the light, and sat down in my chair without removing my coat. Jack was rustling in his office, cheerfully bellowing at some poor sucker who wanted to sign on to our list of clients. I heard him hang up the phone, then call out my name. I didn't move.

Jack came in. "Get a load of this," he said. "That nutty governor from Indiana who thinks he can be president? His campaign manager just called to find out our 'price tag.' Can you believe it?" He sat down across from me, putting his shiny Italian shoes on the edge of my desk. "I think we should avoid him, but hell, you have to admit it's pretty flattering."

I looked at him blankly and wondered, What *is* he talking about? And I thought back to an interview I had seen the night before. Anthony France, gloriously attired in a purple velvet shirt and black leather sandals, explained his pivotal role in the Gold case. When asked, Why did you do it, he had assumed a self-righteous expression, leaned toward the host, and confided, "For a little while, I felt larger than life."

"But weren't you worried about your career?" the host had asked. "There were powerful people saying the exact opposite, still saying the exact opposite."

"My career?" France had laughed. "What is a career? I had this sudden mysterious need for glory, for war, for history, and I got all that. Maybe I'll be on half pay my whole life for this. What does it matter? *I was there*."

Jack waved across the desk. "Hello, hello."

And suddenly I thought, I want a glass of champagne. Not the brands served at restaurants here, the labels that pinch the tongue. Americans never get the real stuff. I wanted the crisp, creamy Grand Cru from the Côte des Noirs, the honest champagne made by the hardworking Boulard family, who had once treated Lili and me to a three-hour tasting. And suddenly I thought, I *desperately* want that glass of champagne, more than anything in the world.

Jack took one look at my face. He had seen it before. "Oh, no, no, no," he said immediately. "Not now, Kate."

But I was already walking out the door, purse in hand. What more did I need? I always carry my passport on me. Some of the weariness fell away then. To be alive at all did require some risk.

It was an hour's drive to the airport. I spent the first fifteen minutes debating whether or not to make the call. There was always the chance he wouldn't answer. Or perhaps he wouldn't want to hear from me. But then I thought, *This is nothing compared to the last few months*. It was worth a try.

Roberto answered his phone on the second ring.

"I'm going to Reuilly to drink champagne," I told him. "Would you like to come?"

"Of course." He did not hesitate. "I will meet you at Charles de Gaulle."

I smiled as I hung up. I drove faster now, cutting into the low Virginia hills, bruised with smoky trees and wet leaves, clouds rolling gray, on my way to limiting my media exposure. Oh, hell, *vacation*. The ticket would be horribly expensive. I might have to stay for some time to make it worthwhile. Maybe I wouldn't come back.

I checked myself in the mirror and wished I had gotten a haircut. After all, I was on my way to see the handsomest man in the world. Half pay, my ass.

Ataturk lit a cigarette; Abdul Haq crossed the border; I drank champagne. Oh, all right, it was hardly the same. But I still sat back and smiled. Come on, you sons o' bitches, do you want to live forever?

ACKNOWLEDGMENTS

I would like to thank, for their hard work, Sarah Burnes, Jennifer Barth, and Ruth Kaplan.

I also would like to thank, for their research skills, David Bernknopf, Bonnie Bertram, Erica Cantley, Simon Dean, Sparkle Hayter, Manny Howard, Jeannie Bonner Kendall, Tim Kopec, Randall Lane, Tim Long, Wendy McCallum, Lynn Marquis, Elena Occelli, Victoria Rowan, Ted Rubenstein, Patricia Sabga, and certain bartenders who serve absinthe (you know who you are).